The Triplet Orphans

*In their search for the truth...
they'll find so much more!*

Identical triplets Rosabella, Isobel and
Annabelle Lennox grew up as orphans in rural
Scotland. On their twenty-first birthday they
receive news of the mystery surrounding their
birth. Now to learn the truth of their parentage,
they must travel to London and make
their debuts!

Bookworm Rose has no interest in the season.
She only wants to uncover the past. Until she
meets cynical James, the Viscount Ashbourne.
He's incredibly vexing—and yet Rose just
can't stay away from him...

As she searches for their birth father,
feisty Izzy encounters arrogant, and
supremely handsome, Prince Claudio...

Eldest triplet Anna is close to discovering where
she came from, and the haughty Earl of Garvald
is getting in her way! Despite his reputation,
Anna is drawn to William. He's clearly hiding
a secret... Will a grand party at his estate
reveal all—including their true feelings?

***Miss Rose and the Vexing Viscount
Miss Isobel and the Prince***

Available now!

*And look out for Anna's story,
coming soon from Harlequin Historical!*

Author Note

Welcome to the second book in my Triplet Orphans series—this time featuring the feisty Miss Isobel and the Queen's distant cousin, Prince Claudio.

Prince Claudio—lately arrived in England—is determined to enjoy life, having gained freedom from the restrictions of his father's court. For Claudio, marriage is out of the question for many years yet.

Izzy, meantime, has decided to find a sensible man to marry, as this season will be her one and only chance to escape from her fate as a schoolteacher or governess. The question marks over her origins mean a titled husband is not an option, so she will have to choose from among the Misters of the ton. But should the chance arise, might she try for one glorious kiss from a prince?

Look out for the third book in the series, coming soon. Of the three sisters, Miss Anna is the sensible one, the dependable one, the responsible one. Yet one man is going to make her forget all reason and common sense—and perhaps help her finally uncover the mystery of her parents' past.

MISS ISOBEL AND THE PRINCE

CATHERINE TINLEY

HISTORICAL

Harlequin®
HISTORICAL

ISBN-13: 978-1-335-59619-2

Miss Isobel and the Prince

Recycling programs for this product may not exist in your area.

Harlequin Enterprises ULC
22 Adelaide St. West, 41st Floor
Toronto, Ontario M5H 4E3, Canada
www.Harlequin.com

Printed in U.S.A.

Catherine Tinley has loved reading and writing since childhood and has a particular fondness for love, romance and happy endings. She lives in Ireland with her husband, children, dog and kitten and can be reached at catherinetinley.com, as well as through Facebook and on Twitter @catherinetinley.

Visit the Author Profile page
at Harlequin.com.

For my husband, Andrew,
with love

Prologue

Scotland,
1796

It was time to leave. Again.

Maria knew it but had been refusing to think about it.
Tomorrow she and her three darlings must uproot themselves from this, their home. The only home her daughters had ever known. A place they had felt safe. Until now.

Briefly, she wondered if she should tell milady the truth,
then dismissed the notion. It was a story too fantastical to
be believed, too risky to be told. Especially now.

Instead, they would leave their haven, their sanctuary,
departing before the guests began to arrive. As she had
done many times before, she bemoaned the twist of fate that
had seen milady—now simply her dear friend Margaret—
seek company for the first time in years. Without letting
Maria know—and why should she, when she was mistress
of the house?—she had invited a group of former friends
to visit. Renton Ashbourne. Thaxby. Kelgrove. All had accepted, and all were even now on their way. Milady Margaret had expected Maria to be pleased, that much was clear,
and had looked decidedly crestfallen at Maria's response.

'But, Maria, you have been encouraging me to move

on, to accept that my dear husband is gone, to focus on my son, and the future. This is a momentous decision for me—to engage again with the people we knew in London.' She frowned. 'I have had little contact with the *ton* since his death, as you know.' She lifted her chin. 'And now I am ready to try again. I could not face going there.' A visible shudder ran through her. 'But inviting them here, for a quiet house party, that I can do—at least, I *think* I can.'

'Of course you can! For you are so strong. We both are!'

'I have learned from you, Maria. Each time I felt my life was worthless I would see you, also widowed, also young, but with no home, no family. Your determination to see your girls safe and well has been my inspiration!'

Safe and well.

A shiver of fear ran down her spine. Those who loved her, those who hated her, those who were indifferent to her... all would be here for Margaret's party, but she would not.

Margaret had been predictably horrified on hearing that Maria and her girls were leaving.

'But why? And where will you go?'

'I am not sure. Somewhere quiet, out of the way. It is better so. Besides, I have relied on your good heart and hospitality for long enough. Five years and more! You are healed enough now from the loss of your husband to start to engage in society again. You no longer need me.'

'But I do! I need your friendship! Are we not friends, Maria?'

At this, Maria had clasped her hand. 'Of course we are! And I promise to write to you. It is just...' She swallowed. 'Margaret, you have never pried into my circumstances. I will always be grateful for everything you have done for me—'

'Oh, stuff and nonsense! What was I supposed to do—

send you outside to give birth in the stable? And you were so shocked to have *three* babies, not one.' She gave a rueful smile. 'My son was a sturdy toddler by then, but I knew enough to help you in those early weeks, along with Nurse.' Her eyes grew distant. 'And then, by the time you were well and managing, you and I were fast friends.' She eyed Maria intently. 'I must confess to a certain curiosity, though. You seemed…frightened. Of someone or something.'

Maria nodded. 'I could not tell you. I still cannot. But know this—I did nothing wrong. Nothing! Those who wished me harm did so for their own reasons.'

Margaret spread her hands. 'I do not doubt it. And I do not mean to pry. But I ask you to reconsider. Stay with me—with us. This has been your home for five long years. Your girls and my son are best friends—as we are. Stay.'

'I wish I could.' There was a catch in Maria's voice. 'But I must think of my safety. And my daughters' safety.'

Margaret gasped. 'Someone would threaten your children?'

'I know not. But I cannot take that chance.'

Margaret was thoughtful, frowning. 'My house guests. You fear one of them?'

Maria eyed her steadily.

'I am so sorry, Maria! Who? Which one?'

But Maria shook her head. 'I have no proof. Of *anything*. So I dare not accuse. I must simply survive in safety and keep my daughters safe. So please, tell no one about me, if you can. And if you must, you may mention me as a friend—the widowed Mrs Lennox and her three children. No one needs to know they are triplets, and no one needs to know my first name.'

'Very well, but I cannot understand it!'

In the end Maria prevailed, as she had to. Tears were

shed on both parts, then Maria, sorrowfully, packed up their modest belongings. Clothing. The books and music sheets gifted to them at Christmastide, and for their fifth birthday earlier this year. Maria's respectable savings—for dear Margaret had insisted on paying her these past years, as her companion, and for helping with young Xander's education. Opening her strongbox, Maria counted the coin within, feeling reassured there would be enough to keep them for many months, until she found a suitable situation.

Other treasures were there, too. Earrings from her grandmother. His last letter to her. And the other thing. The treasure. Carefully she unfolded the velvet cloth, blinking as the jewels within caught the light. So beautiful! So distinctive!

So dangerous, for the piece would be easily recognised by anyone who knew about it. Even now. Wrapping it up again, her brow furrowed, she set it to one side, along with the letter. The earrings, though, those she would take with her. A legacy for her daughters, and a reminder that once, she had had a grandmother who loved her.

Chapter One

Grantham, England,
March 1, 1812

Being born a prince held certain advantages.

Prince Claudio Friedrich Ferdinand of Andernach stretched, yawned, and left his bed. The day was already well advanced, the serving maid who had warmed his bed last night long gone, and Claudio's head was remarkably clear, given the amount of fine wine he had consumed the night before. Having landed in England only two weeks ago, it was remarkable how quickly his title had opened so many doors. Already he had been invited to drink, to dine, and to carouse with a number of new friends, and now this—a brief trip north to see a horse race in the vicinity of Grantham.

The Angel Inn was, his friends had assured him, suitable for people of their class, even though it was also used by commoners. He had seen little of it, admittedly, for after the race yesterday the gentlemen had simply retired to the nearest village hostelry—there to drink, and speak of nonsense, and dally with a couple of saucy serving maids. The maids had been gratifyingly flirtatious, one going so far as to call him *handsome*, but it was only after Eldon had called him *Prince* that the pretty one with the dark eyes had focused her attention on him. It had been well after midnight when he had slipped her up to his chamber in the Angel, and he now only vaguely remembered her fixation on his princely status.

An hour later, having washed, dressed, and partaken of a light breakfast in his chamber, he made his way downstairs to seek his new friends. Sure enough, there they were, in the taproom, already imbibing. *Lord, these English know how to sport!* It was all such a contrast from the decorum and duty that had plagued him at home. A welcome contrast.

'Prince!' Hawkins raised a hand in greeting. 'How is your head this fine day?'

Grinning, Claudio slid onto the long bench beside him. 'Perfectly clear, I assure you! And you should call me Andernach, you know.'

'Well, I would if I could say it!' A look of concentration appeared on Hawkins's ruddy visage. 'Handernack! There!'

Claudio shuddered. 'Actually, *Prince* will suffice. Now, how does a man get some ale around here?'

'Thank the Lord, we are finally in Grantham!' Izzy gazed eagerly out of the window of the coach. 'What is the name of the inn, Anna?'

'The Angel, I think.' Her sister's gaze remained focused on the streets and buildings of the Lincolnshire town.

'Yes, definitely the Angel.' Rose, Izzy's other sister, nodded. 'The coachman said we could stop here for an hour or two for dinner.'

Izzy's frustration rose. 'Can we not stay here tonight? Why must we press on so much each day?'

Anna's tone was even. 'You know our journey has been planned in detail, and at a much easier pace than people usually travel. We must reach Stamford tonight, for a bed-chamber is reserved for us there.' She sighed. 'We are all tired of travelling, Izzy. It has felt like a month since we left Scotland. But we are nearly there. Tomorrow night we sleep in Hitchin, and the day after, we shall finally reach London!'

'There it is!' Rose pointed to a grey stone building, the sign featuring two demi-angels holding a crown. Izzy had a brief impression of an arched entrance before the coach swung into the innyard.

There was a brief silence as they busied themselves with bonnets and reticules. Their matching red cloaks had kept the cold at bay today, thankfully. The farther south they went, the milder the weather. Already the frosts of Scotland and northern England were giving way to warmer temperatures, and in the hedgerows, Izzy had spotted nodding daffodils, replacing the delicate snowdrops and shy crocuses still on display farther north.

We are leaving winter behind, and spring this year holds endless possibilities.

Excitement rose again in Izzy's breast. Until just a couple of weeks ago she and her sisters had lived quietly in a small school for young ladies, which had not suited Izzy one bit. Finally, adventure was upon her, and she intended to relish every moment.

They were handed down from the carriage by the coachman, making their way across the yard and inside the inn. A man dressed in the familiar dun clothing of an innkeeper approached them, his gaze flicking over them in assessment even as he greeted them.

'Good day, good day. And er…good day.'

There it was, the realisation they were identical triplets. Having seen it all her life, Izzy took little notice of the flicker of confusion mixed with surprise. It was as familiar to her as breathing.

'How may I serve you today?' the landlord continued.

He did not say *ladies*, Izzy noted. Their drab dresses, simple red cloaks, and plain straw bonnets had led many inn staff to conclude they were of the servant class—a misapprehension which they had had to frequently correct on their long journey south.

As usual, Anna took charge. Being the eldest of the three, she saw it as her due.

She was born only twenty minutes before me, thought Izzy sourly, then chided herself inwardly. She was not actually cross with Anna—just tired, and a little ill-tempered, and ready for her dinner.

'Good day.' Anna's tone was clipped, and she did not incline her head. 'We require a private parlour, if you please, and dinner. And our coachman will need assistance with the horses.'

The innkeeper's eyes widened briefly. 'Of course, miss! Right away!'

That is more like it!

It was always interesting to note the change in demeanour when people realised they were not in fact servants but young ladies—their educated tones being the usual indication, along with the fact they were travelling by private carriage. Izzy had not been raised to think she was a person of consequence—quite the reverse in fact—but the girls needed the acknowledgement of their status as protection. Three young ladies travelling alone might be subject to all kinds of unwanted attention otherwise. Attentions that they simply were not equipped to deal with.

Izzy looked around her. The place was spotlessly clean and comfortably furnished. A painted notice informed her that the inn had had many royal visitors in its six-hundred-year history, including King John as long ago as 1213 and, more recently, both Charles I and Oliver Cromwell—though not, Izzy surmised, at the same time. To her right she could hear a hubbub through a closed door—the taproom, presumably.

The innkeeper was consulting his ledger and frowning. 'My apologies, ladies. We are busy today, and so I need to find a suitable room for you to dine in. I do have one private parlour that is currently not in use, but it has been reserved by a party of young gentlemen.' He closed the book. 'If you will give me a moment, I shall consult with them. Please, be seated.'

Taking her seat, Izzy became aware of a new noise from the taproom: male voices raised in song.

Lord, they are drunk in the afternoon!

Already she was learning more of the world. Never could she have imagined a life so different from the quietude of Belvedere School. As she listened the chorus ended, a single, clear baritone beginning a solo performance. The innkeeper opened the door, and briefly, the song came to her more clearly.

Why...he is singing in German!

Having an ear for languages, at school Izzy had eagerly devoured Latin and Greek, Spanish and Italian, and then German, making the most of the good fortune that one of the Belvedere teachers had spent ten years near Hanover, tutoring an English family there. Izzy had no difficulty understanding the words the man was singing, a simple drinking song. Something about his voice, though, was disturbing her, causing a feeling almost of pins and needles in her body.

How odd!

After a few moments the singing ceased, and a little later the innkeeper reappeared. Perhaps the singing group were the ones who had reserved the parlour.

'Good news, ladies. You have full use of the parlour for dinner, for the gentlemen do not intend to dine until much later. I do hope that is acceptable, Miss…?'

'I am Miss Lennox. My sisters, Miss Isobel Lennox, and Miss Rose Lennox.'

He bowed. 'Follow me.'

'Thank you.' Anna was every inch the refined young lady as she followed the landlord down a long corridor, her sisters at her heels. Despite their simple clothing, the Lennox sisters were not to be trifled with!

Ten minutes later they were alone, having ordered dinner and used the outside privy before returning to their snug parlour. After divesting themselves of boots, bonnets, and cloaks, Anna and Rose sank into comfortable settees with matching expressions signalling relief. Izzy could not understand it. Pacing about the room, she felt consumed by restlessness.

'How can you sit, when we have been sitting all day?'

Rose groaned. 'Because this settee, unlike the coach, does not bounce or rattle. I declare, my bones are aching!'

'Come, walk with me about the room,' she urged them. 'It is small I know, but at least your legs will get some movement!'

They resisted, and so she continued by herself, walking around the large table a dozen times until she was quite dizzy. It was always this way. Her sisters full of languor while she bubbled with vivacity. Still, at least Anna and Rose had agreed to go to London in the first place. Lord, it had been a close-run thing, though!

Her mind returned to that day a few short weeks ago

when their guardian Mr Marnoch—a lawyer who had been dear Mama's employer before she died—had summoned them to his office. It being the day after their twenty-first birthday, he had informed them that he knew almost nothing of their family background. Mama had come to Elgin with five-year-old triplets, had clerked for him, and had asked him to accept their guardianship during her last long illness, five years later. Mama had died before their eleventh birthday, and so they had spent a full ten years in Belvedere School. Never once in that time had they left the vicinity of Elgin.

In her mind's eye Izzy could recall every detail of the school, the town, and Mr Marnoch's comfortable mansion, where he had bade them visit him occasionally. He was warm and kind and, Izzy reflected, had adapted remarkably well to having three small girls foisted on him. In his office that day, he had offered them the opportunity to visit his widowed sister in London, there to discover what they could about Mama's background and family. He had set each of them a quest, and Izzy's was particularly intriguing.

Your quest is to discover what you can about your father. Your mother rarely spoke about Mr Lennox and informed me she was a widow when she first arrived in the town. Her eyes were hazel while yours are blue, so he may have had blue eyes. Your mama had a London Season, but I am uncertain if that is how they met.

'I am to discover the name of our father? But how?' Izzy had exclaimed on reading the paper. 'How am I to do this?'

Mr Marnoch had shrugged. 'Honestly, I have no idea.

I have written down all I know on the matter. The rest is up to you.'

And so her practical sister Anna and her timid sister Rose, inspired by their own quests, had both agreed to go, and Izzy could not have been more delighted. Going to London, where she might see the sights and dance at a ball and meet people who were *not* from a five-mile radius of Elgin? She could think of nothing more exciting. If only it were not taking so dashed long to get there!

Claudio was happy. Vaguely aware that his happiness was largely due to a haze of ale-induced cloudiness, he was happy nevertheless. In his entire life he had never set out to drink all day with the specific aim of achieving drunkenness, as these English gentlemen did. Never would he have thought to find himself merrily drunk in some random inn in the middle of England, with a bunch of gentlemen he had met only recently, but who seemed to him to be the best of fellows. Yes, travelling to England had been an act of genius on his part—although his father would most certainly not approve of his actions so far. Still, Papa was far away and would never know.

Indeed, it had been Papa's suggestion that he consider making a life in England, given the ongoing machinations aimed at annexing and merging the small German-speaking principalities into larger blocs. Since the fall of the Holy Roman Empire and the work of Napoleon's confederation, the momentum was all in one direction, and it did not bode well for small sovereign states like the one ruled by his father. Claudio's eldest brother would eventually inherit *something*, but it was not currently clear what.

In the meantime, Claudio and his brothers were left adrift, uncertain of their future. Claudio's English was excellent despite never having travelled to this country, and so Papa had urged him to travel here, find an English wife, and settle down. Queen Charlotte—a distant cousin—had introduced him at court on his second night in London, and instantly a group of gentlemen had surrounded him, all keen to befriend the new prince in town.

Some, like Garvald, Ashbourne, and Phillips, had seemed sensible and sober, and remained aloof, if friendly. Claudio however had found himself drawn to Mr Eldon and Mr Hawkins, who had none of the reserve and stiffness he had just escaped from at home. All his life he had played at protocol, adhering to the strictures of his father's court. He had no intention of replacing one set of sensible associates with another. Hawkins and Eldon were fascinatingly different and represented a life as unlike his old existence as Claudio could imagine.

Yes, coming to England must be one of the best decisions he had ever made. Here he could fall down drunk or carouse with comely maids without a disapproving glance from any direction. For the first time in his life, he was enjoying the benefits of princedom, rather than its restrictions.

Rising to his feet he swayed lightly, noting that the room was moving in an alarming matter. Momentarily tempted to sit back down again, he resisted, the need to relieve himself being undeniable. With great focus he put one foot carefully in front of another, determined not to fall down in front of his new friends. Having successfully crossed the taproom, though his head was spinning, he made for the corridor that led to the privies.

Izzy had had enough. Anna steadfastly refused to walk about the room with her, while Rose looked to have actually nodded off on the settee. 'Who will come to the privy with me?'

Rose, naturally, made no answer, while Anna raised a quizzical brow. 'But we went when we first arrived!'

'And? I need to go again.'

'No doubt dinner will be here shortly.'

'Even more reason why I should go now, before it arrives!'

Anna shook her head. 'You should wait, Izzy.'

It was too much. Izzy's chest burned with annoyance. *Anna is not my parent, nor my guardian, nor my teacher!*

'Then, I shall go by myself!'

Anna frowned. 'Very well. But take care.'

Gesturing a vague response to Anna's concerned expression—for surely if she thought there was any real danger she would leave her comfortable settee—Izzy left the parlour and began making her way down the dimly-lit corridor.

Enjoying a brief sense of freedom, she took everything in: the painted walls, low ceilings, the scent of roasting meat rising tantalisingly from the kitchens. The corridor was empty, the only sound the shuffle of Izzy's slippers on the flagstone floor, and a distant murmur from the taproom. In this part now the hallway bent to the right, a window illuminating the scene. Ahead of her a door opened, and a man emerged.

Instantly Izzy caught her breath. She was alone, and this man was an unknown threat. Her gaze swept over him, noting that he was young, not more than two or three years older than she, perhaps. Fair hair, a handsome face, strong figure. He wore the clothing of a gentleman, and Izzy's fear subsided a little. Surely he would behave with honour? Thinking quickly, she decided to simply pass him without speaking. The ladies' retiring room was just past the one set out for the men, and she would be safe there.

Lifting her chin a little, she walked on.

Claudio's head had cleared a little. After making use of the privy he had washed his face and hands using clear cold water from the innyard well.

Perhaps I shall drink a little more slowly when I return, he mused.

After drying his face and hands on a clean soft towel provided by a servant, he left the yard—only to catch his breath. There, walking towards him, was the most divine creature he had ever beheld. Corn-gold hair, deep blue eyes, and a perfect complexion…his gaze drifted downwards. She was perfectly proportioned, her form discernible despite the drab brown gown she wore. A serving maid, he realised, taking in her clothing. Instantly, recalling his success last night, he decided to address her.

'Hail, golden Aphrodite!' He bowed theatrically, but she walked on towards him, avoiding his gaze, without acknowledging his words.

'What?' He sighed dramatically. 'You do not return my greeting?'

Now her gaze flicked towards him—a mix of uncertainty, nervousness, and—was that humour in her eyes? He slapped a hand to his chest. 'You wound me, o fair one.' He frowned. 'At least you could say *good day*.'

She was almost upon him. Boldly he met her gaze. 'Good day,' he addressed her pointedly.

Rose-pink lips pursed in disapproval. 'Good day, sir. Now, will you let me pass?'

He was, to be fair, standing directly in her path, and the corridor was narrow. 'First, a kiss!'

Chapter Two

The golden maiden caught her breath. 'No!'

Claudio was conscious of disappointment. Still, never having kissed an unwilling maid, he was not prepared to do so now. Inspiration came to him. 'Not even if I inform you that I am a prince?'

Now he had her attention. She laughed, scepticism clear in the wry twist of her delectable mouth. 'If you are a prince, sir, then I am the Queen of Sheba!'

He blinked. 'But I *am* a prince!' This was not going as expected. Not at all.

'There is but one prince in England, sir. The Prince Regent. I have seen his likeness many times, and I assure you, you are not he!'

'Well, no. I am not *the* prince—not the Prince Regent, anyway. But I am *a* prince.'

'In your own imagination, perhaps,' she countered, eyes ablaze. 'I do know of princes from storybooks when I was a child, and never did they behave like you.'

'Behave?' His mind seemed slow, befuddled. 'How do princes behave, then?'

She considered this, her head tilted to one side. Amid his confusion, he could not fail to notice again how kissable were her lips: perfect rosebuds that he ached to touch with his own.

She held up her hands, as if to mark off her points on her fingers. 'First, princes should be handsome.' She assessed him directly. 'I concede that you are not ugly.'

Not ugly? His eyes widened at her effrontery.

'But princes are also expected to be *honourable*, sir.'

Now his mind was in sharp focus. Drawing himself up, he gave her one of his father's best disdainful looks. 'How dare you suggest I am anything other than honourable!'

She nodded thoughtfully. 'An arrogant air is a feature of princes, I'll grant you. You should cultivate it. But as to the question of your honour, what else must I think when I encounter someone who, while in a state of severe intoxication, accosts a lone maid in the middle of the afternoon and threatens to kiss her? Now, step aside, sir, or must I scream for help?'

Dumbfounded, he gave way a little. Enough to allow her to pass, but only if she brushed against him briefly.

With a muffled sound of exasperation she did so, and his entire body—despite the ale—thrilled at the sensation of her shoulder sliding across his chest, from right to left.

If only...

He watched as she made for the privy, then made his way back to the taproom in something of a daze. What on earth had just occurred? Never had he been spoken to in such a manner, by serving maid or noble.

And I did not threaten to kiss her.

He had simply *asked* for a kiss, as any man might. And if a maiden said *no*, an honourable man like himself would not force the matter. The accusation rankled, as had her defiant air.

Perhaps the English were not so fond of princes as he had believed.

* * *

Izzy remained in the privy and yard for quite ten minutes, in a high state of agitation. Her sheltered life in Belvedere School had not prepared her for such a situation, and she had to admit to being fairly disturbed by it all. Pacing up and down the innyard, she tried to make sense of it all. The Reverend Buchan, in his sermons at the Holy Trinity Chapel in Elgin, had frequently warned his parishioners of the evils of gin and whisky, although he allowed wine was a civilised drink.

'Take ye not the evil soup,' he had exhorted them, 'for surely it is the devil's buttermilk and leads to all manner of vice and sin.'

The man she had met today must surely have been drinking gin, she concluded, for dear Mr Marnoch regularly had a dram of whisky in the evenings and never behaved inappropriately.

Yes, that must be it.

So what was her own excuse? She had imbibed nothing stronger than tea this day, and yet her mind was filled with visions of kissing the handsome young drunkard she had just encountered.

Reflecting on their exchange, she realised that any fear had vanished very early on. Somehow she had sensed she was in no danger of physical harm from him. Now her mind was filled with his image—his strong handsome face, piercing grey eyes, thick blond hair. And when she had brushed past him…she shuddered, recalling the delicious thrill of her shoulder and upper arm brushing across his firm chest.

Men are shaped so differently from us.

Naturally she had known that, but today she had learned how…how *interesting* the differences were.

Pushing away such shocking thoughts, she concentrated

again on his forwardness. How dare he ask for a kiss from her! No one had ever done so, and it was galling to recall his lazy smile, his confidence that she would oblige him. Still, she thought with satisfaction, at least she had put him in his place.

Despite being unused to the ways of the world, she was not foolish enough to believe his Banbury tale about being a prince. Had she been a gambling person—which of course she was not, having been raised to abhor such vices—she would be willing to stake her new gloves on his having used the *prince* ruse on some other unsuspecting female—and with success. too, given his clear consternation at her rejection of his nonsensical claim.

No, he was no prince—that much was certain. Recalling their brief exchange she wondered now if there had been a tinge of a foreign accent in his speech—although given the ever so slight slurring of his words, it was impossible to tell. The expensive cut and finish of his fine waistcoat and buckskin breeches indicated he was wealthy. A merchant, perhaps.

Satisfied with her own reasoning, she returned to her sisters in a fine state of outrage. When they questioned her, she gave no details, saying only that she had encountered a young man who had behaved in a boorish, arrogant way, but she had come to no harm. Seemingly satisfied, they bade her eat her dinner before it got cold, and an hour later they were on their way again.

The rest of the evening was strangely flat. While Claudio's new friends continued to drink, and jest, and sing, he hugged his cup, only sipping from it now and again. The more sober he got, the more annoyed with himself he became. Why had he just stood there like an idiot and allowed a serving wench to question his honour? He, Prince Claudio Friedrich Ferdinand, third son of the ruling prince of Andernach!

And why had the girl reacted so cuttingly to his overtures? There was no harm in his trying, surely? So why had she been so cold towards him, so judgemental?

Might his Aphrodite be already promised to another? He nodded sagely into his cup. That would explain it. If her affections had already been won—in his mind, he pictured a brawny groom or farmer—then, he would allow her to deny the brief spark of interest he had surely seen in her eye.

But no.

Even if she was enamoured of some coarse servant or labourer—quite unfitting to match her delicate beauty— still she had had no need to turn a light encounter into an assassination of his character. Why, she had acted as though *she* were the princess and he a commoner who had dared to proposition her!

Even worse had been their second encounter. He had chanced to pass the main doorway just as she was leaving, following some other girls out the door to the stableyard. Her drab gown had been covered by one of those red cloaks all young women seemed to wear here, her golden curls peeping out from beneath a simple straw bonnet. It was only when she had turned her head that he had known for certain it was her, his breath catching again at the perfection of her features.

Stupefied, he had simply stood stock-still, staring at her, but when she had fleetingly met his gaze she had looked straight through him, almost as if their previous encounter had never taken place. Taken aback, he had felt his jaw slacken, before tightening it up again grimly. Surely she could have given him a hint of a nod or even a disdainful glare? Instead, her cold emptiness had left him feeling as though she thought him worthless. Worthless…almost like a third son in a tiny principality.

And so his entire evening was spoiled. Spoiled because he had allowed an unknown servant girl to pierce his skin, to interfere with the haze of good-natured carousing he had been enjoying.

When the landlord called them through to their parlour for dinner, he ate his fill and afterwards refused to return to the taproom. Ignoring his friends' raillery, he made for his bed, there to dream fitful dreams where Papa frowned in his direction.

London,
March 17

Lady Ashbourne, Mr Marnoch's sister, proved to be every bit as warm and engaging as her brother. Welcoming the Lennox sisters into her elegant London mansion with great warmth and excitement, she declared them to be pretty behaved, and respectful and seemed to be delighted to be sponsoring them. She was curious as to how to tell them apart, and they had explained they tended to wear specific colours or trim their clothing with such colours— Anna with blue, Izzy with greens and yellows, and Rose with pink.

They each had been given a bedchamber of their own as well as a serving maid. Having shared a chamber with her sisters for her whole life, Izzy was loving having a pretty room of her own. The ladies' maid, however, was taking quite some getting used to. Izzy, Anna, and Rose had always done each other's buttons and hair at school, and it felt distinctly odd to be sitting at a dressing table having her hair pinned by a skilled London abigail. Still, it was all part of the adventure, she supposed.

Today Mary, Izzy's maid, was taking much longer than usual, for today was special. Today they were to leave Lady Ashbourne's house for the first time since their arrival.

Their hostess had been surprised, then delighted, to discover they were identical triplets and had hit upon the notion of revealing this in a dramatic way, when she presented the girls at court. Which meant that for the past two weeks they had all been cooped up together in the Ashbourne townhouse in Grafton Street.

Despite Izzy's usual restlessness, she had quite enjoyed the experience. Lord Ashbourne—Lady Ashbourne's nephew and the current viscount—was often at home, and together they all enjoyed elegant dinners and interesting discourse. But even better was the daytime activity, for they were constantly busy with dressmakers, mantua-makers, and milliners, as well as music and dancing classes. Every day brought new adventures, and after a lifetime of schoolbooks and dreariness, Izzy could not have been happier.

Lady Ashbourne was determined to ensure they were as ready as they could be to make their début at St James's Palace. Mr Marnoch, bless him, had sent money for them to be kitted out appropriately for London society, and Izzy was delighting in the new gowns, nightgowns, pelisses, hats, and shoes that had been made for her and her sisters in just a fortnight.

'That's you done, Miss Isobel.' Mary nodded in satisfaction at her handiwork, and Izzy had to admit the girl was highly skilled at dressing hair. 'I shall place your tiara once you are gowned,' she added, touching the diadem reverently. Izzy's eyes went to it for the hundredth time that day.

Lady Ashbourne had loaned each of them a diamond tiara just for today, and Izzy swallowed at the responsibility.

What if I break it, or lose it? It must be worth a fortune!

But no. Izzy squared her shoulders, determined that nothing bad would happen, for today they would make their curtsy before the queen herself.

Rising, Izzy turned to face the gown. She had of course tried it on already, numerous times, in fact, for a team of dressmakers had been visiting on a daily basis to ensure the Lennox sisters' court gowns were ready in time. Clad only in her shift and stockings, and with her hair now dressed and pinned, Isobel felt a certain solemnity about donning the gown. First, the hoop—for the queen abhorred the current fashion for straight, Grecian-inspired gowns. No, all débutantes being presented to Her Majesty must wear a hoop, and a four-foot train, and feather headdresses with lappets. The tiaras were Lady Ashbourne's own addition.

Next, Mary assisted her to put on the petticoat—a soft cotton half-slip tied at the waist. After that were the stays, which Mary pulled as tight as she could, until Izzy protested that she could not breathe. Following this ordeal Mary tied a padded roll around Izzy's waist—to lift and display the skirts properly, she explained.

Lord! thought Izzy. *I wonder how my mama and her friends managed every day, if this is what they had to endure!*

Sadly, Lady Ashbourne had informed them that the surname Lennox was unknown in the *ton*, and so Izzy's quest to identify their father had fallen at the very first hurdle. They had decided instead to focus on Rose's mission, to discover who Mama's family might have been. It had been something of a relief to Izzy to let go of her quest, for somehow it had never seemed quite real to her. Surely the *fu-*

ture was more important than the past—and for Izzy, the immediate future looked like the most exciting thing that had ever happened to her.

After the hip roll, Mary added the stomacher, a flat piece of stiffened fabric dotted with beads and sparkling thread which she pinned directly to the stays. Finally they were getting to the outer layers which would actually be seen.

The gown petticoat was next, and Mary deftly arranged it over the hoop, moving and arranging it until she was satisfied. At last, Izzy donned the gown itself, and Mary secured it with multiple pins, before deftly stitching it to the edges of the stomacher in three places.

I have literally been sewn into this gown!

The notion was strange, but Izzy was fascinated to be trying the fashions of twenty or thirty years ago—probably the one time in her life she would have the opportunity to do so. The dress was of silk brocade, all in white with silver thread and thousands of tiny stones that made it sparkle and glimmer. It must have taken an entire team of seamstresses the entire fortnight to create three such delightful gowns *à la Française* for Izzy and her sisters.

With Mary's help she put on matching shoes, then the maid carefully placed the tiara and headdress on her head. Eyeing her critically, Mary circled all around her before declaring herself satisfied. In the distance, Izzy heard a clock chime. Why, the whole process had taken more than two hours, and she was supposed to be downstairs by now!

'I wonder how my sisters are faring,' she mused, a frown creasing her forehead. 'Dressing for court took much longer than I anticipated!'

'Never worry, miss, you are ready to go now,' Mary declared—just as the door opened to admit the housekeeper.

'Ah, good! You are ready, Miss Isobel. The others are

waiting downstairs, and the carriage is being brought around, for it is time to go!'

Swallowing against a sudden flutter of nervousness, Izzy thanked Mary, then made her way slowly and carefully down the wide staircase, fearful she might trip or that the tall feathers in her headdress might fall. Thankfully they seemed to be secure, and she was able to walk at a reasonably normal pace through the hallway to where her sisters waited, decked out in matching gowns. Only the tiaras were different.

'Oh, my dears!' Lady Ashbourne seemed momentarily overcome. 'You shall outshine them all, I declare!'

Lord Ashbourne, looking handsome in his formal dress, appeared from his library to bow to them all and tell them they looked beautiful. With a gesture he indicated they should precede him out to the Ashbourne coach.

Beautiful! No one had ever said such a thing to Izzy before, and she could not help but be gratified by it. As the coach made its way across Piccadilly and down the hill towards St James's Palace, she reflected upon this. While she had occasionally seen flashes of what might have been admiration in the gaze of young labourers and tradesmen in Elgin, she naturally could have no dealings with such young men.

Having been raised a lady in an exclusive school for the daughters of gentlemen, she knew herself to be too high for such men. Yet the trepidation in her stomach reminded her that attending court had never been an expectation either. With no known parentage, she and her sisters were too high for tradesmen, not high enough for court. Yet why should she not make her curtsy before the queen? Lady Ashbourne was sponsoring them, and their company manners were good.

So why do I feel like an impostor?

Gazing hungrily out of the carriage window, she tried
to take everything in: the bustling busyness of Piccadilly,
the tall, elegant buildings in St James's Street. Many of the
gentlemen's clubs were located there, including White's,
Brooks's, and Boodle's, they had been told. Certainly Lord
Ashbourne seemed to spend much of his time in his club,
and Izzy eyed the neoclassical façade of White's with interest as they passed it. What on earth did gentlemen do in
there all day and night? Abruptly, the carriage drew to a
halt, and they all looked instinctively to Lady Ashbourne.

'No, we have not yet arrived, my dears,' she chuckled.
'Instead we have joined the queue of carriages for today's
presentations at the palace. We must be patient.'

And patient they were, sitting for more than half an hour
as the carriage moved slowly, slowly forwards—through
the gates and gradually around the courtyard. It was a tight
squeeze within, for Izzy and Anna were seated either side
of Lady Ashbourne, while her nephew and Rose had the
rear-facing seats. Izzy's mind drifted once again to Lord
Ashbourne's describing them as beautiful, and her realisation it was the first time she had ever been described so.

Indeed, the closest she had ever previously come to
receiving a compliment from a gentleman had been that
drunken merchant's clumsy attempt to beguile her at the
inn in Grantham. While she could read nothing more than
politeness in Lord Ashbourne's words earlier, the merchant
had, she reflected, seemed to sincerely admire her—even
if such admiration had been fleeting and expressed in a
highly inappropriate manner. *Fair one*, he had called her
and likened her to golden Aphrodite, no less. Aphrodite,
the goddess of love and beauty, the golden epithet a familiar one from Izzy's studies of Homer's epics.

Golden…rather a trite reference to my hair colour, she thought sourly. He might have done better!

She shook her head slightly, catching the direction of her thoughts.

In the two weeks and more since the encounter at Grantham, on multiple occasions she had had to sternly remind herself not to think of him. She was becoming fairly good at *not* thinking of him—in the daytime, at least. And despite strong urgings, she had so far resisted drawing him in her sketchbook, even though she itched to do so.

Izzy loved to draw and paint and had something of a talent for it. She often gave gifts of sketches and miniatures at Christmastide or on her sisters' birthday.

I should do something for Lady Ashbourne, who has been so good to us.

And perhaps she could send a sketch of Lady Ashbourne to her brother in Elgin. Mr Marnoch had always encouraged her art. Yes, there was an entire list in her head of drawings she should work on. And yet the drawing she truly wanted to make—the one image she could never fully shake from her mind—was of a tall, handsome merchant, with fair hair and piercing grey eyes.

'Here we are, girls!' Lady Ashbourne's brisk tone alerted Izzy to the fact they had finally arrived. 'Veils on!' Their hostess was determined to reveal the fact they were identical only at the last possible moment, and so one of the dressmakers had suggested face veils for use in the palace antechamber. Izzy thrilled at the theatricality of it all, and her heart warmed to Lady Ashbourne who, it seemed, also had a taste for adventure.

Fixing her own veil over the bridge of her nose, Izzy attached it using the ear-loops, allowing it to fall below her chin. Carefully, she then descended from the carriage, trying not to knock the tall feathers in her head-dress. Looking about with curiosity while she waited for the others to emerge, she saw that the palace was of brick, with tall windows and what seemed like dozens of chimneys. While the king and queen no longer lived here all of the time—seemingly preferring Kew Palace and Buckingham House—the court of St James's was still the primary location for levees and ceremonies—including the presentation of débutantes.

'Ready?' Lady Ashbourne asked. They all stepped towards the double entrance doors to the building, when Izzy's attention was caught by some sort of disturbance behind her. Another carriage had pulled up—the last one in the queue, it seemed—and a middle-aged lady was currently scolding a younger lady who was, like the Lennox sisters, wearing a court gown and feather headdress. Another débutante!

About to feel quite sorry for the girl, Izzy abruptly changed her mind when the débutante replied to her mother's scolding in the strongest of terms and using language Izzy had only ever heard in Elgin's market. Her jaw dropped.

Well! Then she chuckled. *Perhaps, after all, I am not an impostor here!*

Chapter Three

Claudio stood rigidly upright, behind and to the right of Queen Charlotte and her ladies, who had the good fortune to be seated on the dais.

Lord, how many more?

The procession of débutantes had been continuing since noon, until it was all a blur of feathers and curtsies and proud mamas.

All his life he had endured occasions like this. He knew the protocol, knew what was expected of him. Yet here in England, following a number of weeks of a life without any protocol or ceremony whatsoever, he found himself inwardly fighting the necessity to stand still, although thankfully he knew his face was a picture of princely impassivity. Ennui such as he had never known threatened to overcome him. None of the young ladies had even had the grace to faint or swoon, which at least might have been briefly diverting.

Why, even now he might be in an alehouse, or at a cockfight, or playing faro with Hawkins and Eldon. His friends were not here today—indeed they had expressed their disgust at the very possibility—but had promised to meet him later, just as soon as he could get away.

Discreetly, he nodded to a servant who had just made

his way subtly up the Council Chamber—the large hall being used today as the queen's drawing room for the presentations. 'How many more?' he asked quietly, knowing the man had come from the antechamber.

'Three families, Your Highness.'

'Very good.'

Just three more! His relief was palpable. There was to be dancing and refreshments after the presentation, but Claudio had no intention of staying for long. No, once these final few high-born virgins had made their curtsies, he would make his escape. Not long now.

Just three families now stood in the high-ceilinged antechamber. As a red-haired maiden and her mama were taken through the ominous double doors into the queen's chamber, Izzy's attention turned once again to the foul-mouthed girl and her scolding mother. Never had she come across anyone quite like them, and her response was part fascination, part horror.

'For goodness' sake, pinch your cheeks, Charity!' the mother was currently demanding. 'You are as pale as paper. And I have told you before, quit slouching!'

Although pouting mutinously, Charity did as she was bade, at the same time taking the opportunity to send a cross glance in her mother's direction. 'I cannot believe I am to be presented last, Mama. It is not *fair*!'

'Indeed, I must agree with you there. Hold—wait one moment!'

Enthralled, Izzy watched as the girl's mother made her way to the door to address the major-domo. Since this personage looked terrifyingly important, Izzy had to admire the woman's audacity. While the palace maids fussed about, straightening her and her sisters' trains and headdresses,

Izzy's attention remained on what was now best described as an altercation. Voices were raised, the lady seemingly alternating between pleading and demanding. Through it all, the major-domo remained unmoved. As the general noise in the vicinity decreased briefly, Izzy, straining, was able to hear some of the man's words.

'As I have told you repeatedly, Mrs Chorley,' he declared evenly, 'débutantes are presented in order of arrival, and Lady Ashbourne arrived before you did.'

This statement, Izzy saw, had also attracted Lady Ashbourne's attention. Her gaze followed Mrs Chorley as, conceding defeat, she made her way back to her daughter. Abruptly, as if suddenly making a decision, Lady Ashbourne moved purposefully towards the major-domo.

Now what?

Frustratingly, Izzy could not hear what passed between them, but a moment later Lady Ashbourne returned, her eyes sparkling with glee.

'Well!' she declared in a low tone, 'I must say I have outdone myself! By dint of a recent fortuitous conversation with the major-domo, I have managed to ensure you will be the very last to be announced. Indeed it was, in the end, a fairly easy task,' she assured them, 'for normally no one wishes to be last, when the crowd may be restless, the queen bored, and the débutantes miserable with anxiety.'

'But—you prefer for us to be announced last?' Anna sounded puzzled, but Izzy knew exactly why Lady Ashbourne had done it.

She is clever, our sponsor!

'Indeed, I do. You will make an impact, girls, I know it. First or last, never the anonymous middle!' She eyed them all. 'Miserable with anxiety? Ha! Not my girls!' she declared, clear pride in her voice. 'Why, you are as serene as a bevy of swans!'

Serene was not perhaps the best word to describe how Izzy was feeling. Dressed in outlandish costumes from yesteryear, they were about to meet the queen, and judging by the anxiety displayed by many of the other young ladies and their sponsors, they had to behave impeccably. Abruptly Izzy was glad that Lady Ashbourne had made them rehearse their walk and curtsy at home. They had walked up and down her ballroom numerous times in the past few days—feathers on their heads and heavy curtains tied about their waists. Now they must perform it for real. Lord Ashbourne—who had been determined not to spend too long in the Council Chamber—now slipped inside, leaving only the ladies, the palace maids, and the major-domo.

Miss Chorley and her mother were called forward, and the major-domo admitted them. Even through her veil Izzy could discern the stiffness of Miss Chorley's shoulders. The girl was clearly nervous and despite her uncharitable behaviour, Izzy was able to feel a little sorry for her. Suddenly she grinned as she put two and two together. The girl's parents had thought it a good idea to christen their child Charity Chorley, and Izzy thought the absurdity of it entirely fitting.

Finally! At the back of the long hall, the double doors opened once again, and Claudio reawakened his attention. The last girl was about to enter, and soon he would be released from this prison of protocol. Apparently this was the third set of presentations this year, with another to follow next week.

Lord, how do they stand it?

The major-domo's voice rang out. 'Your Majesty, Your

Highness, my lords, ladies, and gentlemen. The final débutantes of the day. Lady Ashbourne presents the wards of her
brother, Mr Marnoch. Miss Lennox, Miss Isobel Lennox,
Miss Rosabella Lennox!'

Three of them? Well, this was unusual, indeed. Generally sisters were launched one at a time, the younger ones
waiting until the older ones were married. Sure enough,
instead of a single débutante, three slim figures were now
advancing serenely up the central aisle towards the dais.
They walked in perfect step—a clever ruse, and one which
drew the eye. Their white gowns glimmered and sparkled
as they moved, and Claudio noticed that the sound level in
the room had changed. First, an increase, as people commented on the audacity of launching three débutantes at
once, then a silence, spreading from the back of the hall
and running in a wave towards him. They were approaching steadily, and now he could make out the features of the
girl leading the way, the eldest, he assumed. Guinea-gold
curls, a perfect face—abruptly, he knew that the maiden
before him had eyes blue as cornflowers, and that he had
once compared her to golden Aphrodite. Briefly, his gaze
flicked to Aphrodite's sisters, and his hand tightened on the
hilt of the ceremonial sword by his side. His jaw loosened
in shock. Three of them! And identical in every feature!

His mind could not take it in. Bemused, his gaze flicked
from left to right, as if to check that what he was seeing
was real.

They had reached the dais. The two following flanked
the eldest, then at some unseen signal they curtsied in uni-
son, all the while keeping their eyes fixed on the queen.

'Lady Ashbourne!' said Her Majesty, the shock in her
tone evident.

'Yes, Your Majesty?'

'Where have you been hiding these delectable creatures? I declare I have never seen anything so pretty! Triplets, I declare!' She fluttered an elegant hand. 'La, and I thought only puppies were born in threes!'

Her ladies tittered, but Claudio remained in a state of such shock that he was struggling to know what to think. Not one but *three* golden Aphrodites, all identical.

But which is mine?

Desperately he searched their faces, but their attention was currently given fully to the queen.

Her Majesty rose to speak, and the girls and their sponsor swiftly moved aside. The eldest briefly glanced in his direction, but there were no signs of recognition on her beautiful visage.

Not her, then.

'My friends, I declare we have found our diamond of the Season. And not just one—but three of them!' With a gesture, the Queen indicated the sisters should face the crowd. 'Take your bow, my dears, and then come and sit by me!'

Now Claudio was faced with the sight of the three of them from the rear, again making that curtsy in perfect time with each other. Another realisation dawned. Aphrodite was no serving maid but rather a young lady of consequence, travelling to London to make her début.

What a fool I am! It is no wonder she was so disdainful of me!

Relief warred with mortification within him. Her disdain now had an explanation, and he was an idiot for not having realised she was gently born, and not therefore to be trifled with. But her clothing had been so drab...and of course he had not yet learned to decipher any subtleties of English speech that might have indicated her class.

Also, he belatedly realised, the girl who had afterwards

at the inn behaved towards him as though she had never seen him before was one of Aphrodite's sisters. Who had genuinely never seen him before. His brain felt as though it might ignite in flames as realisation after realisation dawned on him.

The queen's ladies had given up their chairs to Lady Ashbourne and her three débutantes, and as the hubbub in court resumed, Queen Charlotte began quizzing the girls' sponsor about them.

Yes, they were orphans.

No, Lady Ashbourne's brother had no information on their mother's or father's family… *None*—this said with a meaningful nod.

Their dowries were…respectable.

Yes, they had been gently educated and were the *sweetest* girls.

Fascinated, Claudio continued to shamelessly eavesdrop.

'Tell me your names again! And which of you was born first?' the queen demanded.

'I am Annabelle, the eldest.'

Not my Aphrodite.

'By twenty minutes!' the next one clarified, a hint of humour in her voice. 'I am Isobel.'

Is it you?

'And I am Rosabella. I was born a half hour after Isobel.'

Or you perhaps?

'Three babies in one confinement! Your poor, poor mother!' Her Majesty turned to Lady Ashbourne. 'Tell me more, my friend.'

'Well, they were each apparently known as *Bella* or collectively *the Belles* at school,' offered Lady Ashbourne. 'Until I learn which is which, it is how I refer to them.'

'Belle, Bel, and Bella,' repeated the queen. 'Yes, I see. Entirely apt.'

Belles, then, not Aphrodites. Claudio shrugged inwardly. *Belles. Beauties. Yes, just as apt.*

Turning slightly, the queen beckoned him to approach via a raised eyebrow.

Now is the moment. Holding his breath, he stepped forward.

'Claudio, may I introduce Lady Ashbourne, Miss Lennox, Miss Isobel Lennox, and Miss Rosabella Lennox?' Rising, they curtsied to his bow, and he kept his eye on the two younger ones. Miss Rosabella's expression was relaxed and open, while Miss Isobel—

Her eyes were wide, her jaw sagging, and as he watched she threw him a look of utter shock.

Aha! I have you, my Aphrodite!

'It is an honour to meet you,' he murmured, allowing a hint of irony to come through in his tone. Miss Isobel Lennox would know they had met before, and in unusual circumstances.

'Lady Ashbourne, Belles,' the queen continued smoothly, 'this is Prince Claudio Friedrich Ferdinand of Andernach, a distant cousin of mine. He is considering making his home in England. Is that not so, my dear?'

Lord, do not give them expectations of me!

Despite his father's instructions to find an English bride, Claudio knew his priorities for now did not include marriage. His priorities were wine, gambling, sport, bedsport, and more wine. And not always in that order.

'Nothing is as yet decided,' he replied, his tone as neutral as he could manage, and the queen laughed.

'Ah, but I always have my way in the end, Claudio. You know it!' Turning back to Lady Ashbourne and the Belles, she declared, 'Now, you diamonds must all go and mix with the assembly, for how are you to get husbands sitting here with two old ladies?'

'Not *old*, Your Majesty, surely?' returned Lady Ashbourne, a decided twinkle in her eye.

This earned a short laugh. 'Yet not young either, my friend!' The queen patted Lady Ashbourne's hand briefly. 'We bear our trials well, you and I.'

'We do.'

A warm look passed between them, and Claudio realised Lady Ashbourne was likely one of the true friends Queen Charlotte had told him about—a small group of *ton* ladies whom she felt she could trust. Something about the bond between the two women caused a momentary uneasiness within Claudio's gut, something to do with his own friends here. While he was enjoying kicking up larks with them, he could not truly call them friends. Not yet, leastwise. And yet, they were his friends in the usual sense of the word. He sought them out, spent most of his time with them, enjoyed their company.

His gaze searched the room, even though he knew neither Mr Hawkins nor Mr Eldon was there. Recalling his earlier determination to leave as soon as he could, he knew now that he had no intention of leaving. The Belles—the Aphrodites, the triplets, the Misses Lennox, the diamonds—were currently surrounded by admirers and well-wishers, but he knew the first dance was about to be called. He stepped towards the group.

This time, he thought grimly, *she will accept that I am a prince!*

Shock continued to reverberate through Isobel, affecting her ability to think clearly or to focus on the people currently surrounding her and her sisters. Her mind was racing, darting from one realisation to another.

It is him! He is *an actual prince! He is here—just yards from me!*

Her heart was pounding, her pulse fluttering wildly. At the same time, her stomach was sick with mortification and apprehension.

How I spoke to him! Will he wish for revenge on me? On all of us, because of my foolishness?

In the outside world, she was half responding to the group of people who had surrounded them, introducing themselves and making all of the usual comments about just how alike the girls were. *Yes*, she affirmed wearily. *We are identical.*

Vaguely she was aware that to her left some musicians were tuning their instruments, and she remembered Lady Ashbourne saying there would be dancing. Abruptly the crowd around them gave way a little. 'Your Highness,' they bowed, allowing the Prince to approach.

Oh, Lord! Now it comes!

'Good day, good day,' he murmured urbanely, eyeing Izzy and Anna. Those grey eyes, framed by lashes and brows a shade or two darker than his hair, were just as piercing as she had recalled. To their right Rose was busy in conversation with Lord Ashbourne and a dark-haired girl, and the group had clearly not noticed the arrival of the prince in their midst. After looking intently in their direction for a moment, the prince shook his head slightly, turning back to search the faces of Anna and Isobel. Desperately, and knowing exactly whom he was seeking, Isobel tried to keep all emotion out of her expression.

To no avail, for after a pause he bowed to her. 'Might I have this dance?'

Izzy, panicking, gestured towards Anna. 'My sister is the eldest, Your Highness, and by rights—'

'But you were all born on the same day, were you not?'

She nodded helplessly, and he held out his hand. 'Come, Miss Isobel. Dance with me.'

Her eyes widened.

He knows my name!

People usually took months if not years to tell them apart—particularly without the clues of coloured embroidery. Somehow she found herself walking with him towards the dancing area, her hand held in his. She could feel his warmth through her thin glove, and now the kaleidoscope of emotion within her gained a new colour: something golden, and bright, and sparkling. Something unwanted, and frightening, and wonderful.

He knows me!

They had reached the dance floor. Mimicking the other ladies, Izzy wound the long train of her gown twice around her left arm, then took a breath.

I am ready. Now, what will he say to me?

The musicians had not yet begun, and so the hum of conversation was continuing. To Izzy's relief a gentleman addressed the prince, and while he was busy replying, Izzy stole a glance at her dance partner. Yes, he was just as handsome as she remembered—and being sober improved his looks immeasurably, she thought dryly. Yet, even foxed, he had caused her heart to pound in the same way it was pounding now.

His conversation was ending, and instantly she looked about her as though she had been doing so the whole time. Rose, she noted, was in the next set being partnered by Lord Ashbourne, while Anna's hand had been claimed by a tall gentleman who was handsome in a rather forbidding sort of way. The entire situation was beyond belief.

We are in the queen's drawing room, dancing with titled gentlemen, and the queen has singled us out for favour, it seems!

Yet she could not enjoy their collective success, for standing before her was a man she had thought was a merchant, a man who had told her of his princely status and she had laughed.

I laughed at a prince.

Mortification rose within her again but, thankfully, the musicians had finally struck up the first dance.

I shall get through this, then escape.

It was the only strategy she could think of.

Curtsying to his bow as the dance began, she lifted her chin.

I can do this!

He fired the first arrows almost immediately. 'We have met before, Miss Isobel.'

Now, this was an easy feint to counter, for the triplets had all their lives made the most of being identical. Pausing as the dance took them apart for a few steps, she affected puzzlement when they came back together. 'I do not think so, Your Highness. I am certain I would recall—'

He chuckled. 'That will not do, Your Majesty, for I know it was you.'

She tossed her head. 'I am sure I do not know what you mean, Your Highness.' His words registered fully. 'Why did you call me *Your Majesty*?'

'Am I not addressing the Queen of Sheba?'

She flushed as his words hit home.

Oh, if only I had not been quite so scathing that day.

Laughing lightly, she frowned as if confused. 'The Queen of Sheba? What on earth are you talking about?'

When next the dance brought them together, his expression had changed. Now he looked grim, angry.

Oh, dear.

'You may deny it all you wish, but we both recall what happened that day. You were determined to deny that I might possibly be a prince, and you questioned my honour.'

Faced with such a direct accusation, Izzy felt rage rise within her. Ignoring the voice of caution in her mind—a voice that she associated with Anna's calm good sense—abruptly she abandoned all pretence. 'Well, think of it from my perspective. How likely was it that I would meet an actual prince in a random inn in—in *Grantham*, for heaven's sake!'

'You should have accepted my word,' he returned stiffly.

'Aye, and kissed you on your say-so, no doubt!' she returned scornfully and had the satisfaction of seeing a faint flush across his cheekbones.

'I—I did not know of your station when I said that.'

'So it is your habit to proposition maidens of a lower station, then? Always ensuring they know of your royal status? Have you had much success, *Your Highness*?' Her tone dripped with venom, and she felt his hand tighten on hers.

'I shall not deign to answer such a question.' His tone was low, but she knew she had riled him.

Oh, such dignity!

'So the answer is *yes*, then. And so, my *honourable* prince, are you ready to apologise to me for speaking to me in such a manner?'

'*I* apologise to *you*? You are the one who questioned my honour, without evidence or just cause!'

'Evidence? Just cause? You tried to kiss me, a defence-less female, alone in a hallway!'

Now anger flashed clearly in those grey eyes.

Have I gone too far?

'I did not!' he retorted. 'I asked for a kiss and accepted your refusal!'

'I—' To be fair, this was true. Momentarily speechless, yet still the anger within her flared higher at the sight of his self-satisfied expression.

'So are you planning to apologise for your wrongful accusation of dishonour?' he pressed, sure of his advantage.

No! The answer came instinctively. He might not have forced a kiss upon her, but he had made her feel decidedly uncomfortable, and even now it was clear he was not prepared to back down from his pillar of righteousness even a little.

The dance took them apart again—this time for him to turn every other lady in their set, and by the time he returned she was stonily determined. 'I suggest, Your Highness, that we endeavour to put this...*incident* behind us. We are clearly not destined to be friends, but London is surely large enough that we might avoid one another.'

'Agreed.' His tone was clipped, his expression disdainful. In silence they completed the dance, then went their separate ways.

Rose approached her as she left the dance floor, and alarm crossed her face as she read whatever expression Izzy was currently wearing.

'What happened?'

'Insufferable man!' Izzy could barely contain her anger.

'Who? Who is insufferable?' Rose glanced about, a perplexed expression on her face.

'That prince person! He thinks a great deal of himself, that one.'

He dared to ask me *for an apology!*

'As does the Viscount Ashbourne!' Rose retorted. 'He dared to try and advise me, as though I were a junior girl at Belvedere!'

Anna joined them, wearing a slight frown. 'Izzy! Rose! What has got you both in such high dudgeon?'

Briefly, Izzy gave her to understand that Prince Claudio was superior and conceited and thought very highly of himself, while Rose made her opinions of Viscount Ashbourne clear.

As ever, Anna remained calm. 'Izzy, he *is* actually a prince, you know. He may think as highly of himself as he wishes!' While she added some soothing words to Rose, Izzy's attention went inwardly.

He is *actually a prince.*

Well, yes, but did he need to be so lofty and condescending? Vaguely, she was aware that her outrage was tinged with both guilt and mortification, both of which were serving only to reinforce her current anger.

Rose glanced her way, bringing Izzy's attention back to her sisters. 'Still,' Rose declared cheerfully, 'we are here at the palace and dancing in court dresses. Who would have thought it possible just two months ago?'

Izzy snorted. 'Well, I should much rather be back at school, sewing, than suffering such arrogance!' Even as the words were spoken, she knew they were a lie. Coming to London was the best thing that had ever happened to her—despite the arrogance of a certain gentleman—er, prince. 'And Anna,' she continued hotly, 'you are wrong. Just because he happens to be a prince does not mean he can treat others with disdain!'

'Izzy!' Anna breathed in warning, making Izzy stiffen in horror.

Sure enough, the prince had joined them. Bowing, he smiled politely, his face a mask of impassivity. There was no doubt he had heard Izzy's words. She felt herself shrink in mortification.

'Having already danced with Miss Isobel,' he declared urbanely, tilting his head unerringly towards Izzy, 'I should now like to dance with each of her sisters.' He looked from Rose to Anna and back again. 'Which of you is Miss Lennox the eldest?'

Anna identified herself and walked away in step with him, her hand on his arm, while Izzy died a little inside. *Lord!* An instant later two other gentlemen came to claim Rose and Izzy for la Boulangere. Automatically Izzy accepted and was relieved when her partner—a fairly handsome gentleman who introduced himself as Mr Fitch—took her to a set at the bottom of the room, far away from the prince, who had clearly won their latest bout.

As the first couple linked their way around the circle Izzy stood impassively, pretending to watch, but in reality her mind was on Anna's current dance partner. Not by so much as a quiver had he revealed he had heard her insults, and his very composure demonstrated his royal quality. It was *she* who was lacking, she who had been rude, she who had let herself down—and in doing so she had let down her sisters, and Lady Ashbourne, and even Mr Marnoch and the Belvedere teachers, though they were far away in Scotland.

Mr Fitch tried to speak to her and, conscious of the need to redeem herself, she was more than polite to him. As the dance continued, she positively encouraged the man to converse with her.

See? she asked an invisible judge. *I am a lady of quality. I am not always rude or uncivil.*

Yet at a deeper level she was conscious of something that felt suspiciously like shame.

Claudio played his part in la Boulangere, his mind awhirl. The lady beside him was exquisite—the Belles, in his opinion and no doubt in many others, were the most beautiful maidens in the room. Moreover, Miss Anna was demure, polite, and pleasant. They enjoyed easy conversation about his journey to England, and he even told her of his father's pleasant memories of the country from his own visit more than twenty years ago.

Like Miss Rosabella, the youngest of the sisters, Miss Anna was the embodiment of an ideal. So why was Claudio's attention so caught by the middle sister? Why, when he could be enjoying a pleasant dance with a lady who was *exactly* as beautiful as Miss Isobel, was his mind still repeating and repeating the sound of her voice as she described him as arrogant, spoke of him treating people with disdain?

Is it true?

Instantly, he rejected the notion. Being mindful of one's position in life was not arrogance, it was simply a recognition of reality.

I was born a prince.

He could no more change that fact than he could his height or his eye colour. Thus reassured, he completed the dance, made his farewells to the queen, and departed from court without a backwards glance.

Chapter Four

Gradually, Claudio became aware that he was awake. Opening his eyes, he focused on a beam of bright sunshine streaming through a tiny gap in his curtains. Instinctively he glanced towards the clock on the mantel and gave a wry smile. Waking at midday was becoming quite a habit with him, and one that would have been abhorred back home. But then, many things were different here.

Since the clock had been striking four when he sought his bed, his late awakening was hardly to be wondered at. After the court presentations yesterday he had gone directly to White's, there to meet Eldon, Hawkins, and a group of merry young men. While Hawkins and Eldon were a little older, they behaved just as young men ought and indeed at times led the merriment. Together they had drunk copious glasses of wine, played cards, and talked of everything and nothing, before gradually drifting away to seek their rest.

Sitting on the edge of the bed Claudio yawned and stretched, absent-mindedly scratching his bare chest as he recalled yesterday's presentation at court—and in particular the realisation that his golden Aphrodite was part of the *ton*. He had thought to never see her again and had built around the Grantham memories a scaffold of impossible things. Yes, the reality of her was far removed from his romantical notions, for she was pert and judgemental, and her wasp-ish words had stung. Having falsely accused him of being dishonourable—an accusation that still rankled—she had gone on to accuse him of treating people badly. Something tight within his chest burned at the memory.

Dishonour.

Such an accusation went deep, for he had been raised to value honour above everything.

He shook his head, laughing softly at his own foolish-ness. All those times in his imagination where he had man-aged to persuade her for a kiss in that Grantham hallway now seemed absurd, for it seemed she heartily disliked him—a lowering notion. He was not accustomed to being disliked. He was, after all, a prince.

Ugh! Annoyingly, his thoughts had already gone to Miss Isobel, and he had only been awake for a few minutes! But he had much to think about. Miss Isobel and her sisters had been the talk of the club last night, with those who had been present at court regaling the others with tales of the impact they had made.

That entire conversation had left Claudio feeling strangely uncomfortable. When they were speaking of the triplets' beauty, he had felt a mix of pride and…*possessiveness*, al-most. As if by meeting Miss Isobel in Grantham, it had given him some sort of prior claim on her.

How odd!

It meant, too, when there had been deprecating com-ments made about their dowries—no better than *respect-able*, apparently—he had felt the strangest urge to come to their defence. Surely a person was worth more than their wealth? Naturally money mattered, but did it perhaps mat-ter too much to some of his new friends?

He shrugged, then used the chamber pot before crossing the room to wash before calling for his valet and fully opening the curtains. He himself had an adequate settlement from his father. If he did decide to live in England, it would undoubtedly be clever of him to marry an heiress, but he was in the fortunate position of not needing to do so.

Should I stay in England, I will need a townhouse.

Today he and his friends were to begin the Season tradition of house calls, and from what the others had said most of the *ton* lived within a three-mile radius of St James's Palace. Inwardly he admitted to a growing curiosity about the *ton*, their houses and traditions, their way of life.

This place, these people, might become my home.

Buckingham House, his current residence, was well-known amongst the *ton* as it was Queen Charlotte's favourite residence. Although the Queen herself always travelled by carriage, the distance between here and St James's was no more than a ten-minute walk, and living here suited Claudio very well. It would not do as a permanent home, however. Having grown up in his father's *Schloss*, he had a strange hankering for a different sort of residence, a different way of life. Something proportionate to a man, not a prince. Yes, a townhouse seemed appealing after a lifetime of castles and palaces. *If* he stayed.

His attention was drawn to movement in the gardens below. A gardener was conversing with a middle-aged kitchen maid amid box hedges and daffodils. The woman had a trug on her arm filled with vegetables and was clearly on her way back to the scullery door. As he watched, his mind still elsewhere, the maid happened to glance to where he stood in the first-floor window. Instantly her jaw dropped, a look of shock crossing her face.

What?

A moment later he remembered. English prudishness

meant they were uncomfortable with nakedness, unlike his own countrymen. In his father's principality, the doctors had recommended sun therapy and enjoyment of nature as health-giving. People swam in the lakes and rivers in the summertime, and there were not the same puritanical attitudes as he had been informed were common here. Sighing, he stepped away from the window, and was already donning his shirt when the valet arrived.

As he dressed, his mind returned to last night's conversations about the Belles—which, it seemed, was to be society's name for the Lennox triplets. The most difficult moments for him had been the scathing comments made by some about the girls' parentage. Apparently the sisters had been raised as ladies and were accepted as such, yet no one could say who their parents had been. This seemed to be a matter of some importance to the *ton*, though Claudio was uncertain why this was the case. Of course one's lineage was important, but outside of royalty or matters of inheritance, surely it should not matter that the Belles did not know the names and backgrounds of their parents? The girls were making no claims on anyone, and were surely entitled to be part of the Season without their names being bandied about so critically.

Although Miss Isobel had royally irritated him and had chosen to dislike him—why, he could not fathom— he was man enough to separate that from the inappropriate tittle-tattle being flung about. What had been her other wounding words? Oh, yes. She had accused him of *treating others with disdain.* Since this was something he had not nor would ever do, he was trying to dismiss her tantrum as being motivated by momentary anger. So why did the memory still sting so?

He had come to London for the chance to be himself.

Not Prince Three of Four in his family. His brothers were all that was admirable, but at court, the four sons of the ruling prince had been seen as something of a set. All well-behaved. All respectful of their father and of their positions within the principality. All lacking in individuality, in passion, in distinctiveness. Here, he could be Claudio.

If only he knew who Claudio was.

Miss Isobel certainly believed she knew. Her judgements were based upon the briefest of acquaintance, and it bothered him that she had formed such a damning impression of him. Yes, he had spoken to her in Grantham in a way that had not been appropriate for her station. But he had done her no harm.

I am not a bad person.

Acknowledging briefly the uncomfortable feelings now swirling within him, with determination he pushed them away, diverting his attention elsewhere. The treatment of three sisters who were almost strangers to him was none of his concern, and the opinions of one of them certainly had no relevance to him. His energy would be better spent considering his activities for the coming week.

While there would be visits to the *ton* at-home where he might be in the company of débutantes, there were also plans for fencing and boxing sessions at the hands of London's finest teachers, a card party in Hawkins's bachelor apartments, a trip to see a horse race at Hampstead later in the week, and of course, endless nights of wine and ale.

Life is good.

Striding out of Buckingham House, Claudio's step was light and his heart lighter.

Izzy was in alt.

This is why I came to London!

Yes, she had a quest to try and discover the identity of her father, but since they did not even know who Mama was, and the surname Lennox was unknown, she had no realistic starting point to begin. Sensibly, she thought, she had decided to shelve the matter for now. And besides, it was the *ton* who likely had the information she and her sisters needed. And so mingling with the *ton*, getting to know everyone, was the best way to advance her cause.

Satisfied with her own logic, she turned her attention back to the present. This afternoon Lady Ashbourne was hosting callers, and callers had come in droves. The large drawing room of Ashbourne House was full to bursting with gentlemen of the *ton*, many of whom had brought or sent flowers for the Belles. Many ladies had come too, and the place was thronged.

Growing up in a school was all very well, but for years Izzy had craved company and excitement and a place where one had a wide circle of acquaintances. The Belles would be here until the summer, and Izzy intended to make the most of every moment.

Scanning around the room, it thrilled her to think these were all people she would get to know but did not know yet. And they were all so stylish! With a silent prayer of gratitude for her guardian's generosity, Izzy smoothed her hands over her pretty muslin gown. She tended to wear greens and yellows, and this gown had tiny printed flowers and leaves all over the fabric, the hem trimmed with not one but two ruffles.

Such extravagance!

The court gown yesterday had been astonishing, but to Izzy's eye, today's dress was both prettier and more flattering.

As the afternoon progressed Izzy lost count of all the

people she conversed with. Having desired new company for years, she was eager to become acquainted with as many people as possible. Mr Fitch, who had danced with her at court yesterday was there, as was a Mr Kirby, and both of them offered her flattery and flimflam, which she managed to take without rolling her eyes. Both seemed solid, sensible gentlemen, and while Mr Fitch was rather better-looking, Mr Kirby had kind eyes.

The flattery was novel, though not unwelcome—even if she did not quite believe their outrageous compliments. These past couple of days had given her the impression that she and her sisters were considered good-looking, and such attention was new to her. Briefly her mind flicked to a certain gentleman likening her to Aphrodite, but she pushed the thought away. He had not come, and she was not particularly surprised. Her words last night had been harsh, she knew, and spoken in anger…but she could do nothing about that now.

Excusing herself, she left Mr Fitch and went to greet Miss Chorley and her mother, who had just arrived. They were, she thought, a perfect example of what her teachers had called *vulgar*, and Izzy was gleefully interested in them. She knew herself to be something of a rebel, but never would she behave in a way that was vulgar. To meet people who were so unaware or uncaring of their demeanour was fascinating to her.

'I told you the gentlemen would all be here, Charity. Look, the Earl of Garvald!' Mrs Chorley was muttering to her daughter as Isobel approached.

'Welcome, welcome!' declared Lady Ashbourne, bustling across to them before Isobel could get there. 'Mrs Chorley, it is lovely to see you again. And your pretty daughter! I trust you are well?'

'I am well, thank you. And are you well, Lady Ashbourne?'

Lady Ashbourne confirmed it, and Mrs Chorley continued in a rush, 'I wanted to thank you again for kindly allowing my dear Charity to precede your *delightful* charges yesterday!'

The word *delightful*, Izzy noted wryly, was uttered as if through gritted teeth.

Stepping forward, she exchanged greetings with the pair, then offered to take them to the other part of the room, where there was a vacant settee. 'Just there, can you see?' she said, pointing. 'Next to the Earl of Garvald.'

'Indeed!' Mrs Chorley's gaze swivelled instantly to the Earl. 'How fortuitous! I mean, that there should be *any* settee free, for you have no shortage of visitors!'

'Indeed we are very fortunate,' Izzy replied noncommittally, leading them to the settee and seating herself alongside the pair.

To her no great surprise she was promptly ignored by the Chorleys, whose attention was fully given to conversing with the taciturn earl, whose good looks, Izzy thought, were almost spoiled by his closeness. He answered every Chorley query with equanimity, politeness, and brevity, and Izzy felt an unexpected giggle bubble within her.

Why, this is as good as watching a play!

Not that she had ever seen a play—not in real life, leastways. The scenes she and the other Belvedere girls had played out occasionally at school did not count.

Perhaps I can visit the theatre, here in London.

Oh, it was such an adventure to be here! A pang went through her at the realisation that her visit would inevitably end, but she pushed it away.

After a few moments Garvald bowed and left them, and

the Chorleys, seemingly undeterred, began finally to engage in conversation with her, their gaze flitting around
the room all the while. They were clearly in search of a
better option—which might have been a deflating thought
to anyone more sensitive than Izzy. But she cared nothing
for what such people thought of her. In that regard she was
armoured against hurt. Unlike—

'Sit up, Charity!' Mrs Chorley's tone was almost a hiss.
'He has arrived!'

Startled, Izzy froze as she put together what was happening. She had no need to turn her head to see who had
just entered the drawing room. Keeping her eyes fixed on
her companions, she noticed that the hum of conversation
in the room quieted for a moment then increased, as though
time had briefly stood still and was now rushing to catch
up with itself.

The cynic within her curled a lip at the sycophancy of the
ton, despite the woman in her being foolishly desperate to
look at him. Thankfully she had enough strength of character to resist, maintaining her attention on Miss Chorley.
Unfortunately the latter was gazing hungrily towards the
door—or, more accurately, the person who had just entered.

'Scotland,' she murmured, drawing both Chorleys back
to her. 'You asked where my sisters and I grew up,' she reminded them, amused by the identical blank looks they
were giving her. 'In Elgin, actually. It is near Inverness.'

'How sad for you!' Mrs Chorley's tone dripped with false
sympathy. 'So far away from everyone and everything of
importance. We live in London, naturally, and my husband
has also purchased a *darling* little country estate for us to
take refuge in during the hotter months. No more than forty
acres, you understand, but it is in the heart of Kent. It cost
a pretty penny, I assure you!'

She went on to add the exact amount paid by Mr Chorley, and an uncomfortable feeling settled in Izzy's chest on hearing Mrs Chorley's words. One did not speak so plainly of such things! It was simply not…polite.

Distaste, she realised. *I feel distaste.*

Then, a moment later, the understanding that somehow, between Mama and Mr Marnoch and the Belvedere teachers, she genuinely did have a sense of what was appropriate behaviour and what was not. Vulgarity was indeed real and embodied in Mrs Chorley and her daughter.

How strange!

She caught her breath. Without conscious thought, as her attention had been briefly diverted by Mrs Chorley, her head had slowly turned, and now the prince was in her line of vision. Instantly her stomach seemed to flip, her mouth went dry, and her heart began thudding loudly. Abruptly, it dawned on Izzy that she had been hoping for his arrival—or awaiting it, at least.

It must be because he vexes me so much.

Hungrily she took everything in at a glance. His fair hair and strong profile. His broad shoulders, trim figure, and strong legs perfectly displayed by the current fashion for tight coats and breeches. Lord, it was unfair that any man should be so handsome…particularly when his good looks were matched by his arrogance!

This day is not for him, she reminded herself. *It is for me and Anna and Rose to finally experience being out in society. I refuse to let him spoil everything.*

With some effort she dragged her gaze away from him lest he catch her looking, instead focusing on his companions. Both gentlemen were older; perhaps in their early thirties, so around ten years older than the prince. One was portly, with a round red face, while the other was tall and gaunt. They had clearly arrived together. She frowned. Why on earth would a young man such as the prince seek the company of men who were so much older? Perhaps he was more sober than she had imagined. Strangely this elevated her impression of him, suggesting a gravitas she had previously thought lacking. Did she *wish* to think well of him? She shook her head, rejecting the notion. She would do better to not think of him at all. Besides, it was entirely possible that the other two gentlemen had coincidentally arrived at the same time as Prince Claudio.

'Who are those gentlemen with the prince, Mama?'

Instantly her attention swivelled to the Chorley ladies. *Yes, I should also like to know this.*

'The tall one is Mr Eldon, and the other is Mr Hawkins. They are the prince's closest companions, by all accounts. Let us go and speak with them.'

With the briefest of farewells to Izzy they were gone.

It is a good thing, she thought wryly, *that I am not easily put out by such behaviour.*

And yet the prince himself had also managed to stir her to an unexpected degree. Because she was still cross with him, no doubt.

Mr Kirby returned to sit with her and engage in empty conversation. It took very little to reply to him, while at the same time her mind was busy ruminating on her response to the prince. Undoubtedly he had been arrogant in Grantham, and his ruse of trying to get a kiss by telling her he was a prince still enraged her. Surely a man should stand on his own merits and not by any unearned plaudits, such as royal birth? And yet, did she not also expect others to treat her with particular respect simply because she had been raised a lady? Oh, it was all too complicated! One thing was certain, though: the *ton* was determined to fawn over him. Which strengthened her resolve to do exactly the opposite.

Lord! I have done it again!

Having resolved earlier not to even *think* of him, she had in fact been lost in thought for quite a number of minutes. With determination she turned her attention back to Mr Kirby who was still talking. Stifling a sigh—for poor Mr Kirby was dreadfully dull—she focused on his words.

'And so I would be honoured, Miss Isobel, if you and your sisters would join me in my box at Drury Lane.'

Suddenly she was all attention. 'The theatre? I should like that!' She frowned. 'But I do not think we can go without Lady Ashbourne.'

He laughed. 'Well, naturally! I shall of course invite a couple of gentlemen to make up the numbers...' He considered the matter. 'The *right* gentlemen. Not—but perhaps—yes, I must think on this.'

All the while, the prince had been standing near the fireplace, fully within her line of vision. With half an ear on Mr Kirby's deliberations, she could not help but notice that Mrs Chorley and her daughter were still with the prince and his friends, and the five of them seemed to be getting along famously. As she watched, the prince turned his head slightly, and their eyes met. Instantly she stiffened, her breath catching in her throat and her heart skipping a beat. After a long moment during which she was trapped by his gaze, she came to her senses.

Lord! I am caught looking at him!

Turning away, she laughed as though Mr Kirby had said something full of wit and wisdom. 'Oh, Mr Kirby, I am certain you will invite exactly the right people!'

Thankfully her companion seemed not to notice anything amiss, and they continued to converse for another ten minutes, Isobel acting as though Mr Kirby was the most interesting person in the entire world. It was only when he commented how delightful and unusual it was for a young lady to remain in extended conversation that she suddenly realised she was perhaps encouraging him in a way she had not intended. 'You are right, of course, and so you must go now, Mr Kirby. I should not wish anyone to think I was paying you particular attention!'

Much struck, he replied with great animation. 'Indeed, no! I would not for the world compromise your reputation in any way, Miss Isobel.' He rose and bowed over her hand. There was a light in his eye that gave Izzy a momentary discomfort.

Oh, dear! Does he think I have a particular liking for him?

Briefly alone again, Izzy's uncomfortable thought was that she did not wish for…*anyone* to think her unpopular. Rising, she made her way to where Anna and another lady were in conversation with the Earl of Garvald. Lady Mary Someone, she recalled. Deliberately, she kept her back turned to the prince and his friends, and when she next looked he was gone.

After that, the party felt oddly flat. Was she really so focused on one arrogant man that she might allow it to detract from this wonderful day? Sadly, it seemed she was. Still, at least he was gone, and she no longer had to worry about inadvertently meeting his gaze or, worse, having to make polite conversation with him. Yes, it was so much better without him.

Having worked out some of his frustrations in Gentleman Jackson's boxing saloon, Claudio prepared for another night out in London. From now on, his friends assured him, their evenings would be taken up with soirées, musicales, theatre performances, and balls as the Season got properly underway. Claudio also had a responsibility to his cousin the queen, who had requested his attendance at some of her own gatherings. Still, at least for some of the time he and his friends could choose their own diversions.

Tonight, Hawkins was taking them to a discreet club off St James's, a club where, he was assured, the stakes were higher than the usual fare. Undoubtedly there would also be good wine, possibly ale, and perhaps even good French brandy. All of the elements were there for another night of drinking, gambling, and generally being free of the sort of scrutiny and expectations he was subjected to at home.

So why was his mind hankering back to the tea and conversation he had endured earlier in Lady Ashbourne's drawing room? Surely those were exactly the sort of tedious events he had so abhorred back home? And yet… something within him had welcomed the familiar rhythms of social chit-chat. Meeting new people, observing others… He had engaged in relatively interesting conversations with some of the gentlemen: Garvald, Ashbourne, Phillips. All had seemed sober and sensible…and dull as ditch-water in comparison to his own merry friends.

All three Lennox sisters had been present—well, naturally they would be, given that Lady Ashbourne was their sponsor for the Season. While he had initially struggled to identify which was Miss Isobel, he had worked out before long that the one in the pink-trimmed dress and the one in the blue gown were unlikely to be her, as they had both greeted him in an unaffected way. The one in the yellow-and-green print muslin, however… He stifled a grin. She had made such a show of *not* looking at him that it had to be Isobel.

And then there had been that moment when they had locked eyes and the world had seemed to pause for a moment. Deliberately he released his breath, shocked by the realisation that this young lady was beginning to become something of an obsession with him.

Perhaps tonight he should seek a bed-mate, someone to distract his mind and return it to the evenness he had taken for granted. Yes, that was a good plan. Most of the clubs had courtesans working for them or serving maids willing to earn extra coin. Deliberately, he took a guinea from his strongbox, the golden colour exactly like her hair. Kissing it, he slipped it into his watch-pocket rather than his purse. Yes, that would banish the ghosts that haunted him, the intrusive thoughts he did not choose to think. A night on the town, some wine, and a willing bed companion, and he would be like a new man!

'Move over, then!'

Izzy shuffled up to the top of the bed, leaning against the wall and rearranging the pillows behind her. Anna and Rose had come to her chamber for a night-time chat. They were getting used to their individual bedchambers here in London, though it was the first time in their lives they had slept apart. Izzy would never have admitted it, but she missed their company: Anna's wise counsel, Rose's dreaminess, the sound of their breathing as they slept. And so they had developed the habit of coming together each night to exclaim at their new experiences and share their impressions of London. Tonight, Rose was sharing novel information, having discovered that the whole aim of the Season—including being presented to the queen—was so that débutantes could attract husbands.

'And so, we are to hope for vouchers to an assembly

room called Almack's, which is the height of this *marriage mart.*' Rose's opinion on this was evident from her grimace and her scathing tone.

'So the whole thing is one enormous social whirl, designed to fire off their daughters?' Anna sounded as incredulous as Izzy felt.

How sordid!

Instantly, her mind reviewed the behaviour of the gentlemen at court and in Lady Ashbourne's drawing room. Given this shocking new information, their behaviour— even that of Mr Kirby and Mr Fitch—suddenly had new significance.

And as for Miss Chorley and her mama, who marched straight up to...

But no, it was the gentlemen who were the buyers in this unsavoury Marriage Mart.

She shuddered. 'And as for the gentlemen... I suppose they circle about, making judgements on the worthiness of the young ladies?' In her mind's eye she could see the prince, loftily judging every young lady in the room. She also now recalled that the queen had sent them off to dance, asking them how they were to get husbands otherwise. At the time she had thought it an idle jest—the sort of thing unmarried ladies were used to hearing. 'I can just imagine... Ugh! How appalling!'

Anna was, as always, leaning towards the practical and calmly pointed out it would actually make sense for them to marry. And it did. Of course it did. Married ladies had more security and more freedom than spinsters. And it would prevent them from being dispatched back to quiet Elgin at Season's end... The thought was an interesting one and worthy of more consideration when Izzy had time to think.

Hmmm...

Regardless, even if she did decide to marry, Izzy could not but be outraged at the thought of being an item for sale in a marketplace.

If I marry, it will be to a man of my choosing, and I shall choose with care.

This led to another thought—a worrying one.

Can we choose husbands from among the ton*?*

Mama had been a lady; that much was clear. She had had a Season. But that knowledge was not enough. For many reasons they needed to discover exactly who her family had been, not least because it would not do to accidentally marry someone who turned out to be a relative! Lightly, she mentioned the possibility.

'Let us only flirt with gentlemen who cannot possibly be closely related to Mama or our unknown papa,' she declared lightly, and they all laughed. The very notion of flirting seemed odd. And yet, Mr Kirby might reasonably believe that was what she had been doing this very afternoon.

Is he, then, on the hunt for a wife?

Lord, but life here was so much more complicated than in Elgin!

'But seriously, how are we to do so, when we have no idea of Mama's maiden name?' Anna frowned, then an idea seemed to come to her, for she added, a hint of slyness in her tone, 'I suppose foreign princes must be a safe option, eh, Izzy?'

Izzy's mouth was suddenly dry. 'Not at all' she managed, 'for the prince in question let slip that his own father lived here for a few years, more than twenty years ago.' *Ha!* He had told Anna exactly this during their court dance, so she would know it was true. 'Besides—' she adopted a nonchalant air '—I could never consider aligning myself with anyone so arrogant.'

Thankfully Anna did not labour the point, and the conversation moved on to their quest to find out about their origins. It all went back, Izzy knew, to Mama's decision to leave England and live quietly in Scotland. Had she run away from home and family because of her situation?

Anna had clearly wondered the same. 'To be with child is ruinous for an unmarried lady of the *ton*. Perhaps Mama ran away—'

'Or was rejected by her family—' Izzy interjected.

'Because she was with child.'

'With child…us?' Rose's hand went to her mouth. 'Oh, poor, poor Mama!'

'That may not be what happened,' Anna returned, ever cautious. 'We simply do not know. Our first step must be to discreetly discover who she was.'

'That will then lead us to *him*—our father, I mean. If any of his family are here, we should confront them!' Izzy declared, a sense of righteous anger flooding through her. 'I would know the truth, and soon! Why was she abandoned so? Was it her family's fault? Or does the responsibility lie at our father's doorstep? Perhaps these Stuarts—?' Rose had been informed the surname Lennox was associated with the Stuarts of Scotland.

Anna's tone was scolding. 'Lord, Izzy, quit being so devilish, and take your head out of those Gothic novels. This is not a story in a book.' Izzy made to answer, but Anna talked on. 'This is *real*. And real life is always more…'

'Practical?' offered Rose, with only a hint of wryness. Anna was always practical.

'Yes, more *practical* than a storybook. Our papa died, remember? And Mama always described him as a good man. The truth may be entirely prosaic. She may have simply married someone her family disapproved of. But speculation is useless, so I suggest we quit guessing and instead focus on finding out if anyone in the *ton* remembers Mama.'

They left soon afterwards, and as she blew out the candle, Izzy knew sleep might prove elusive tonight. Her head was full of evil relatives throwing Mama out in the cold, of prospective suitors judging her as though she were a prize ewe, and supercilious princes who would no doubt enjoy every moment of the Marriage Mart. After tossing and turning in her comfortable bed, Izzy finally dozed off, only to dream of a dreary life as Mrs Kirby or Mrs Fitch.

Chapter Five

'Sir! Sir!' The voice was relentless, insistent, annoying. Finally though, it pierced his slumbering. 'You have to wake up! It is time to go!'

Groaning, Claudio opened his eyes, wincing as morning light sliced painfully into his skull through his eye sockets. '*Ja, ich stehe auf!* I'm getting up!'

The young woman's face was vaguely familiar. 'Good,' she retorted, 'for I must go to work soon!' Turning away, she finished fastening the buttons on her bodice, and he established that she was fully dressed.

What happened last night?

Turning onto his back, he groaned again as his head throbbed with pain. Closing his eyes, he let memories wash over him. Following his friends through a discreet archway in Mayfair. Gambling in the club in Pickering Court. Flirting with the maid. Her taking him by the hand up some winding stairs. Then—nothing. Nothing at all.

'What happened last night?' he managed, propping himself up on his elbow.

She sniffed. 'You fell asleep. Too much wine.' She raised an eyebrow, adding pertly, 'Your spirit was willing…'

But my flesh was weak. Damnation!

'I thought that quote referred to one's ability to *resist* temptation, not indulge in it!'

She sniffed again. 'Then, wine is surely the solution to the so-called evils of decadence, sir.'

Too much wine.

Shock was now shuddering through him as he realised that for the first time in his adult life he had failed to make the most of a promising situation.

'And now you must go, sir.' Her tone was firm.

'Yes, yes of course!' Lumbering to his feet, he felt woolly-headed and exhausted, while his head was thumping a dull ache with every beat of his heart.

Lord, I am wine-sick!

Never had this happened to him before. Oh, he had seen it in others—occasionally at home, and many times since arriving in England. Hawkins and Eldon were normally incapable of coherent speech before noon, and he had learned not to call on them in the morning, even should he himself feel fresh as a daisy. Which he usually did. Not today, though.

Must have been the cheap wine.

Half an hour later he was back at the palace, his watchpocket lighter and his head still heavy. It was barely nine o'clock and only servants were about, thank goodness. What he needed was a few hours' more sleep, then he would be right as rain. He stiffened. Was that judgement he was seeing in the eyes of the queen's servants? Stiffening his shoulders, he continued through the lofty hallway with eyes directed straight ahead until he reached the sanctuary of his chamber. There he closed the curtains, summoned his valet, and a little later sank down onto the bed into welcome oblivion.

Izzy was once more in her element. Today they were making social calls, and her mind was dancing with dazzling details of people and places: society families and their beautiful mansions. Tea was *de rigueur*, served in delicate china and with delicious pastries. Lady Jersey had been welcoming and entertaining, the Andertons a little dull, and the Phillipses kind and friendly. Oh, and there had been Lord and Lady Wright, too. It was all a long, long way from Latin lessons in the Belvedere School for young ladies.

And now they were drinking tea yet again—this time in the delightful home of Lady Kelgrove. Izzy stifled a happy grin. The elderly lady had a spark of devilment in her eye that was calling for Izzy to match it. When they arrived she had pushed herself out of her armchair with the aid of a sturdy stick, which was now resting by her chair. Oak, Izzy guessed, with a silver handle.

Lady Kelgrove already had visitors when they entered— a middle-aged couple called Mr and Mrs Thaxby. Sneaking a glance at Mrs Thaxby, Izzy was amused to see a sullen expression on the lady's face. The source of her discontentment was clear: Lady Kelgrove was much more interested in the Lennox sisters than in the Thaxbys.

Human nature is no different here than in Scotland.

Quizzing Lady Ashbourne at length about their presentation—which she had clearly heard about but had not herself attended—Lady Kelgrove wished to know every detail of the queen's conversation about them. At this, the Thaxbys recalled another engagement and took their leave.

They were barely out of the door when Lady Kelgrove gave a self-satisfied chuckle, banging her stick on the floor and declaring wickedly, 'They can take a hint, it seems! Good, for if I was forced to bear their company much longer I might have had a sudden fainting fit or bad turn. Nothing, I assure you, can clear a room more quickly than illness!'

Lady Ashbourne laughed, shaking her head. 'You are a wicked, wicked woman, Lady Kelgrove.'

'Ah, but you know me well, Sarah,' she replied, leaning across to tap Lady Ashbourne's hand with clear affection. 'I am eighty-four,' she informed the triplets. 'And when one is eighty-four, one can say and do almost anything.'

Izzy could not resist. 'Then, I can barely wait to reach eighty-four, for at twenty-one, one can say and do almost nothing at all!'

'Is that so?' Lady Kelgrove's tone was sharp, but Izzy was undaunted.

I have the measure of her, I think.

'I see you have some opinions, Miss Lennox. Which one are you, again?'

'I am Isobel,' Izzy replied evenly. They held each other's gaze for a moment, Izzy understanding she was being thoroughly examined, then Lady Kelgrove cackled with mischievous delight. 'Ha! I predict you will do well, Miss Isobel.'

Turning back to Lady Ashbourne she resumed her questioning, asking about their dowry and family.

'Are there any clues as to their parentage?'

Lady Ashbourne pressed her lips together. 'None. There is no Lennox listed in *Debrett's*.'

'Hmph. Not good. A tradesman or servant, perhaps?'

'Perhaps.'

'It would not be the first time. Nor will it be the last. Still, they are pretty as well as being pretty behaved. They should attract some offers at least.'

Offers.

The Marriage Mart again. Earlier, Lord Ashbourne had told them that with small dowries and the possibility of illegitimacy, Izzy and her sisters might not attract what he referred to as *stellar offers*. Speaking plainly, he had advised that realistically they should look for husbands among the older gentlemen or what he had described as 'those at the fringes of society desirous of a marriage to someone who will appear ladylike'.

Izzy had flinched then and felt her insides clench again now at the notion that in this Marriage Mart, she was less of a prize ewe and more an untried gimmer, a young female with no history of safe lambing behind her, and therefore of less value. And all because of the possibility their birth had been somehow scandalous. That Mama had been un-married and possibly thrown out by her family.

Not that Izzy wished to marry, anyway. She consid-ered the matter. Leaving school to come to London was the greatest adventure she had ever had, and it had left no space in her mind to think of her future. Perhaps she would marry, one day. Maybe she would fall madly in love, like the heroines in some of the Gothic novels. But no, for she could never be so insipid, swooning and crying over some man. Yet she would like to be a mother someday. Yes, the question bore consideration.

She brought her attention back to Lady Kelgrove. 'Who knows, Sarah?' she was saying. 'They might even outgun the Gunnings!'

The Gunnings? Izzy didn't recall meeting anyone with that name.

Lady Ashbourne then explained that the Gunning sis-ters had taken the *ton* by storm sixty years before and had both made impressive marriages despite their dubious back-ground.

'Maria Gunning had a tremendous rivalry with Kitty Fisher, as I recall,' Lady Kelgrove said thoughtfully, 'once Kitty became involved with Coventry. They even argued

in the park one day. How I should have loved to have witnessed it!'

Involved?

Izzy, realising what Lady Kelgrove must be referring to,
felt a sense of shock laced with fascination.

Ladies of the ton *sometimes take lovers. I wonder, if I
married Mr Fitch, or Mr Kirby, could I perhaps...?*

'Yes, well, perhaps we should not speak of such matters,'
said Lady Ashbourne primly, with a nod to the triplets. 'At
least, not in present company.'

'Stuff!' declared Lady Kelgrove bluntly. 'I firmly believe
that girls should know of the real world once they make their
debuts. I wish I had known more than I did. And I wish
I had been more open with my own daughter and granddaughter.' She shrugged. 'But I can do nothing now about
might-have-beens. Let me advise you, Sarah. Ensure these
girls are well-informed and well-prepared. They have good
faces and fine figures, their manners are good, and they have
you as sponsor. The Gunnings had no dowries to speak of
and had even performed on the stage before their debuts. If
anyone asks me, I shall say that your protégées may look as
high as they wish for a husband!'

As high as we wish.

Shaking her head against the absurd notion that had
just popped into it, Izzy reminded herself that certain men
might *look* beautiful, with sculpted features and intense
eyes and fine figures, but if, sadly, they were arrogant it
mattered not a jot!

They left soon afterwards, and in the carriage Lady Ashbourne warned them that her nephew had the right of it.
For all that Lady Kelgrove wished them well, without more
details of their parentage she believed they were unlikely
to marry well.

If we marry at all! Izzy thought defiantly. And yet...

Somehow a seed had been sown within her. The alternative was what? Returning to rural Scotland to become a spinster teacher or marry a clergyman or farmer who had never gone farther than Inverness or Aberdeen? She shuddered. That would most certainly not do. Having had a taste of *ton* life, she already knew that here was where she wanted to be. And so logic dictated she should give consideration to other possibilities.

Gentlemen like Mr Kirby and Mr Fitch were clearly flirting with the triplets despite being aware of their lack of known background and dowries that were no better than *respectable*. With a ring on her finger Izzy could remain here at the centre of society, avoiding banishment back to Scotland at the end of the Season... Yes, the notion definitely required more thought.

Lady Ashbourne was still explaining why Lady Kelgrove's optimism was, in her opinion, unfounded. 'The Gunning sisters had their Season sixty years ago. What happened then was highly unusual and has never been repeated. I fear my nephew has the right of it when it comes to London society today.'

'So we should not expect offers of marriage from anyone of note?' Anna's voice was low.

Their hostess grimaced. 'I cannot lie. It will be highly unlikely with the possibility of illegitimacy hanging over you. You may look perhaps among the professional classes, but not the *ton*. Or at least, none of the titled gentlemen.'

And certainly not a royal prince.

'Well, that is a good thing,' declared Izzy brightly, 'since we have not come here to search for husbands but to search for information about our parents.'

Which was true, and yet Izzy's brain was currently fired

with speculation. What might be the benefits of a marriage
to someone like Fitch or Kirby? Both were gentlemen without a title. Both were clearly part of the *ton*. Both seemed to
admire Izzy and her sisters. Could they—could *she* perhaps
bring one of them up to scratch? And did she even wish to?

The weeks went on, and Izzy and her sisters became lost
in a whirl of excursions and musicales, theatre trips and
routs. Izzy loved every minute of it: the fashion, the excitement, the large circle of acquaintances they were building. Naturally, as in any group, there were people she was
more drawn to, like the indomitable Lady Kelgrove and the
vivacious Lady Jersey. Their own dear Lady Ashbourne
was a darling, of course, and some of the other débutantes
were warm and genuine, like Lady Mary Renford and Miss
Phillips. Both were a little too quiet for Izzy, but Rose had
befriended them, and so Izzy counted them in her inner
circle of intimates.

Among the gentlemen, Izzy had categorised them into
distinct groups, spending quite a bit of her time honing her
thoughts and thinking about the categories.

'Miss?' A gentle knock on her bedchamber door alerted
her to the fact it was time to dress for tonight's ball at the
home of Lady Cowper. This would be their first proper
ball, and Izzy could barely wait for the gowns, the dancing, the excitement of it all.

As Mary dressed her hair, adding a pretty silver band
at the last, Izzy considered the matter of gentlemen afresh.
Firstly, there were the older men, married men, and committed bachelors. These tended to take an avuncular atti-
tude towards all the débutantes and could be relied on for
interesting conversation without ogling—always a benefit.

Standing, she stepped into her glittering ballgown, a

delight of white crêpe and satin fringed with gold and featuring a golden satin bodice ornamented with three rows of embroidered leaves. The sleeves were short, full, and edged with the gold satin, while the gown was completed by a short sash of shaded ribbon in a paler gold tied in a fetching bow under the bosom. The maid was adjusting the gown with great reverence and sighed with delight as she finished doing up the buttons. 'You look beautiful, miss!'

'Thank you, Mary.'

Izzy returned to her reverie. Then there were the poets and would-be poets. These were invariably young, romantical, and resoundingly silly. They gave extravagant compliments and pretended to fight for the honour of finding a lady a seat, or procuring a glass of too-sweet ratafia. The poetry they produced was laughably trite, and Izzy often felt that it mattered not to them of which young lady they were currently enamoured, for they listened only for a chance to speak and seemed to be in love with the *idea* of love, rather than with anything to do with the reality of the ladies they were complimenting. Rose and Anna seemed to tolerate them much more readily than Izzy, for she could not help but reflect that if a young lady behaved in such a silly manner, she would receive universal criticism.

Looping her painted fan over her arm, Izzy made her way downstairs, accompanying Lady Ashbourne, Lord Ashbourne, Anna, and Rose out into the carriage. Lord Ashbourne, she thought now, glancing at his handsome face half-revealed by flambeaux, was in a different group to the others. He and Rose were sitting opposite her, and momentarily Izzy had the strangest notion they were *aware* of each other in some way.

Lord, my imagination is running away with me!

To divert her attention from such foolishness, she considered the viscount dispassionately. He, like Garvald and a few of the married men, formed a distinctive group. These men were sensible, intelligent, and—mostly—respectful, although even the cleverest of men tended to underestimate the wit and wisdom of the female sex. However, despite their undoubted good qualities, neither Viscount Ashbourne nor the Earl of Garvald were of particular interest to Izzy, for it had been made clear to the triplets that such unmarried gentlemen—titled, well-respected, and at the heart of the *ton*—could never give serious consideration to marrying a lady whose parentage was unknown.

For the past few weeks they had been making concerted efforts to discover Mama's identity, having decided to investigate all ladies called Maria who had made their debuts around the right time period. Sadly, they had already eliminated most of the options, including Maria Craven who was now Lady Sefton and Maria Berkeley—Lady Kelgrove's granddaughter—who had died of smallpox.

They had arrived. Izzy's heart skipped a little. Receiving an invitation to one of Lady Cowper's events was an achievement in itself. It also meant that tonight, there would be dancing—proper dancing, not like the dances at court, while trying to manhandle a four-foot train over one's arm. Nor would it be like the spontaneous dancing she had enjoyed at some of the less formal soirées, which generally involved no more than four couples taking to the floor at once. No, all night long tonight there would be dozens of couples dancing all at once. *Dozens!*

Having been welcomed by their hostess, Lady Ashbourne and the triplets made their way through the throng— the viscount swiftly taking his leave of them to seek out Garvald and his other friends. Izzy looked around with interest. This was surely the biggest crowd she had ever seen in a house before! The word *house* was of course inadequate in describing the elegant and enormous mansion tucked into the corner of St James's Square. All of the *ton* was here, it seemed. In all directions were people Izzy knew, mixing with elegant people she had yet to meet.

How wonderful!

Her eye fell upon two familiar figures, Mr Hawkins and Mr Eldon. She pressed her lips together. Over the past weeks she had formed a fuller impression of the two gentlemen and their set. In her mind she had dubbed them the pleasure-seekers. They were frequently drunk and liked nothing more than sport, wine, cards, and—in some cases—lechery. Instinctively she checked the group they were standing in, checking helplessly for blond hair and a handsome, sculpted face.

He is not here.

Her heart, a traitor to all rationality, sank in clear disappointment.

Over these past weeks, she and the prince had maintained something of a truce, in that they no longer insulted one another directly—though each time she recalled his arrogance during their early encounters, it still had the power to make her blood feel as though it boiled in her veins. But now she could greet him with an appearance of equanimity, could even make passing conversation. The fact that her senses ignited each time she was in his presence was both unwelcome and extremely puzzling, but she could do nothing about it. Her strange fascination with him continued, despite all common sense.

Their arrival had been noted, and instantly the Belles were surrounded by gentlemen asking for the promise of a dance later. Calmly, Izzy and her sisters allocated some of their dances—but not all of them. Inwardly, Izzy squirmed a little in recognition that, despite his vexing her, she might quite like to dance with His Highness if he were to make an appearance tonight.

Well, he is a good dancer!

Not that she had been able to properly appreciate his skill during their dance at court, being overcome with anger at the time.

I wonder who my sisters are holding spaces for?

Rose, spotting Lady Mary and her family, excused herself, making her way across to her friend. That left just Lady Ashbourne, Izzy, and Anna.

'Now, girls!' said Lady Ashbourne bustling, 'shall we attempt to find a seat, or are you content to wander about for a—Oh! Your Highness!' She sank into a graceful curtsy, and Izzy and Anna followed, Izzy's heart predictably skipping to a new rhythm.

With a conscious effort, she turned, lifting her eyes to meet his.

It is you! something within her declared, a thrill of recognition firing through her.

Quite against her wishes, her mouth went dry, and she could feel her pulse throbbing insistently as she made her curtsy and exchanged pleasantries.

'Miss Lennox, Miss Isobel,' he addressed them, directing his gaze unerringly to the correct sister. *How does he do that?* 'Might I please have the pleasure of dancing with each of you tonight?'

They agreed—well, how could they not?—Izzy's dance with him being fixed for the second one of the evening. Of course, now that he was here and had asked her to dance with him, Izzy's mind was full of righteous indignation. 'It is a sad truth,' she declared once he had joined his friends, 'that politeness does not allow us to decline a dance without good reason.'

'Oh?' Lady Ashbourne raised a knowing eyebrow. 'I quite thought you wished to dance with him.' It was not a question, and yet Izzy, stammering, tried and failed to reply. Mostly because Lady Ashbourne was entirely correct. Lady Ashbourne frowned briefly, then added briskly, 'Let us speak to Lady Kelgrove!'

She swept ahead, leaving Izzy and Anna to follow in her wake. Anna, a hint of a smile at the corners of her mouth, made to speak, but Izzy cut her off.

'Do not, Anna, just do not say it!' While she could not know exactly what her sister had been about to say, she was sure she could guess at the general tenor of it.

The dancing began soon afterwards, and Izzy made sure to sparkle and dazzle her way through the set. Mr Fitch was suitably overcome, and Izzy took his compliments as a balm to her disordered senses. As they left the crowded dancing area when the music ended, he offered to procure for her some ratafia or punch, whichever she should prefer. As he spoke, his left hand was playing with a signet ring on his right, something she recognised as a habit of his. For some reason, it irritated her a little.

'Oh, thank you, Mr Fitch. I should like some—'

'Punch.' It was the prince, two glasses of punch in his hands. 'You always prefer punch, Miss Isobel. As the next dance is mine, I thought to procure your drink in advance. Now, was that not clever of me?'

'It might have been,' she responded sweetly, 'had I wanted punch.'

And there it was—the slightest hint of consternation. She laughed—genuine amusement overcoming her. 'I am jesting, Your Highness. I shall accept the punch.'

Taking it from him, their eyes met, and she was relieved to see similar amusement in his. 'You *almost* convinced me, Miss Isobel.'

'Almost?' Arching a brow, she took a sip from her drink, her eyes never leaving his face.

His gaze dropped to her mouth, then back to her eyes. 'Almost,' he repeated firmly. 'But you have a distaste for ratafia, I think.' His voice lowered and deepened. 'It is too safe for you, too sweet. No, better the thrill of punch for you, Miss Isobel.' His words were rippling through her, stirring feelings she had never felt before. Entranced, she stood there, trapped by his gaze, his nearness, his words. 'Punch is stronger, more potent,' he continued. 'You could never be satisfied with ratafia.'

Yes! she wanted to say. *Yes!*

'Er… I shall take my leave of you, Miss Isobel. Your Highness.'

They both turned to say farewell to Mr Fitch, Izzy having quite forgotten he was there. His interjection reminded Izzy to try and maintain a semblance of normality, and yet something within her continued to thrum in celebration of standing so close to Prince Claudio, of having his full attention. And she had his *full* attention. She was sure of it.

Mr Fitch was barely gone when the musicians struck up for the next dance. Keeping his eyes fixed on hers, the prince raised his glass to her, then emptied it in one swallow. Mesmerised, Izzy took it all in—the strong line of his throat, the lines of his handsome face, the cool challenge in those grey eyes.

'Well?'

Knowing exactly what he wanted, Izzy lifted her chin. *I can do this!*

'Very well.' Taking a breath, she raised her glass, then

tipped it back. As the potent liquid trailed fire down her throat, a recklessness came over her, a desire to *feel* every moment, every sensation, every thrill.

He bowed and held out a hand. 'The waltz is common-place in my homeland, Miss Isobel. Have you danced it before?'

The waltz!

'No, I have not.' She tutted at herself. 'That is to say, I *have*, but only in dancing lessons.'

He bent his head to murmur in her ear. 'Then, prepare for a singular experience, Miss Isobel.' The way he said her name, with a hint of his accent, seemed to her in that moment a caress, and her entire body now tingled with... *something*. Whatever spell of madness had briefly over-taken her persisted yet.

In something of a daze, she took her place alongside him, forming a set with another couple, Miss Chorley and Mr Kirby. The music began, and Prince Claudio took her hand, turning her under his arm. For an instant, during the turn, she was within an inch of him, his firm body aligned with hers. Then she completed the turn, and they all four formed a circle, stepping forward and back in time. The other gentleman then turned her, and Izzy was astounded to find there was no thrill at all in his doing so. None.

She took a breath. The next hold was the one. His gloved hands came to rest on her shoulders, and she raised her arms to rest on his. This was the first time she had ever touched a man in such a way—or been touched by one. Together they moved, spinning around in time with the music, their eyes locked upon one another and their hands and arms en-suring they were held in each other's embrace.

Embrace?

Yes, for that was exactly what it felt like. Dancing les-

sons had not relayed to Izzy the full impact of this part of
the waltz, for she had felt no discomfort when practising
with her sisters or the middle-aged dancing master. They
had reached the next couple. Once again, the Prince turned
her, once again they completed the circle and the visitor
turn, and then it was time for them once again to embrace.
This time she was reaching for it, waiting for the delicious
moment when she felt the warmth of his hands on her shoulders, sensed his upper arm muscles flex and harden as he
led her around to the next place in the set.

Ten times they repeated the pattern, and ten times she
felt as though she were in heaven. On the last repetition, he
slid his hands down from her shoulders to the bare skin of
her upper arms. Izzy had no idea he was going to do it, and
when he did so she thought she might die from sheer sensation. Her eyes, still held by his gaze, widened in shocked
delight, and he swallowed hard.

'Isobel!' he groaned, so softly she could barely hear him.
Oh, Lord!

What on earth was happening to her? They had returned
to the beginning, with Miss Chorley and Mr Kirby. Miss
Chorley, Izzy noted absent-mindedly, was currently eyeing
the prince coquettishly. Just for an instant, Izzy wished she
knew how to flirt with a man, then dismissed the notion.

I can only be Izzy. No one else.

The prince, she observed—with more than a little satisfaction—seemed not to notice Miss Chorley's efforts. He
had turned her proficiently and now returned to Izzy for
the last turn of the dance. As the music ended he bowed to
her—a deep bow, his eyes once again locked with hers. She
curtsied gracefully, maintaining his gaze, no words passing between them.

The formal salute completed, Izzy felt at a loss. Unable

to move for the shocking sensations coursing through her, she simply eyed him helplessly, as all around them chattering couples began moving away in search of refreshment.

'So, how did you like the waltz?'

'I-I liked it very much.' Her voice trembled a little. Most unlike her.

Ah, Izzy, quit being such a weakling.

She tossed her head. 'I shall enjoy dancing it again—perhaps with a different partner.' A flicker of something that looked suspiciously like hurt flashed across his expression, and remorse flooded through her. 'I mean—of course I enjoyed dancing with you, Your Highness. I—'

'Enough with *Your Highness*!' he growled, bowing again, this time a curt farewell. 'I wish you well, Miss Isobel.'

Pain arced through her, almost physical in its intensity. *I should not have—*

But it was too late. He had rejoined his pleasure-seeking friends. Lifting her chin, Izzy made for Anna.

The next two hours passed in something of a haze. Izzy danced and drank more punch and laughed gaily at the slightest of witticisms from her various dancing partners. After the cotillion, Lady Renton cornered her, asking bluntly, 'Which one are you?'

Momentarily taken aback, Izzy instantly rallied to declare coldly. 'I am Isobel, Lady Renton.'

Though you are not behaving in a very ladylike manner at present.

'Ah, yes.' She waved a hand at Izzy's gown. 'Wrong colour.' Rose must have told Lady Renton's daughter about their preferred colours. With a smile that did not quite reach her eyes, she added silkily, 'Rumour has it the prince is promised to some Prussian princess, you know.'

Already braced for a fight, Isobel did not let any inner shock deter her, although something in her chest twisted in pain.

He is to marry?

'Really?' she smiled. 'I do feel sorry for the poor girl, whoever she is!'

'*Sorry* for her?' Lady Renton's voice was low, her tone sharp. 'When she is to marry a prince?'

Suddenly, Izzy had had enough. Enough of the fawning. Enough of the attention. Apparently all people could see was his title. They seemed not to notice the *man* and all his qualities—good or ill. 'Yes, I am sorry for her, whoever she is. For she is to marry a man-child with no thought for anyone other than himself!' Izzy retorted hotly. 'It is not a fate I would wish on any maiden!'

Pointedly, Lady Renton looked over Izzy's shoulder. 'Your Highness,' she crooned, 'such a delightful evening, is it not?'

Lady Renton must have known he was approaching when she said that!

The woman had timed her barb perfectly, clearly hoping Izzy would say something indiscreet. Which, because of her own dashed hot-headedness, she had. Izzy had fallen neatly into her trap.

Gritting her teeth, Izzy turned. There he was, his gaze fixed on Lady Renton. 'Indeed, yes,' he declared, 'although not all of the company is what I am accustomed to.'

A direct insult. Measure for measure he had met her challenge. Shock stopped Izzy's throat for an instant—but only an instant. 'I *so* agree, Your Highness.' She sighed mournfully as his eyes met hers, too lost to turn back now. 'It is *such* a disappointment to find people are much, much less than their status would suggest.' Her heart was racing, her fists clenched with ire. The truce, such as it was, had ended.

'Like the fools who hang about you with flowers and poetry, I suppose?' His eyes flashed fire.

'Lord, no!' She gave a small laugh. 'They are among the most gentlemanlike of my acquaintance.' She adopted a thoughtful air, belying the rage pulsing through her. 'Indeed, some of them are becoming like friends to me. I do think friendship is a strong basis for any connection, would you not agree?' Her eyes flicked sideways to where Mr Eldon was currently meandering drunkenly through the crowd, apologising each time he clumsily knocked into someone. 'And a true friendship must call to similarity, or affinity, I think.'

His jaw hardened as he glanced briefly towards his friend. 'Much as I would love to continue this delightful conversation, I must go, for I see they are striking up for the next dance. Miss Anderton is waiting!'

He bowed curtly just as, with perfect timing, Mr Fitch came to claim Izzy's hand. Giving the man a smile warm enough to make him blink and stammer, and bidding Lady Renton an insincere farewell, she accompanied him to the dancing area, serene as a swan.

Joining her sisters for supper, Izzy noted Rose seemed uncharacteristically exuberant tonight. She herself was filled with energy—passionate anger thrumming through her.

This place—the dancing—it is all going to our heads, I think.

And she refused to let the thrill of her first proper ball be ruined by a certain royal gentleman—one who had been bestowing glittering smiles on multiple débutantes this evening. Let him carouse himself to death if he chose. And his Prussian princess alongside him. Izzy cared not.

When she and Anna quizzed Rose, though, the youngest triplet gave an unexpected explanation for being in alt herself. Lady Mary Renford had accepted an offer of marriage from Mr Phillips.

Is that why her mother was so odious to me earlier?

Mr Phillips was a perfectly nice gentleman, but Lady Mary's mother had probably hoped for a title for her only daughter. Even as she exclaimed with Anna, abruptly Izzy felt a pang of something that felt suspiciously like panic.

Lady Mary has made her match!

Time was marching on, the Season was well underway, and those from suitable families, like Lady Mary, were able to make matches with the men of their choice.

Not us, though.

Everyone had been most clear. Choices for the Lennox sisters were limited due to their lack of known parentage. Turning away from a strange and unexpected ache in her heart, Izzy focused instead on the prospects that were more rational, more achievable. Mr Kirby. Mr Fitch. Not Mr Phillips—who, to be fair, had made his preference plain a number of weeks ago. Options would likely narrow further over the coming weeks, and Izzy would have to decide very soon whether to marry, and if so, to whom. Something within her shuddered at the very notion, but she suppressed it. Returning to rural Scotland at the end of the Season to become a teacher was unthinkable. She was Miss Isobel Lennox, and she would do what she must.

Chapter Six

Claudio strode to the window and opened the heavy curtains to admit the morning light. The rowan tree outside his chamber was now in full bloom, an abundance of creamy blossoms adorning its branches and creating a soft carpet beneath.

Having woken before ten—uncharacteristically early for his London life—he stood for a moment in the long window, pondering his options. Last night had deeply unsettled him, and he knew exactly why. After Miss Isobel's cutting comment at the end of their dance together, he had done his best. Had danced with half a dozen simpering maidens, eaten a poor supper, and—shockingly—had drunk very little. The appetite for getting thoroughly foxed had left him, as gently and subtly as the blossom petals drifting to the ground. A temporary aberration, no doubt, but Miss Isobel had once again prevented him from doing something he had wished to do.

Not for the first time, last night he had found himself feeling strong irritation at the antics of his own friends. Their teasing about his possible marriage was not new, but it was becoming more of a theme with them. They themselves had not married and seemed determined to make him commit to a similar fate. And he would not.

Last night their teasing had galled him into lying to them by saying he was already promised to a maiden back home. At the time, he had thought only to gain some respite from their relentless appraisals of all the débutantes in London—with the aim, they said, of helping him select his target. Yet the repercussions had been immediate, and he had found himself having to deny the story to multiple people.

'Oh, no!' he had stammered. 'My papa wished for me to marry a certain lady, but nothing is agreed.'

As if that had not been bad enough, he had then been given a very clear understanding of Miss Isobel's opinion of his supposed Prussian princess—a person to be pitied, apparently, since he was a *man-child*. Anger rose within him again as he recalled her scathing tone and her level look towards the extremely bosky Mr Eldon. Such a man, he knew, would not be long tolerated at his father's court, and yet Eldon and his set were Claudio's closest acquaintances here in London.

He closed his eyes, feeling the warmth of the morning sun through the window bathing his body in light. Of course, no sooner had he done so than there she was, in his imagination. She was all golden, her smooth skin glowing with fiery warmth, and he ached to kiss her, to hold her, to—

Hastily, he opened his eyes, stepping away from the window before he mortified himself. Oh, the servants all now knew of his habit of greeting the morning in his skin. He even suspected that some of the maids who happened to be passing through the gardens around noon each day might deliberately tarry there, hoping for a glimpse of the foreign prince who had a tendency to be shockingly naked. Members of the *ton* often walked in the gardens in the afternoons, so he knew to be more circumspect if he rose particularly late in the day. Thankfully, at ten in the morning no one was around—neither aristocrats nor servants—and so he turned back to the room, calling for Jenkins, his valet.

The hours ahead stretched before him with dreary emptiness. His friends he would see later, to discuss nothing but drink and sport and wenches. Yet again. He sighed. Such a life had seemed to him to be so much better than strictures and expectations of his father's court. And now, after only a few short weeks, was he already tiring of it?

Perhaps I shall never be satisfied.

As the clock struck ten, Izzy made her way downstairs to the morning room, a frown on her face and concern lurking within. Something was not right. There was a strange, uneasy air in the house, the servants were acting strangely, and Izzy simply could not figure out what it was about. She had not slept well, her dreams a parade of faceless Prussian princesses, each one more gentle, more refined, more graceful than the last. And now this…whatever it was. Hearing someone behind her on the staircase, she turned.

'Anna!'

'Izzy! What is amiss? My abigail barely spoke to me just now, all the while wearing an air of—of *knowingness* or something.'

'And mine!' She lowered her tone, adding confidentially, 'The maid's mouth was clamped shut the whole time as she helped me dress. I cannot account for it!'

They paused, thinking it through.

Anna spoke slowly. 'It seems as if they know something—'

'But are forbidden from speaking of it.'

Izzy's heart lurched. It had to be something bad, as her maid's demeanour had not suggested a pleasant secret or unexpected treat was on the horizon.

Has Lady Renton complained about my being rude to the prince?

Still murmuring together, they opened the door to the morning room. Inside was Rose, along with Lady Ashbourne, and one look at their faces told Izzy instantly that something was terribly, terribly wrong—something much worse than plain-speaking at a party. Rose was pale, her expression closed and pinched, while Lady Ashbourne's mouth was a grim, narrow line.

Having dismissed the servants, Lady Ashbourne looked to Rose, then turned to Izzy and Anna. 'My brother, your guardian, is unwell,' she began. Izzy froze.

Dear Mr Marnoch, who has been so good to us since Mama's death!

Lady Ashbourne was continuing, 'And so Rose has kindly—'

'No.' Even as Izzy's brain tried to take in the bad news concerning dear Mr Marnoch, Rose interrupted. 'Everyone else may hear that tale,' she stated, her voice low. 'My sisters deserve to know the truth.'

The truth?

What on earth—?

Lady Ashbourne nodded. 'Very well. But you must both swear to repeat this to no one.'

'Of course!'

'Naturally!'

Even as they made their promises, Izzy's mind was racing, desperately attempting to think what might be happening.

Rose swallowed. 'Yesterday, I allowed…a gentleman… to—to kiss me. In a public place. And we were seen.'

Izzy gasped. 'Rose!' A hundred thoughts flew through her mind. Shock at Rose's situation. Disbelief.

Can this really be true?

Dawning horror at the realisation this could be terrible for poor Rose.

Rose nodded grimly. 'If word gets out about this, I am ruined. And unfortunately—' her voice trembled '—you would be ruined along with me, for society judges all three of us as one. I am so sorry. I have failed you. Failed you all. Failed Mama. Failed Mr Marnoch.' She buried her face in her hands, clearly distressed.

Stupidly, all Izzy could think of was Rose's evident happiness at the ball. 'Lord, Rose! Last night I thought you seemed—'

I recognised it because I felt equally happy too, for a time.

A flash of memory came to her. His hands on her shoulders. Their eyes locked together. How wonderful it had been, before all had crashed about her.

A Prussian princess.

Shaking it off, she brought her mind back to her sister and to the true reason for her evident happiness last night. 'So it was not Lady Mary's betrothal, then.'

'Lady Mary is betrothed?' Lady Ashbourne's tone was sharp. 'To whom?'

Izzy's mind, still sluggish from Rose's announcement and with her own waltz memories and quarrel memories tingling through her, made her only stare stupidly at her hostess.

'Never say she has managed to catch Garvald!' Lady Ashbourne declared. 'That is to say, Lady Mary is a sweet girl, but she has not the strength of character for the earl.' She continued, musing thoughtfully. 'Not the prince either, for his passionate nature would terrify her.' She stopped, an arrested expression in her eyes. 'Mr Phillips?'

Rose nodded. 'He spoke with Lord Renton yesterday.'

'I see.' Lady Ashbourne rubbed her chin. 'And I begin to see so much more...'

But Izzy was not listening.

His passionate nature.

She shivered.

How I should love to be kissed by him!

Rose had kissed a man. Or been kissed by him, perhaps. Rose—the quietest, most timid of the sisters. She knew what it was to share a kiss, and yet Izzy, who had long seen herself as the most adventurous, the most passionate, the most headstrong, had not one single adventure to show for all her time in London.

Quit this foolishness! she admonished herself. Rose's situation was a reminder that to be caught kissing a man was a heinous crime for a débutante and not something to be wished for. Lady Mary's footman, it seemed, had witnessed the incident and told Lady Renton.

That woman!

'But my lady, what is to be done?' Anna took Rose's hand.

'Done?' Lady Ashbourne shook her head. 'I have already had this conversation with Rose. She must either marry the gentleman in question, or she must go away.'

'And I have decided to go away. That is why we are pretending that dear Mr Marnoch is ill.' Rose's eyes were suspiciously bright. 'So much deceit! And all because of me!'

Go away? Banished from London?

Izzy's heart stilled at the severity of Rose's punishment. Having decided that she strongly wished to make London her home, Izzy could not in this moment think of a worse fate than to be forcibly banished. With Anna's support, she objected strongly to the plan, but Lady Ashbourne was adamant. She hoped for discretion from Lady Renton, but it could not be assured. Yes, Rose might return at some point in the future perhaps, but for now she needed to leave. Immediately.

Today?

'Oh, Rose! I shall miss you so much!' Izzy hugged her fiercely.

'We have never been apart,' added Anna, wrapping her arms around both sisters. 'How shall we do without you?'

'And I you! Oh, Anna! Izzy!'

Touching her head to Izzy's and Anna's, Rose cried bitterly, and her sisters joined her. All their lives they had been together, even sharing a bedchamber until their arrival in London. Now their bond was to be sundered, and life would never be the same again.

The uneasy feeling within Claudio would not go away. Surprisingly it had been assuaged a little by the fact he had spent more than an hour this morning reading in the Buckingham House library. He had always had a good mind, yet it had astonished him to discover how much enjoyment he had gained earlier from reading a couple of well-crafted essays collected by a man called Dobson.

I have missed using my brain, I think.

Today was four months to the day since he had landed in England. Four months of drinking and gambling, of sports and bedsports, of fencing and boxing. He had been enjoying his body all this time, subjecting it to the effects of wine and ale, exercise and activity—although the desire for bedsport had not returned since his abandoned attempt with the tavern maid that time. *Why?* He shied away from the answer, not wishing to look at it too closely.

Perhaps then, he had not given enough time and attention to the needs of his intellect.

Very well.

Reading—one of his favourite pastimes at home—would return to his days. The book of essays now rested on his nightstand, and he would make time to read more later, before tonight's soirée at Lord and Lady Sefton's.

He glanced at the clock in the long hallway as he passed through. Nine hours until he would make his bow at the Sefton soirée in Arlington Street. He was promised to the queen for dinner, and even with bathing, dressing, and now his plan to read, he estimated he still had five or six hours to kill. His friends would not yet be at the club, and the thought of going directly there, to inhale the odours of stale smoke, spilled wine, and stale bodies from the night before held no attraction. Sighing, and feeling decidedly unsettled, he decided to take a long walk through the Green Park. Perhaps that would assuage the strange restlessness within him.

Rose is gone.

An emotion that felt rather like grief surged through Izzy. She and Anna had left Ashbourne House soon after seeing their sister off in the carriage and were hoping that a brisk walk might distract from the wrenching separation. Even now Rose would be on the outskirts of London on the first stage of the long, long journey back to Scotland. Mr Marnoch was there, and Rose hoped to gain a teaching post in their old school, Belvedere.

Izzy shuddered. Such a fate lay before her, too, should she fail to take this opportunity to make a match.

Poor Rose!

Some young ladies, she knew, dreamed of a love match, but Izzy's options did not now include such luxuries. No, she wanted only a sensible husband with a steady income, who was fixed in the capital. Someone who could be relied upon. Always her mind circled back to two names: Mr Kirby or Mr Fitch. Both were a little dull, to be sure, and she certainly had no desire to kiss them. But then, kisses were not a good measure for a suitable husband. Rose had been near ruined by kisses!

'Izzy,' Anna ventured now, drawing her out of her reverie. 'The gentleman Rose kissed… Have you considered who it might be?' Rose had steadfastly refused to reveal the man's name earlier.

Izzy snorted. 'Who it *might* be, Anna? There can be only one possibility!'

'Viscount Ashbourne?'

Izzy nodded. 'Looking back, it is clear to me that he and Rose share some sort of…' She searched for a suitable word.

'Affinity?' Anna suggested.

'Yes. It is plain to me now. Even last night, in the carriage, I sensed something between them.' She laughed lightly. 'Of course, in my foolishness I did not see what was in front of my face. Not until Rose said someone had kissed her. I do wish she had told us about him. We have never had secrets from one another before.' She sighed.

Affinity.

'We have not the luxury of making eyes at gentlemen who are beyond our reach, Anna.'

Anna slid her hand into Izzy's arm. 'I know. And I never thought to see the day when *you* are the one saying sensible things!'

'These are peculiar times. All manner of strangeness surrounds us.' Like feeling an affinity for someone who had behaved arrogantly towards her. Someone who was as far out of her reach in rank as the stars. Someone who was already promised to another.

And other strange things, now. Like choosing a husband as though he were a new hat. She squirmed uncomfortably at the notion. No, she would be respectful of her future husband. Anything less would be unprincipled. Dishonourable, even.

Even more strangeness. Having a mind that endlessly focused on one person, every day, every night, even though one did not wish it. Did not choose it.

'Oh, my goodness!' Walking towards them was a familiar figure, tall, proud, and handsome—just as though her thoughts had conjured him.

I even recognise the way he walks!

Her heart, naturally, was now pounding, and she even felt a little dizzy.

She swallowed. 'Am I imagining it, Anna, or is that truly the prince before us on the path, strolling through the Green Park alone, like any commoner?'

'It is certainly the prince, Izzy. Now, pray do not—'

'I shall be all politeness, I assure you!' Yet inwardly, Izzy's mind and heart were in chaos. Last night, she had been quite rude towards him, in speaking of pitying his princess. One should not say such things. Unless one was Izzy, who frequently did. She had also snubbed him a little after their dance, earlier in the evening. But why should he care? And why should she not enjoy dancing with different gentlemen?

He had seen them. Izzy knew it from the way his shoulders suddenly stiffened, ever so slightly. His coat today was of blue superfine and… Oh, how it drew attention to the breadth of his shoulders, the colour making his eyes look more blue than grey in the June sunshine. He stopped to make his bow, and as she gave the required curtsy, his handsomeness made Izzy catch her breath briefly. Only her inner determination ensured she managed to play her part in the polite conversation that ensued.

Their health, the weather, and the delights of last night's ball dispensed with, there was a brief pause.

'Are you often about in the mornings, Your Highness?' Anna's tone was polite.

'Actually no, but this morning I rose unexpectedly early.' He grinned. 'I have even managed to read two of the Dobson essays before venturing out.'

'My sister has read that collection. Were we not speaking of it just a few days ago, Izzy?'

Izzy was still trying to control her thumping heart and feeling of joy in her stomach.

Why did he have to smile? I might have coped if he had been dour today.

'We were,' she managed. 'A most interesting volume.'

There was another pause, then he opened his mouth to say something else. With sudden dread, Izzy wondered if he was about to ask after Rose and so jumped in hastily.

'Do you make a habit of strolling in the Green Park, Your Highness?'

'I enjoy walking in natural surroundings as much as any man, Miss Isobel.' His gaze pierced hers, a hint of challenge in those eyes. 'Why do you ask?'

She sniffed. 'I would have thought such activity too… *commonplace* for such a person as a prince.'

His brow furrowed. 'Indeed? Well, it pleases me to inform you that, despite being a prince, I am clearly sadly commonplace.' He turned to Anna. 'Miss Lennox, I shall hope to see you at Lady Sefton's soirée tonight. I shall wish you both good day.'

His bow was stiff, Izzy's curtsy shallow, and then he was gone.

'Insufferable man!' Izzy declared behind closed teeth as they resumed along the path. 'Highness? High-handedness, more like! Did you see how he cut me just now?'

Anna was frowning. 'Enough, Izzy! You were *rude*, as you must realise! And for no good reason! That is not how we were raised to behave, and I am sorry to say it.'

'I—' About to defend herself robustly, Izzy was suddenly overwhelmed with something that felt like regret, laced with a strong dose of shame. 'You are right, Anna. It is just— Being rude to him is all I can do to…'

'To protect yourself?' Anna's voice was low. 'Because you are drawn to him?' At Izzy's gasp, she shook her head. 'I am not bird-witted, you know. While Rose's *tendre* for the viscount is only apparent to me now, I have known all along that you and the prince only behave as you do because you—you *like* one another.'

'I do not think he likes me! And sometimes I do not like *him* at all!' Izzy returned, an image of him laughing with his vacuous, hedonistic friends coming to mind. 'But I cannot be indifferent to him, no matter how I try. And yet I must try, for he is not for me, and if I allow him to take all my attention, it may prevent me from making a sensible match.'

'Then, you will marry?'

Izzy shrugged. 'I wish to remain part of the *ton*, and the only way to do that is to marry. Teachers and governesses are not permitted to dance at balls or sing at musicales. I cannot sit by the side and watch others *live* when I cannot.' She squared her shoulders. 'So yes, I should marry. And there are gentlemen who will consider us, despite our small dowries and our dubious parentage.'

Anna sighed. 'Lady Ashbourne has had a letter from her friend, confirming that Miss Maria Carew is not our mama, for she is alive and well and living in Pembrokeshire.'

'But she was the last possibility! All of the other débutantes called Maria from around the time of Mama's Season are either married or dead. And I have made no headway on my own quest, for how can I discover who our father was if we do not know Mama's maiden name?'

'I know. Lady Ashbourne says we are unlikely now to ever discover the truth. She believes *Maria* may have not even been Mama's true first name.' She shook her head. 'Mama must have been truly frightened, for she went to great lengths to hide her true identity.'

'Secrets. Mama's secrets. Rose's secrets.' Izzy turned to her sister, stopping in the middle of the path. 'I am glad you know of mine—the prince, I mean,' she declared fiercely. 'Let us try not to have secrets from one another from now on, Anna. We never did before.'

They hugged briefly, and when they parted, Izzy noticed that Anna's eyes were bright with unshed tears. 'What is it?'

'Ach, I am as foolish as you and Rose, if you must know! For I, too, have an affinity for someone who is not for me.'

On they walked, sharing secrets and tears, hopes and dreams. Finally they turned towards home. 'You know,' Izzy said slowly, 'I think that the delights of London— wonderful as they are—have distracted me from what is truly important. My quest. My sisters. Family.'

Anna nodded. 'I, too, have been too distracted. And now Rose is gone.'

There was another silence, then Izzy frowned. 'What are we to say to everyone tonight? At the soirée, I mean?'

'About Rose? Lady Ashbourne's tale is a good one— Rose has gone to care for Mr Marnoch, who is ill.'

'It does not sit easy with me to lie.'

'Nor with me. Perhaps we should not go tonight. By tomorrow the worst of the shock may be over for us, and we shall lie with ease!' Her laugh held a great deal of cynicism. 'I told you off for rudeness earlier, but lying to everyone is a much greater sin. And yet we must.'

Lying. Dissembling. Hiding her true feelings. Every hour of every day Izzy had been doing these things. She had even been lying to herself. Well, no more. Having shared her burden with Anna, she knew what she had to do. The prince was not for her, but she should not need to be rude to hold herself at bay. What had happened to Rose was much too serious for her to risk a similar fate.

I shall be polite to him, and distant. I shall protect my heart and allow my logical brain to choose a husband.

The plan was a good one, even if it made her feel a little sick inside. But she was her mama's daughter, and Mama had had worse trials to face.

Chapter Seven

'**O**ut!'

It was the morning after Lady Sefton's soirée—which they had *not* attended—and Izzy was with Anna and Lady Ashbourne in the dining room. The viscount had joined them earlier at the breakfast table, and Izzy had been relieved when he had left. He had been the cause of dear Rose's banishment, and he neither knew nor, it seemed, cared about her sister's fate.

Oh, how she had longed to rail at him, to accuse him and berate him and scream at him. He was a gentleman about town, a *viscount* for goodness' sake, while Rose was an innocent girl just out of a schoolroom in rural Scotland. And yet he had kissed her, and been seen, and now poor Rose was gone. *Ach!* Izzy could barely look at him.

'Out!'

The viscount was standing in the doorway, his face contorted with rage. Both footmen were already fleeing, the viscount stepping into the room to let them pass.

'Leave us, girls,' Lady Ashbourne sounded wearily resigned. 'No,' she waved away their protests, 'I should like to speak to my nephew alone.'

They went, Izzy throwing him a disdainful look on her way out. A half hour later, Lady Ashbourne joined them upstairs in the drawing room, astonishment in her demeanour. 'Well, my dears, he is going after her. He intends to marry her, despite her objections!'

They were all bewildered, and it took some time, but eventually they were persuaded that the viscount had, after all, true regard for Rose and was determined to marry her if she would have him.

'I told him Rose does not wish to marry him.' She laughed, shaking her head. 'I must say I have never seen him so shocked. Still, it will no doubt do him a world of good. He has had things his own way for much too long.'

'So what will happen now?'

'He is following her to Scotland. He is forced to take the old carriage for she is in the new one—and she is almost two days ahead of him. He will likely not catch her until she is already in Elgin. As to whether she will marry him, I know not. That part is between them.'

'It seems,' Izzy remarked thoughtfully, 'as though he may be worthy of Rose, after all. And so I do hope she will have him.'

'We must say nothing of this, girls,' Lady Ashbourne reminded them. 'Our story stands, and my nephew is often away from town. We must hold fast and hope for a good outcome.'

'And in the meantime, we stand together,' said Anna firmly.

'Indeed. Oh, my dears!' Lady Ashbourne reached for her lace-edged handkerchief. 'How lovely it is to think we may become family!'

They embraced then and discussed their plans. Tonight there was to be another ball, and before that they would stay at home. Unusually for Izzy, her feelings on being denied the opportunity for company leaned more towards relief than disappointment. Leaving the others, she made for her chamber and drew out her sketchbook.

It has been a while.

As she found her pencils, she realised how much she had missed her art. In order to be polite and distant with Prince Claudio in public, it was important that she give vent to these unwelcome feelings in private. Taking a breath, she seated herself at the window and began to draw.

The queen was in a querulous mood. Nothing would do. She had apparently not enjoyed her dinner, her gown was decidedly uncomfortable, and she was now regretting accepting tonight's invitation to Lord and Lady Wright's ball. Claudio made sympathetic noises as the carriage rolled through St James's, bracing himself for the evening to come. He sympathised entirely with his cousin's mood, since he himself was feeling decidedly unsettled.

London was not what he had hoped for. No, that was not quite right. He genuinely liked the city and liked England. He was certainly enjoying the freedom of being his own man, away from the strictures and expectations of his father's court. And yet…

'Ach! The truth is, Claudio, that I am finding this Season dreadfully dull.' The queen made a sharp gesture with both hands. 'There has been no scandal, no intrigue, apart from the usual antics of my sons! A few solid matches, but nothing to excite my interest.' She adopted a teasing air. 'Will you not take an English wife, cousin?'

'What?' Matching her tone, he raised an eyebrow. 'Just to alleviate your ennui? I think not!'

'You are an ungrateful pup, and so I shall tell your father when I next write to him!'

Resisting the urge to squirm in his seat, it occurred to

him for the first time that the queen's account of his carousing and drinking his way through England might not
present him to his father in the most flattering light. 'Ah,
pray do not, for I assure you I am truly grateful to be here,
and I thank you for welcoming me.'

Abandoning her teasing tone, she patted his hand. 'And
I am glad to have you, for there is no substitute for family.'
Cocking her head to one side, she regarded him thoughtfully. 'It has sometimes seemed to me as though you are…
discontented. Am I wrong?'

He shrugged, maintaining an air of nonchalance. 'Everyone may be discontented at times, but I have not regretted my decision to come here.'

But I am beginning to question my choice of friends.

'Good! For you cannot abandon me now. Indeed I quite
rely on you, you know!'

'You do?' He could not hide his surprise. 'But you are
always so poised, so self-reliant…'

'A queen must play a role, Claudio. As must a prince.
And yet underneath the mask, we may be as unhappy or
as cross or as uncertain as we please.'

A prince. Does she refer to my father? Or to me?

Nodding slowly, he thought for a moment. 'We hide our
true selves from the world.'

'But not from certain people. It is important to have
people we can be true with—people who truly know us
yet remain by our side. For me, as I told you before I have
certain of my ladies, my daughters, those few close friends
among the *ton*, and—' she patted his hand with affection
'—now I have you. Sadly, my sons are largely a disappointment, and my husband is lost to me, his mind gone in a fog
of fear and confusion.'

They talked then of the king's madness, of the brief moments of lucidity when Queen Charlotte could see again the man she loved.

My trials are nothing compared to hers.

They had arrived. Feeling decidedly off-balance, Claudio stepped down from the carriage, offering his hand to the queen.

'*Danke*, Claudio.' Their eyes met briefly, then he saw her stand up straighter, mentally applying her mask.

But she is formidable! Just like—

Leaving the thought unfinished, he walked towards the house, the Queen of England on his arm.

'The queen has arrived! Look, she is even now entering the ballroom!' Mrs Chorley's countenance was twisted with excitement. 'And the prince! Charity, for goodness' sake, do not look! And stand up straight, girl!'

Resisting the urge to square her own shoulders, Izzy kept her eyes firmly fixed on the Chorleys. Miss Chorley tonight was glittering with diamonds, an elaborate necklace around her throat and a matching bracelet on her right wrist. Her gown was of white silk, dotted with beads, with the same beads threaded through her glossy brown curls.

Beside her, Izzy felt like an absolute dowd in her pale gold gown—although, she had thought it pretty an hour ago, when checking her reflection in the mirror in her chamber. The gown was unadorned save for some subtle beading on the bodice, sleeves, and hemline, nothing like the elaborate ornamentation on Miss Chorley's gown, which must have cost a fortune. Izzy wore no jewellery and was suddenly convinced she must appear like a pale candle in sunlight next to Miss Chorley.

'Good evening, ladies!' It was Mr Fitch. Conscious that here was one of her most loyal suitors, Izzy gave him a warm smile. As greetings were exchanged, she took a quick glance towards the new arrivals. Naturally they were surrounded, ladies and gentlemen alike coming forward to greet the queen and her cousin.

Let them! I am quite content here and shall pay my respects in good time.

As Mr Fitch drew her aside to request her hand for the supper dance, Izzy remained half-aware of the conversation between Mrs Chorley and her daughter. Miss Chorley seemed to be distressed about something, but her mama was having none of it.

'We have been through this a hundred times, Charity,' she hissed. 'You simply play your part, and we shall have the prince by the end of tonight!'

Have the prince?

What did that mean? Glancing briefly their way, Izzy saw that Miss Chorley looked genuinely anxious, her mother cross. But there was no more time to think, for Mr Kirby had approached, his brow furrowed as he spied Mr Fitch.

'Good evening, Miss Isobel! At least, I assume it is you!' He indicated her golden gown. 'This is one of your colours, is it not? I confess I am not the most quick-witted of men, but I can remember a thing when it is repeated to me often enough.'

Izzy beamed at him. 'Mr Kirby! How delightful to see you! And yes, it is me.' Turning slightly to include her other suitor, she addressed them both. 'You two are among the few gentlemen to unerringly find me and recognise me.'

And they both rely on the colour of my gown. The prince, though, seems to have been able to recognise me from the start...

The two gentlemen were eyeing each other with a degree of hostility, she noted.

'Fitch.' Mr Kirby nodded his head slightly.

'Kirby.' Mr Fitch matched him for coolness. Opening his mouth to address Izzy again, he found himself forestalled by the newcomer.

'Miss Isobel, may I please ask you to save a dance for me?'

'Of course, Mr Kirby. It is always a delight to have you for a partner. And you, of course, Mr Fitch. I know one is not supposed to have favourites, but if such a thing were permitted, you both would be on my list.'

There! Encouragement for both of them, without leaving myself open to accusations of favouring either one.

Mr Fitch gave a sly smile. 'If you are hoping for Miss Isobel's hand for the supper dance, Kirby, you are too late, for she is promised to me!'

Kirby was undeterred. 'Not at all,' he replied serenely. 'I should like to claim the fourth dance tonight, if I may.' He leaned forwards, his tone now confidential. 'For I happen to know it will be a waltz.' At Mr Fitch's sceptical expression, he declared, 'It was a great success at Lady Cowper's ball, and it is nigh on impossible to get a dancing master these days, for everyone is desirous of learning it!'

Mr Fitch was eyeing him sourly. 'Are you sure you wish to risk it, Kirby? After all, one might easily make a fool of oneself if one gets the steps wrong.'

'I have no worries on that score, I assure you. And with such a graceful partner as Miss Isobel—I saw you waltz with the prince that night—I shall be the most fortunate of men!'

Both gentlemen, Izzy realised, were now fairly agitated, and so she set out to smooth ruffled feathers as best she could. By the time she had done so, the Chorleys were long gone, having joined the other sycophants currently surrounding the queen and the prince. Isobel had nothing against the queen, who had been kind and welcoming to her and to her sisters.

But the longer Izzy was about the *ton*, the more she wished that character meant as much as station. As the lowest possible rank tolerated within society—a girl without parents or lineage—she must attract friends and admirers based on her own God-given gifts of intelligence, looks, and character. In addition, she acknowledged wryly, the fact she and her sisters had dear Lady Ashbourne as a sponsor did not hurt...particularly when contrasted with the encroaching Mrs Chorley.

Izzy's gaze drifted to the Rentons, who were currently standing with Anna and Garvald at the long windows. Lady Renton behaved in very similar ways to Mrs Chorley—her ambition for her daughter being no secret—yet was not sneered at, for her birth and title protected her from judgement. As Izzy watched, Mr Phillips, his mother, and his sister approached the party. Lord Renton welcomed them warmly, his lady less so. Lady Mary's engagement to Mr Phillips had not come as a great surprise to people, once they thought about it, for the young gentleman and young lady were clearly partial to one another. The only speculation was around Lady Renton's clear displeasure at this outcome.

The musicians struck up for the first dance, and Izzy realised she had no partner. Having neither the expectation nor the desire for popularity, this did not bother her in the slightest, but as the Earl of Garvald led Anna to the dance floor and both Kirby and Fitch made their farewells, leaving to seek out their promised partners, Izzy found herself standing alone. Despite herself, she could not help but search out a tall, blond, royal gentleman. *There he is!* He had Miss Chorley by the hand, his head bent to listen to something she was saying on their way to the dance floor, and as he straightened, his gaze met Izzy's.

She stiffened but was unable to tear her gaze away. It was not just his looks that compelled her—there were other gentlemen present who were, some might argue, just as handsome—but something more. Something decidedly unwelcome. Briefly, her memory flicked to her sketchbook—drawing after drawing of one man, one face. All day she had tried to capture his likeness, and more. The essence of him.

Power. Strength. Passion. Unhappiness.

The last had surprised her, for he had never before seemed unhappy to her. In public he was assured, smooth—arrogant, even. Yet she had learned over the years to trust her instincts when drawing or painting. And her instincts were telling her something more lurked in the depths of his soul.

Tonight he will dance and laugh with his empty-headed friends and drink as much as he wishes. And it will not be enough.

He was *more* than the others, somehow. The likes of Eldon and Hawkins were both stuck in the shoes of a very young man, caring only for drinking, gambling, and wenching, no doubt. Prince Claudio was perfectly at liberty to enjoy such a life—being an actual young man. But if he had, as she suspected, more depth, then surely it would eventually begin to pall.

The dance had begun, and now he was entirely focused on his partner. With determination Izzy looked away—directly into the eyes of the queen, who was now seated on a raised chair with a commanding view of the room. Never taking her eyes from Izzy, she leaned her head to the right, speaking to her lady. Izzy swallowed.

What on earth—?

A moment later, the lady approached Izzy.

'Her Majesty wishes to speak with you, Miss Lennox.'

Oh, no! Have I offended her?

Racking her brain to try and understand why she was being singled out, Izzy approached the queen with outer calm, curtsying deeply.

'Come, Miss Lennox, sit with me.'

Miraculously a chair appeared, one of the hovering footmen clearly being charged with satisfying Her Majesty's every demand. Izzy sat, folding her hands in her lap and awaiting the queen's pleasure.

'First things first, my dear. Which one are you?'

'I am Isobel, Your Majesty. The middle sister.'

The anonymous middle. Wasn't that how Lady Ashbourne had described it? 'Always first or last', she had said, the day of their presentation.

'Isobel.' She repeated Izzy's name as if committing it to memory. 'I am told you each have preferred colours. Is that correct?'

'It is.' She indicated her gown. 'I tend to wear greens and yellows. Golden yellows, occasionally, like this gown.'

'Noted. How do you like London, Miss Isobel?'

Izzy replied in the positive and conversed with the queen for quite half an hour—just as if it was the most natural thing in the world. After a time, feeling reassured that she was not in any trouble, she relaxed a little, allowing her character to shine through a little more. Before long the queen was asking her opinion of the people and places she had encountered and laughing aloud at some of Izzy's responses. Izzy tried to be kind and couched her witticisms in guarded language, but Her Majesty was both quick-witted and ready to be entertained.

'You are a keen observer, Miss Isobel. I like it!' was her verdict. 'Now, who else must we discuss?' Her eyes drifted around the crowded room. 'Ah, yes, my cousin, Prince Claudio. What do you make of him?'

Izzy stiffened. 'You must know, Your Majesty, that I cannot possibly comment on someone so closely connected to you.'

The queen's jaw hardened. 'Your queen commands you, Miss Isobel Lennox.'

Izzy held her breath for a long moment, then nodded. 'Very well. The prince is not easily categorised. I have spoken of the pleasure-seekers as a group.' Her gaze moved about the room, seeking him out. He had not danced since partnering Miss Chorley and was currently imbibing a long glass of something. 'He is part of their set, yet does not properly belong.' Returning her gaze to the queen, she shrugged. 'I cannot say why. It is just a feeling.' Taking a breath, she decided to share her notion from earlier. 'I think he is…he is *more* than he shows to the world.'

The queen's gaze was unfocused. 'More than… Yes, I believe you are right. I have seen young men become stifled—staying at the hedonistic stage of life when they should be growing beyond it. For now, this is who he chooses to be.'

'But is it not frustrating to you? To see someone limit themselves to—to drinking and sport, when they could be something more? He has every advantage. Birth, position, looks, a good mind. Yet as far as I can make out he spends his days and nights in pursuit of nothing but pleasure.'

The queen chuckled. 'Patience, child.' She patted Izzy's

hand, then catching the prince's eye she beckoned him to join them. Izzy felt tightness rise within her as he approached. *Now what?*

'Ah, Claudio. I do believe the waltz is next. May I commend Miss Isobel Lennox to you as a dance partner?'

Oh, heavens! Even as mortification flooded through her, Izzy noted the tightening of his jaw, the grimness with which he nodded his acceptance.

'Of course!' He was all politeness, but it was clear to her he had no wish to dance with her. 'Miss Isobel, if you would kindly do me the great honour—'

But Izzy was already on her feet, the need to flee pulsing through her. 'Unfortunately I have already promised the waltz to Mr Kirby.'

The queen frowned. 'Well, of course you must not let Mr Kirby down, child.'

'And there he is!' Izzy gestured to her right where, thankfully, she had spotted her suitor, wearing a rather forlorn expression. 'I must not keep him waiting. Your Majesty. Your Highness.' A swift curtsy, and she was gone before the queen should finagle the prince into offering her a different dance.

A wide smile broke across Mr Kirby's pleasant face as she approached. 'Miss Isobel! I had wondered if all was lost when I saw you talking with Her Majesty. A great honour, yet selfishly all I could think of was our waltz.'

He held out a hand, and she took it, conscious that she was being subjected to scrutiny from many people around her. Talking with the queen, she supposed, would be noticed. Particularly being shown such favour for half an hour and more.

And why should she not speak with me, if she wishes?

Lifting her chin, she walked serenely to the dance floor, there to execute the waltz with particular grace.

* * *

Claudio, having hastily approached Miss Anderton for the waltz, could not prevent dissatisfaction from rising like bile within him.

What ails me?

Why should it matter to him what a certain young lady had said? Or what she believed of him? The same questions had been tormenting him since Grantham. Miss Isobel Lennox was a nobody—one of many débutantes, and not even particularly eligible in terms of dowry and parentage. There was no point being cross about it. He was, after all, a prince.

Setting himself out to be charming, he had Miss Anderton blushing and stammering in no time and was forced to stifle a wave of ennui.

Afterwards, his duty briefly done, he took a glass from a footman and downed it with a feeling of defiance. The servant remained nearby, knowing well what was required, and so Claudio set down his empty glass and took another, this time swirling around the golden liquid therein and contemplating it meditatively. His friends were in the corner to his left. He knew their exact location without looking as they were rapidly achieving a state of raucousness that would no doubt have Lord Wright casting them meaningful glances in the next hour or so, indicating it was probably time for them to retire to their club. Having himself drunk very little so far tonight, Claudio knew he would have to make some effort to catch up or be left frowning soberly at his friends' antics.

His gaze searched the room, pausing as he spied the golden hair of one of the Lennox triplets. She turned, and he dropped his gaze.

Not Isobel.

He needed no clues from the colour of their gowns these days. By now he could tell Anna apart from Rose if he looked carefully, but Miss Isobel's visage was instantly recognisable—just as though she was simply their sister, not part of their likeness. On he searched, pausing when he finally located her, bestowing brilliant smiles on the unedifying Mr Kirby.

Still, at least she is here.

Last night he had searched constantly at the soirée, but the Lennox sisters and Lady Ashbourne had not attended, leaving the entire evening dreadfully flat.

Catching the direction of his thoughts, he cursed inwardly. Why should it matter to him whether she was here or not? Setting down his untouched glass, he turned away from Miss Isobel Lennox and made his way across the room to where Mr Phillips was standing with his shy sister. At least Phillips was capable of sensible conversation, and besides, the man had to be congratulated on making a good match with Lady Mary Renton.

Isobel, half-listening to Mr Kirby's enthusiasm, noted the prince's progression across the room towards the Phillipses, and also Mrs Chorley's hawkish stare. She shuddered, uncertain as to why, then turned her attention back to Mr Kirby, who was in alt that he had performed the waltz without mishap.

'Having such a graceful, sure-footed partner is doubtless the reason for my good fortune,' he declared, and Izzy was moved to protest.

'Oh, no! For I have danced with many gentlemen much less agile than yourself, Mr Kirby, I assure you!'

At this he beamed, a generous smile spreading across his homely face.

I could do worse than Kirby for a husband, she mused, *for he is both kind-hearted and amiable*.

They conversed on for another few minutes, then, making her excuses to Mr Kirby, Izzy made for the ladies' retiring room. As she moved silently down the grand hallway, her thoughts on Mr Kirby's amiability, a door opened farther ahead, and Mrs Chorley and her daughter emerged, deep in conversation. They moved ahead of her, perhaps themselves seeking the retiring room, but something about the set of their shoulders, the hissed speech between them, drew Izzy's attention. Without considering the inappropriateness of eavesdropping at a *ton* ball, Izzy skipped silently to catch up, her sharp ears picking up tantalising snatches of conversation.

'But Mama, I cannot! It would not be right!'

'Nonsense! You are simply securing your future, Charity. Do you not think every other maiden would not do the same?'

To this, Charity replied with something unintelligible, to which her mother replied, 'Oh, fiddlesticks! Do not try my patience, my girl! Now, do as you are bid. That library is perfect for our plan, but we must wait a little longer, for all the young men are becoming nicely wine-befuddled.'

Our plan?

Whatever it was, it involved the prince, and Izzy had a strong notion it would not be to his benefit. Stopping, she allowed the Chorleys to enter the retiring room before turning back, making her way unerringly to the room they had recently vacated. Checking left and right, Izzy opened the door and slipped inside. It was indeed a dimly-lit library, with floor-to-ceiling bookcases, a fireplace, and armchairs upholstered in reddish-brown leather.

The room was empty.

Closing the door behind her, Izzy moved forwards, trailing her fingers along a line of books on the nearest shelf, pausing as she recognised a particular title, *Dobson's Essays*. A gleaming side table held a branch of candles and something else: a lady's painted fan.

Standing still for a moment, her brow furrowed in deep thought, Izzy tried to recall whether Mrs Chorley or her daughter had been carrying a fan just now. Abruptly she came to a decision. Scanning the room, she selected a particularly large armchair, the sort with comfortable wings at the top, against which to rest one's head if one fell asleep while reading. It was heavy, but she managed to tug it into a new position—one turned away from both the door and the side table. Quickly she took the book from its shelf—grateful for her good fortune in finding exactly the book she needed—and placed it on the chair, then took one final look about her before departing. With Rose's disgrace fresh in her mind, she had perhaps jumped to a false conclusion, but it did no harm to be prepared, just in case her absurd notion proved to be correct.

Thankfully the hallway was empty when she emerged. Exhaling slowly, she resumed her journey towards the retiring rooms as though nothing had happened.

Claudio spent a good quarter of an hour with Mr Phillips, enjoying a conversation that included multiple topics, not least Mr Phillips's recent betrothal to Lady Mary. The man was beaming with happiness. Indeed he seemed to exude it from every part of him, almost as though there were a glow about him.

Claudio was at once fascinated, uncomfortable, and, truth be told, a little envious. What must it be like to know love and to have one's love reciprocated? He had never thought on such matters before. Beyond fleeting infatuations with unattainable ladies in his youth, he had never felt anything as deep or as all-consuming as that which was clearly currently affecting Mr Phillips.

As always, his mind flicked to Miss Isobel—his image of her, as always, surrounded by golden light. She was a glowing candle, a blinding ray of sunshine, a blazing fire… Could it be?

But no.

It must not be. He would never choose to fall in love with someone so…*difficult*, and challenging, and direct. Someone who could see clearly every one of his flaws and hold them up for inspection in the clear light of her soul. Someone who knew her own worth, and his. He pushed away the uncomfortable thoughts, focusing his attention once again on the newly-betrothed gentleman beside him.

Afterwards, instead of returning to his friends, he stood there, vaguely unsettled. Where should he go next? Viscount Ashbourne was not present, having apparently gone out of town on a matter of business.

Where can I find sensible conversation?

Looking about, he espied the Earl of Garvald, and before he had even thought about it, he found himself making his way across the room.

Supper was called, and Izzy allowed Mr Fitch to accompany her, following their dance together. 'I noticed,' he began carefully, 'that you have been enjoying the queen's favour.'

Izzy shrugged. 'The queen has never before fixed her attention on me and probably will never do so again.'

'It is a singular honour, and one which many here must envy.'

'I had not thought much about it. The queen is, naturally, the Queen, but she is also a person like everyone else.'

His eyebrows shot up. 'How absurd! She cannot be a person like everyone else, for she is always the Queen.'

About to deliver a heated retort, Izzy decided to give the man a chance to redeem himself. 'Whatever can you mean?'

'Just that Her Majesty must be treated with…a certain *reserve*. As a sign of respect. No—' he held up a hand '—I will not hear an opposing view. My own mama reminds me constantly that the royal family are truly appointed by God to rule over us, and as such I cannot see them simply as— as *people*. The very notion offends!'

'I see.'

Respect?

A hundred words were on her tongue—not least the shocking profligacy of the Prince Regent and, by all accounts, his estranged wife. 'And I have no intention of arguing with you, Mr Fitch.'

There was no point in arguing with such a person. Still, the conversation had been enlightening. Mr Fitch was better-looking than Mr Kirby and had probably a quicker mind, but a habit of being dogmatic would not bode well for marital harmony. And his putting a hand up towards Izzy's face to stop her from talking had not been well-received. Not at all. No, if she had to choose between them right now, Mr Kirby would have the upper hand.

As she ate, idly making conversation with Mr Fitch, she tried to imagine her life a year from now, should she marry.

Is this what my future holds? A husband who tells me what to think? Or—she pictured the amiable Mr Kirby—*a husband who acknowledges he is not quick-witted?*

She stifled a sigh. These were the limitations of her choices. She could no more choose a different husband than become Queen of England. Glancing towards the large table at the top of the room, she saw that Her Majesty had been joined by the prince, and they were currently deep in conversation. Unable to resist, she allowed her eyes to linger on Prince Claudio's handsome features, then looked away before she should be seen. The Chorleys, she noted, were seated at the next table to hers and Mr Fitch's. Mrs Chorley was currently attacking a well-filled plate with gusto, while Miss Chorley seemed to have little appetite.

After supper the retiring rooms were busy for a time, but once the dancing was underway again, the ballroom was soon crowded. Those not dancing were ranged around the edges of the dance floor or sitting and standing in groups. The noise level had increased, no doubt down to the increasing effects of the wine, ratafia, and strong punch being offered by Lady Wright's footmen. Having danced a quadrille with Mr Phillips, Izzy thanked him and made her way to the side, where the open windows gave some relief from the heat of the packed room. Most of the ladies were at this point making good use of their fans, and it reminded Izzy to observe the Chorley ladies. There they were—and Mrs Chorley was making for the prince!

Someone passed in front of Izzy, blocking her view, and by the time she moved to a better vantage point, Prince Claudio was in conversation with Miss Chorley, her mama having left them to converse. Miss Chorley, from what Izzy could see, had no fan.

Claudio was fighting the urge to yawn. To do so at a *ton* party would be the height of rudeness. To do so while in conversation with a young lady would be unforgivable. He was not drunk enough to take Miss Chorley's giggled inanities with any forbearance. Indeed he was not drunk at all, which was probably a mistake. If he were, he would probably be able to bear Miss Chorley's clumsy attempts at flirtation a little more easily.

'Do you like to dance, Your Highness?' Her tone was arch, and quickly he reminded himself he had done his duty by her earlier. Indeed—he ran through a list in his head—he had danced once with nearly all of the eligible maidens, as well as a few of the married ladies. Nearly all. Despite the queen's machinations he had yet to dance with Miss Isobel tonight—an omission that was bothering him much more than it should.

'I do. I think an appreciation for music is one of the higher arts.'

'Well, I know nothing of such matters, but I do love to dance!'

He ignored this, having no intention of asking her for a second dance. His own comment, had he directed it to Miss Isobel—or indeed to Ashbourne, Garvald, or Phillips—would likely have resulted in a lively debate as to the place of music and dance in the civilised world, but with Miss Chorley there was no such opportunity, for she was among the most hen-witted persons of his acquaintance.

Yes, Miss Chorley, and Eldon, and Hawkins…all alike in that respect. He frowned. That was not quite correct. Hawkins and Eldon had the benefit of thirty years and more on this earth, and so had gained knowledge that younger persons like himself could not yet possess. However, it seemed to him his friends used their worldly wisdom simply for their own advantage: to bet on a likely fighter, or to contrive an invitation to a race meet. And why should they not?

His thoughts were interrupted by the realisation that he had been standing in glowering silence next to Miss Chorley, and as he focused on her again he saw that she was bringing a hand to her head.

'Oh, dear,' she said weakly, triggering all his gentlemanly instincts.

'Miss Chorley! Are you unwell? May I be of assistance to you?'

'Yes, I… I feel unwell. The heat…'

'Indeed it is extremely warm in here. Can I fetch your mother for you?' He looked around but could not see Mrs Chorley's plump form anywhere.

'No! Please do not!' Her tone was forceful, and he reflected that Miss Chorley might be quite nervous of her mother. The woman was formidable—and *not* in a good way. Before he had the time to consider who might actually be formidable in a good way, Miss Chorley swayed slightly, so he applied a steadying hand to her elbow.

'Thank you,' she murmured, looking up at him.

'How may I assist you, Miss Chorley?'

'My fan… I left it on a table…' Vaguely she gestured toward the door leading to the hallway.

'Then, I shall fetch it for you! In the meantime, shall I find you a chair?'

She laid a restraining hand on his arm. 'No…please do not make a fuss. If you try to find me a chair they will all be looking at me, and my mama will be displeased.' She squared her shoulders. 'I shall fetch the fan myself, but thank you.' She stepped forwards, swaying ever so slightly.

With a muffled expletive, he started after her. What if she collapsed in the hallway?

'Miss Chorley! I shall accompany you.' His sense of responsibility would not allow her to go alone. Something about her behaviour was a little strange, and he wondered if she was overcome by ratafia as much as by the heat of the packed ballroom.

Izzy could not keep her eyes away from the prince, but this time, instead of an idle or intense perusal of his form and features, her senses were on full alert to his conversation with Miss Chorley. As she watched, she saw Miss Chorley put a hand to her head, and a moment later the prince took her elbow.

Is she unwell?

He looked around, as if seeking someone. Miss Chorley's mama, most likely.

Izzy's eyes widened. He would not find her, for Mrs Chorley was currently hiding behind a pillar to Izzy's right—and seemed to be leaning slightly as if peeping around to watch discreetly. Whatever the Chorleys' plan was, they were clearly currently executing it.

Swiftly, Izzy made for the far doors to the hallway. Time was short, for if her suspicions were true, Miss Chorley and the prince would imminently be on their way to the library.

The hallway was empty, apart from Claudio and the apologetic Miss Chorley.

'I cannot thank you enough, Your Highness! Now, where did I leave that fan? Oh, I remember now!' She paused, opening a door to her left. 'It is in here, I believe! They have the most amazing collection of books—just look! Not that I am a great reader, you understand. You must not think me bookish!'

He frowned. Now was not the time for visiting a library in someone else's house—particularly when it was so dimly-lit in contrast to the bright hallway. Just as his awareness began to send a warning, she half collapsed inside the room, grasping the back of a leather sofa for support.

'Oh! Oh, dear! I feel most unwell!'

'Let me assist you, Miss Chorley.' Gently, he guided her round to the other side of the sofa, bidding her sit. She did so, her breathing agitated and her face flushed.

I must find her mother.

But when he made to move away she reached for his hand, preventing him from leaving.

'Oh, please stay with me, Your Highness. I shall be well in just a moment, I promise.'

Reluctantly, he stayed, his discomfort growing. Her hand gripped his tightly, as if he was saving her from some danger by his very presence. But, *Lord*! It would look bad if someone came upon them. And the hallway outside was the main route to the retiring rooms. He glanced towards the door, which was slowly swinging from open to half-open.

The devil take it!

What if someone should see him? Yet he could not leave Miss Chorley, for she was clearly in some distress. His mind was racing, but for now he could see no way out of the dilemma.

His heart sank as he detected a surge in noise as the doors to the ballroom opened, then closed again. Was someone even now making their way down the hallway?

Thankfully the door had closed farther and was now ajar rather than fully open, so hopefully whoever it was would not even notice but continue to make their way to the retiring rooms. Now he could hear voices. He tensed as he recognised the tones of their hostess, Lady Wright, who seemed to be directing someone. 'You see, the room set aside for ladies is just along here.'

'And what is this room, Lady Wright? Such a delightful house!'

Everything happened at once. As the door began to open he snatched his hand from Miss Chorley's vicelike grip, even as he recognised her mama's voice and realised the trap that they had sprung between them. A trap from which there could be no escape.

'Charity! Your Highness! What on earth are you doing in here, all alone?' Mrs Chorley's manufactured outrage was belied by the delight in her eyes.

Almost, he could feel the blood draining from his face. His mind was frozen. Oh, he had heard of such plots, but never would he have thought himself foolish enough to be caught in such a snare.

And I am not even drunk!

His gaze swung to Lady Wright, who was frowning. Oh, she might suspect that he had been deliberately ensnared, but she would be forced to confirm that he had indeed been alone in the library with Miss Chorley.

His gaze flicked back to the mother. As he looked her expression changed, her jaw sagging—this time in genuine shock. A familiar voice from behind him declared sunnily, 'Oh, but they are not alone, Mrs Chorley. For we are all here together!'

He swung around—to meet the innocent gaze of Miss Isobel Lennox.

Chapter Eight

Izzy's heart was pounding so loudly she could swear Lady Wright might hear it all the way across the room. Having barely made it into the library before the prince and Miss Chorley had opened the ballroom doors, she had hidden herself in the armchair, remaining stock-still and barely able to think. Thankfully, Miss Chorley's histrionics had covered up the sound of Izzy's own ragged breathing.

What if I am wrong? What if they walk straight past the door?

But only a few seconds later her worst suspicions had been confirmed. The door had been pushed open and in they came, Miss Chorley saying she was unwell and the prince—very properly—assisting her to sit. Izzy could hear the rustle of Miss Chorley's silk dress, her dramatic, fast breathing.

Lord! She is really going to do this thing!

Doubts suddenly assailed her. What if the prince *wanted* to be alone with Miss Chorley? Was she to remain here, hidden in a large armchair, while he kissed another maiden? Pain knifed through her at the thought, and abruptly she realised since the day she had met him she had considered his request for a kiss to be an unfinished matter between them. One that could only be resolved by—

Voices in the hallway had distracted her from the thought,

and as she became aware of who was approaching, suddenly she knew that Prince Claudio must not be compromised by this cheap trap. No, she had the power to save him, and save him she would! So when she heard Mrs Chorley's faux outrage, she rose from the chair like an angel of justice, declaring, 'Oh, but they are not alone, Mrs Chorley. For we are all here together!'

The effect was instant. Mrs Chorley's jaw was sagging and her visage turning a sickly grey. Lady Wright was eyeing her approvingly. Miss Chorley's mouth was opening and closing silently. And as for the prince—even now he was turning to face her. Anxious that he not given himself away, she continued brightly, 'And here is the collection we were speaking of, see?'

She held out the book, and he took it, saying, 'Dobson? A most excellent collection.' His face was deathly pale, but as his eyes met hers again they softened a little at the corners, making her heart melt and her knees tremble.

Swallowing, she moved away from him, turning her head left and right as if seeking something. 'Miss Chorley, your fan is here!' Walking across to the side table, she picked it up. 'We came in to look for it, but I then got distracted when I saw the very collection of essays His Highness and I talked of recently. I simply had to sit for a moment to look at it.' Handing the fan to Miss Chorley, whose mouth was still opening and closing in the manner of a goldfish, she turned back to the prince.

'And now, if I am not mistaken, Your Highness, I am promised to you for the next dance.' She waited, her breath caught in her throat. Had she managed to pull the thing off?

He bowed, placing the book back on the shelf, while behind him Lady Wright declared, 'Yes, go and dance, Your Highness. I think you could not find a better partner.'

Turning back, he took Izzy's hand, murmuring, 'I quite agree. Ladies.' He bowed formally to all three of them, then led Izzy from the room.

Claudio could barely take in what had just happened. Disaster had been averted, and by the intervention of the one woman who was rapidly becoming an obsession with him. His mind awhirl, he walked beside her down the hallway towards the ballroom, the warmth of her gloved hand on his arm the only anchor in a world that suddenly seemed much more dangerous than it had a half hour ago.

'I must thank you, Miss Isobel.' Turning his head slightly to meet her gaze, he found her expression to be one of amusement, mixed with a strong dose of relief.

'Well, I was not certain I could carry it off, you know. I am glad you were quick-witted enough to follow my nonsense about the essays!'

He grinned. 'Mr Dobson to the rescue! But no, I can give him no credit, for this was all your doing.'

They had reached the doors. Lifting her gloved hand to his mouth, he pressed a kiss there, and as he lifted his gaze to meet her eyes a shudder of desire powered through him—desire that was surely reflected in her eyes?

'Isobel!' he breathed, as their gazes caught and held.

Beside them, the doors began to open. Instantly both donned matching masks of nonchalance, unconcern, and polite distance, nodding politely towards the gentleman who emerged, clearly seeking the retiring rooms.

'Another waltz!' Claudio declared, as the sound of the musicians' opening bars came to them. 'Perfect!'

Leading her straight to the dance floor, he tried to manage the maelstrom of emotions within him. Relief, yes, and outrage at what the Chorleys had tried. But mostly, he found himself thrumming with warmth and gratitude towards her.

'You are formidable, you know,' he told her as they began to move. 'In a good way,' he hastened to add, conscious that she often put the worst possible interpretation of his words. 'Like the queen.'

Glancing towards Her Majesty, he saw that she had been joined by Lady Wright and was listening intently to whatever their hostess was saying.

Lord! My cousin will have the whole story in a moment.

Still, Lady Wright was discreet, and so he had every hope that the incident in the library would not become common knowledge.

As he moved through the waltz in harmony with Miss Isobel, he felt decidedly strange. All of the usual feelings were there—desire and fascination chief among them. For once, though, there was no argument between them. Instead they talked about what had just happened...and *almost* happened. Isobel had, it seemed, heard the Chorleys making plans earlier.

'Then, it was not just serendipity that brought you to the library?'

'Lord, no! I had to run to get there before you both left the ballroom. Through those far doors.' She frowned. 'I could not know with certainty what they were planning. Indeed, it was only when I heard Mrs Chorley's voice in the hallway that I was sure.' She shook her head. 'I still cannot quite take it in!'

'Nor me,' he replied grimly. 'Even now, I might be informing the queen of my unexpected betrothal.' He thought for a moment. 'So it was all play-acting. No wonder I could not find Mrs Chorley when her daughter first told me she was unwell!'

'As to that—' Isobel's eyes were dancing '—she made certain of it by secreting herself behind a pillar!'

'No! Really?'

'Yes—a very *large* pillar, I must say!'

On they danced, talking and laughing together, oblivious to the attention they were drawing. Claudio knew only that his fascination for her had reached new realms, for their present harmony contained an unexpected addition, the connection of something that felt oddly like friendship. Like, yet strangely unlike. For never before had friendship been so intense, so all-consuming, so…magical.

'I cannot believe it!' Anna's face was a picture. It was almost three in the morning, they were in Izzy's bedchamber, and Izzy had just told her sister the full, sorry tale. 'That Miss Chorley would do such a thing!'

Izzy grimaced. 'It was her mother's plan. My impression is that Miss Chorley was a reluctant participant.'

Anna snorted. 'Yes, but she carried it out regardless.' She shook her head slowly. 'This place… The Marriage Mart…'

'It is all rather sordid, is it not? They reward the *appearance* of goodness, not goodness itself.'

'Yes. Rose must go away, while Miss Chorley might have finagled a prince for a husband!' She sent Izzy a piercing look. 'When you danced with him tonight, you seemed to be getting along famously.'

'Yes, we had just returned from the library and were caught up in what had just happened. I would not read anything into it.' Yet inwardly, her mind kept playing again and again certain memories. The kiss upon her hand. The feeling of connection with him as they danced. The way his eyes had softened when he looked at her that time… She shrugged. 'A temporary truce, no doubt. But I—I asked

Lady Ashbourne about his father's visit to England all those years ago.'

'And?'

She shrugged. 'Prince Claudio's father was apparently devoted to his wife. The *ton* always knows,' Lady Ashbourne said, 'for gossip, *on-dits* and the latest *crim. cons.* are the currency of every *ton* conversation.'

Anna's eyes widened. 'I have certainly seen shocking behaviour from some of the married gentlemen and ladies. I must say I should prefer to marry someone who would not behave in such a manner.' She frowned. 'But I suppose if a man were tricked into marriage, then he might not feel the same respect for his wife.'

'Or vice versa! Remember that Rose might have been forced to marry Ashbourne—although we know the case is different, for she loves him. I am sure of it.'

'What did the Chorleys do after you foiled their dreadful plan?' Anna was frowning. 'I do not recall seeing them in the last hour or so of the ball.'

'They left early.' Izzy grinned. 'Apparently Miss Chorley had a headache!'

'And what of the queen? She spoke to you not once, but twice!'

'Indeed.' Briefly, Izzy summarised her first conversation with Her Majesty. 'She seemed genuinely amused by my observations. I do hope I did not inadvertently offend her.'

'And the second time?' Anna prompted.

'Ah. Lady Wright told her about the library, so she summoned me again. That time our conversation was brief. "I believe I have reason to thank you, Miss Isobel Lennox," she told me. "You have the gratitude of your queen."'

Anna put a hand to her chest. 'My goodness!'

'I know!' She grinned. 'Who would have thought that a

trio of unknown girls from Elgin with small dowries and no known parents could come to the notice of the queen!'

'And do not forget we are her diamonds!' Anna sighed. 'Such a pity Rose is gone. She should be here, hearing this tonight.'

They hugged, and Anna departed for her own bedchamber. Alone in the darkness, Izzy allowed herself to remember other moments. The rush of desire she had felt with him in the hallway. The swell of possessiveness she had felt in the library. Yes, she would marry a London gentleman—Mr Kirby had the upper hand at present—but before that, she had another task to accomplish. Somehow, somewhere—discreetly and safely and avoiding scandal—real (Rose) or contrived (Miss Chorley), she would find a way to kiss the prince.

Lady Kelgrove was in fine form. Having summoned Claudio to sit by her, the elderly lady was now regaling the prince with a mix of anecdotes, biting observations about members of the *ton*, and piercing questions, which she would throw at him at the most unexpected moments. They were ensconced near the fireplace at Lady Kelgrove's elegant mansion, drinking tea and observing the other guests. Lady Kelgrove was today at-home to visitors and was clearly enjoying every moment.

'And of course Mr Phillips managed to catch Lady Mary Renford—an impressive feat, do you not think?' Her black eyes held a clear challenge. Would he say something banal and meaningless, pretending to not understand her implication?

He decided to match her. 'Given her mother's ambition, yes.' Throwing her an equally challenging glance, he added, 'The most impressive feat of the Season, perhaps?'

'Perhaps—or perhaps not. The queen's diamonds are not yet betrothed, and they are discerning enough, I think, to wait.'

Feeling rather as though he were playing chess with a master, he managed to maintain an unchanged expression. 'The Lennox sisters?'

She chuckled. 'Why? Are there yet more diamonds of which I am unaware? Yes, of course I mean the Lennox sisters. They are quite my favourites, you know.'

'They are? And why so?' Perhaps by keeping the attention on Lady Kelgrove he might be able to manage the disquieting flutters currently tormenting his innards.

No, he would not look towards Miss Isobel again. She was currently by the window, enjoying an animated conversation with Kirby or Fitch. He could never remember which gentleman was which, for to him there was no difference between them. Neither were leaders of society, with nothing of note about them—not their opinions, nor their appearance, nor even their fashion sense. They dressed conservatively and—he would wager a pony on it—used the same tailor. What they also had in common was their devotion to Miss Isobel Lennox, a devotion which entirely grated on him.

'They have been fêted for their beauty, and their manners, and their lively minds. But it is more than that. The Lennox girls are not just admired, they are well-liked. They have *countenance*, my dear. And unlike beauty, countenance is not lost with time.' She sighed. 'So few young ladies have that firmness of character when they have their Season. Often they are too ready to obey their elders unquestioningly. Or, worse, to behave in the silliest way possible.'

Her words were resonating within him, more powerfully than he wished. He knew himself to be drawn to Miss Isobel, knew also that it was for more than simply her beauty, for her sisters—almost identical in looks—did not attract him in the same way.

'I had a granddaughter, you know. She died a long time ago.'

He frowned in sympathy. 'I was not aware. I am sorry, Lady Kelgrove.'

She waved this away. 'My Maria had countenance. I often wonder how she would have fared as she matured. But no matter, for we are speaking of the Lennoxes. So alike, and yet so different. Rose, deceptively quiet. Anna, deceptively commonsensical.'

He waited. 'And Miss Isobel?'

The chuckle came again. 'Not deceptive in any way. Headstrong, obstinate, and opinionated. Just as I like her!'

Something like pride began burning within him—which was nonsensical as he was not connected to the Lennoxes in any way. 'Then, you can tell them apart, my lady?'

'As easily as you can,' she retorted. 'Oh, I am aware there are many who claim to believe they are so identical it would be impossible for anyone other than their mother to know the difference. Now, to be fair, I had the benefit of knowing their preferred colours to begin with, but now it seems to me their faces are different enough to make them seem like sisters only, not triplets.' She sent him a searching glance. 'And you share this, too, do you not, Your Highness?'

He shrugged. 'I do. It is strange to me when people appear to genuinely mix them up.' And yet he could not tell Isobel's suitors apart. 'Of course, Miss Rose has been gone for a few weeks now, so there are only the two of them.'

She pressed her lips together. 'I am told Rose may not return this Season. I am most displeased that Lady Ashbourne allowed her to go away. Surely someone else can take care of Lady Ashbourne's brother? Has he no servants, for goodness' sake?'

He had no answer to this, although inwardly he wondered yet again if Isobel was missing her younger sister. It mattered to him, somehow.

'She may opt for Kirby rather than Fitch, I think.'

Now Lady Kelgrove had all his attention. 'Miss Isobel? You think she will *marry* one of those fools?'

She raised a quizzical eyebrow. 'You have reason to think otherwise?' At his dumb silence, she continued. 'I thought not. From what I know of Miss Isobel, she is practical enough to know she needs a husband. And since many of the *ton* are foolish enough to bemoan the lack of information about their parentage, a Fitch or a Kirby is exactly what she needs. What? You disapprove?'

'Why must she marry at all? Or why can she not wait a few years?' His heart was suddenly pounding in a most distracting way, and there was a sick feeling in his stomach.

'Did you not know? Lady Ashbourne's inestimable brother—the one who has become unwell at quite the most inconvenient time—has paid for a single Season for the girls. He is, I understand, a solicitor and, as such, has limited funds. If they are not betrothed by summer, they may have to return to wherever they have been living. Somewhere in rural Scotland, I understand.' This last was said with a scathing tone.

'Then—she—they will not return after the summer?'

'Unlikely, unless at least one of them marries.'

'But—but we are already well into June! The Season is almost done!'

'Indeed. Once July arrives, the *ton* will start making for their country homes for the summer.' Eyeing him closely, she waited.

'I see… I see.' And he did. A little, at least. For the first time, he tried to understand what it might be like to have options restricted by one's level of wealth. Oh, not abject poverty. That, he understood, albeit from a distance. Both at home and here in London, he gave alms and carried out good works, as he had been raised to do. No, this was altogether different. The Lennox triplets had the *appearance* of wealth—gowns and fripperies, the benefits of a good education—but, he reflected now, no jewellery. So enough wealth for one Season, but no more. Instantly a wave of something like fear rippled through him.

She should have all of it. Everything she wants.

'So why must Miss Isobel limit herself to gentlemen such as Kirby and Fitch?'

'Because no titled gentleman has offered for her. Yet.' She eyed him levelly.

He swallowed.

I am not ready for this!

'And if they do not, then she will do what she must, Your Highness.'

What she must.

He could not like it. And if he had been a few years older, perhaps things might have been different. As it was, how could he think of marriage—even with someone as wonderful as Isobel—when he did not yet know who he was?

Chapter Nine

'What a glorious day for it!'

The sun was shining, Greenwich was sparkling, and a cavalcade of carriages was currently dispensing its *tonnish* occupants out into nature.

'Delightful!' was the reply, the same sentiments being echoed among the rapidly increasing group of lords, ladies, and gentlemen spilling out into bright sunshine, cerulean skies, and lush, green grass.

Izzy played her part, meandering through the throng with Anna, parasol resting delicately on one pale shoulder. Her dress was of buttercup-yellow muslin, with a fine line of ivy leaves embroidered at the hem. Carefully she angled her parasol as she walked, ensuring the blazing sun should not touch her face, for there was nothing worse than to be sunburnt. The gentlemen, she guessed, would be uncomfortable in their jackets and waistcoats, and she could only be grateful for the current fashion for loose muslin gowns for ladies. How her mama would have managed in the stiff brocade gowns of twenty-five years ago she could only imagine.

Today had been appointed as the day for a casual luncheon on the grass, on the hill above Greenwich. Those attending had agreed which foods they would provide, with

Lady Ashbourne's cook contributing five blancmanges, which were even now being unstrapped from the back of the carriage, still in their copper moulds. The food was being gathered in a central location, whence servants would distribute it to each cluster of elegant persons. The Ashbourne servants had also packed cutlery and crockery, along with cloths for them to sit on and ale and orgeat for them to drink. The carriage was the hired one they had been using for weeks now, as both Ashbourne carriages were currently in Scotland.

Rose had written to say she had arrived safely and was to begin teaching at Belvedere on the morrow, but at that point the viscount had clearly not yet arrived.

Will she have him?

Lady Ashbourne was dubious, but Izzy privately thought she would.

I believe she loves him. I only hope he loves her.

She and Anna had spoken briefly of what it might mean for them, should Rose become a viscountess. Surely then, they would be more acceptable to the high sticklers, as sisters-in-law to Lord Ashbourne, rather than orphans with no known family? While they still could not expect similar good fortune—for Rose's marriage, should it happen, would be seen as surprising, and probably assumed to be related to propinquity, since the Lennox ladies had been living in the Ashbourne townhouse all Season. Still, it might reassure Mr Kirby or Mr Fitch about the advisability of offering for Izzy.

To be fair, neither gentleman seemed to need such reassurance, for both—possibly fuelled by dislike of the other—were becoming marked in their attentions towards her, to the extent that she was beginning to avoid them a little. Once a proposal was made, she would have to decide, and she was not quite ready to do so. Stifling a sigh, she continued to greet the various ladies and gentlemen. The notion of being actually married to Mr Kirby—or Mr Fitch—was beginning to feel all too real, and she was developing an understanding that it would take an inordinate amount of courage to make vows of lifetime devotion to either gentleman. Thankfully, neither was to be present today, as Mr Kirby had an unavoidable appointment with his man of business, while Mr Fitch was apparently visiting his elderly mother somewhere south of London.

Her heart skipped, for finally she espied the blond hair and strong shoulders of Prince Claudio. He had his back to her, but she knew every line of his shape. Excitement fought with relief within her, for events always seemed flat when he was not there. Oh, she knew he was to marry his Prussian princess—although the gossips could not agree on just how fixed his betrothal was. It would always have been impossible for a prince to consider a maiden such as herself, but still, she dreamed. Even when he frustrated her. Even when he vexed her.

Hearts are not minds, she told herself. They are permitted to be foolish.

So for now she would allow herself to dream. Would indulge her foolish heart, a little. Soon the time would come when her dreams must be overruled, when she would agree to marry someone—anyone—for safety, for security. For the chance to remain here.

I shall have to be honest, she reminded herself.

Mr Kirby—or Mr Fitch—must know that she did not love him. And from what she could understand of *ton* marriages, this would not be a particular barrier.

Love matches were apparently rare. And she must not yearn for *rare*. She must accept *common*, *normal*, *ordi-*

nary. Once again, she sighed inwardly, bringing her attention back to the present.

This was real. Being here now, with the sun shining, her dreams intact, and Prince Claudio in her eyeline. Her heart lifted.

Claudio looked around surreptitiously, knowing he could not settle until he had established where she was. Thankfully, his friends—who had just been commencing their card games when he had left the club last night—would not be here today. No doubt they would sleep for many more hours yet. Good, for that gave him the opportunity to be himself without their ribbing, which was constant.

It seemed he could not speak to a young lady without being teased about courting her, although that had decreased a little since his fiction about a Prussian princess, which was now, he hoped, suitably vague enough to avoid speculation about her identity. Nor could he speak to a sober-minded gentleman or an older lady without his own set accusing him of being staid and dull. And yet, he enjoyed their company, too, when in the mood.

Why can I not be more than one person? he wondered as he and the queen made the rounds, glad to stretch their legs after the journey out from London. *Why can I not be the drunken gambler on occasion, while still remaining my father's son, with an interest in all sorts of people and activities?*

No answer came to him, and so he pushed the conundrum to the back of his mind. The day was bright, Eldon and Hawkins were snoring in their beds, and Miss Isobel was here. He could wish for nothing more.

Isobel remained in a sunny mood. She had managed to spoil the Chorleys' abhorrent scheme, Lord Ashbourne was on his way to Scotland to offer for Rose, and she was determined to steal a kiss from Prince Claudio before accepting her fate as Mrs Kirby or Mrs Fitch. Having—for now at least—given up fighting her mysterious *tendre* for the prince, it was astounding how it had spread through her, as if sunlight had penetrated every part of her. It seemed concentrated behind her breastbone, with a fierce glow that made everything in her life seem better.

As the servants laid out the cloths, she kept a subtle eye on the prince, willing him to approach. He had greeted them briefly in the initial melée, but she hoped he would return for a more meaningful conversation. *Yes!* Finally, he was heading in their direction.

Her heart skipped.

Soon I shall speak to him, and our eyes will meet again, and perhaps I will feel again what I felt in the hallway, when he said my name...

The sun was shining and life was good, and she was determined to avoid thinking of future storms. Today was today, and she would simply enjoy every moment.

The queen wished to sit with her ladies, and so Claudio had decided to make one more circuit of the gathered assembly, wondering if he might secure an invitation to join Miss Isobel and her family. Most of those present would probably welcome his company, not because of who he was, but because of *what* he was. Today, he wanted Miss Isobel and her companions to welcome him because he was *Claudio*, not because he was a prince. The notion was unsettling, challenging him to look more deeply into it, but for now he shoved it away.

In all directions cloths were being laid out, with elegant people of all ages and sizes arranging themselves on the ground. Lady Ashbourne and the two Misses Lennox were to his left, standing beneath the generous canopy of an oak tree as their servants made everything ready, but as he approached he saw that a gentleman had just joined them. His heart sank, for really he could not bear another half hour of hearing Mr Fitch—or had it been Kirby?—extolling the virtues of his horse.

He had, of course, already greeted them all, during that first frenzied ten minutes—Miss Isobel's dazzling smile seeming to be momentarily brighter than the sun. Aphrodite! he had thought again, recalling her effect on him the very first time he had laid eyes on her golden beauty.

Indeed he had greeted everyone bar the Chorleys, whom he had avoided—not precisely cutting them, but making it clear he was not inclined to welcome their company. Both mother and daughter were present today, and as he approached Lady Ashbourne and her party, he saw with horror that his path would take him directly towards Miss Chorley and her mother. Since their attempt to trap him into marriage in Lady Wright's library, he had had nothing but disdain for the pair of them but was well-bred enough not to give them the cut simply because they deserved it. Besides, a gentleman should never deliberately insult a lady. Briefly, his mind flicked to some of his previous encounters with Miss Isobel, generating a flash of shame.

What should I do?

He had only a moment to decide, for already he was near them.

'Your Highness.' The Chorley ladies curtsied, and he made his bow.

'Good day, ladies.' No enquiry after their health. No comment about the weather or the occasion. His words delivered in a hard tone. He moved on, satisfied, making for

Lady Ashbourne's area. To his great relief, the gentleman with them was neither Fitch nor Kirby, but—

'Garvald! Good to see you.' Pumping the man's hand with genuine pleasure, he realised that men like the earl, and Ashbourne, and Phillips—sober, sensible gentlemen—were becoming just as much his favourites as his drinking set.

Perhaps I should make the effort to get to know them better.

He made his greetings to everyone, then graciously accepted Lady Ashbourne's invitation to join them for luncheon—an invitation which seemed genuine. *Ah, yes*, he thought as he seated himself beside Miss Isobel, being careful not to sit on her skirts. *This is where I wished to be.*

Izzy was in alt.

This is heaven!

A beautiful summer's day, the joy of eating delicious food out of doors, and the best company. If only Rose had been here, it would have been perfect.

'May I offer you some of the beef, Miss Isobel?' Prince Claudio asked, his grey eyes meeting hers and sending a shiver of delight through her. Garvald was deep in conversation with Anna, and Lady Ashbourne was directing the servants at length about what further food to bring from the central area, where masses of shared food awaited. No one was paying any attention to Izzy and her prince.

'Yes, please.' She held out her plate, allowing her eyes to meet his and linger there. Instantly, breathing became difficult—or unimportant, perhaps. The only reality was his eyes on hers, his face so close… She swallowed, adding, 'Just a little, if you please.'

Watching as he served her, she studied the lines of his

face, the way his hair fell across his brow, his expression as he concentrated on the food...

Oh!

He looked up unexpectedly, and she gave him a sunny smile. He blinked, causing a wave of remorse to ache through her.

He is not used to pleasantness from me.

But things were different now. Following the incident with the Chorleys, there was now harmony between them. Dangerous harmony.

Dangerous?

Her heart quickened at her mind's use of such a powerful word.

Yes, dangerous.

To her peace of mind. And to her heart. For the first time she allowed herself to look forward to the day when she would be Mrs Whomever and he would marry his Prussian princess. Pain lanced through her, hot and fierce and searing. She gasped.

Concern flitted across his features. 'Isobel—Miss Isobel? You are unwell? May I be of assistance?'

'I am well, I assure you.' She took a breath. 'Indeed, I am *very* well at this moment.' Her look was intent.

He seemed to take her meaning. 'As am I.' His voice was low. 'Once you have eaten your fill, perhaps we could walk a short way together? These surroundings are idyllic.'

She nodded. 'I should like that.' *Like* it? She would love it above all things.

Sure enough, once a good half hour had passed, Garvald rose, helping Anna to her feet. The prince, a warm glint in his eye, performed the same service for Izzy, and their hands remained clasped just a moment too long.

Lady Ashbourne, a thoughtful expression on her kind

face, declined to go with them, stating she intended to find Lady Wright and Lady Jersey, if someone would help her to rise. And so the gentlemen offered her a strong hand each, and she made a breathless comment about enjoying the attentions of not one but two handsome young gentlemen. The two handsome young gentlemen exchanged a wry glance and assured her they were happy to be of service.

After seeing Lady Ashbourne off, the four of them— Izzy and Claudio, Anna and Garvald—strolled towards the tree-lined patch at the side of the hill. Just two ladies and two gentlemen, with the sun shining and nature sharing an abundance of delightful sights and aromas. No additional chaperones were needed, for who could object to a group of young people walking together in broad daylight?

Entering the blessed shade of the woods, Izzy resolved to fix the memory within her. The sound of birdsong. Sunlight shafting through gaps in the canopy, dappling the undergrowth here and there as if to say *Look here—foxgloves! Or here—wild garlic!* Some late bluebells were even dotted here and there, nestling amid the ferns with tenacious beauty. The scent of the garlic soon gave way to honeysuckle and hawthorn as they made their way through the woodland. Deliberately, Izzy noticed it, too.

But most of her attention was given to the man by her side. His height and strength. The way he moved. The way his arm felt beneath her gloved hand.

Anna and the Earl of Garvald were behind them, and frankly, Izzy wished them both at Jericho. If only they would vanish, she could perhaps contrive to get the kiss she craved. A kiss from a prince—just like in the old stories…

By unspoken agreement, Izzy and Prince Claudio maintained a brisk pace, allowing the others to fall behind a little. Still, Izzy felt watched. If she were to kiss the prince, she wanted no possibility of them being seen. Trapping him into an unwanted marriage was an abhorrent notion. It still made her shudder to think how appallingly the Chorleys had behaved. And as for poor Rose, she had undoubtedly kissed Ashbourne because she loved him, not because she wished to compromise him. Indeed, Rose had left London rather than force the viscount to offer for her. No, Izzy's wish was simple: one secret kiss from the prince before resigning herself to a life with Mr Kirby. Or the other one.

And Prince Claudio wanted to kiss her. She knew it with absolute certainty. From the way he looked at her. From her awareness of this thing—whatever it was—that thrummed between them.

Frustratingly, she could still hear Anna and her beau behind them and knew that the privacy she craved was not within her power to achieve. Still, the opportunity might not be entirely wasted. Here was the chance for private speech at least.

'Your Highness, I—'

'Please do not call me that.'

She eyed him quizzically. 'Then, what should I call you?'

He sighed. 'I should like you to call me Claudio…but that would cause a scandal, would it not?'

She nodded, her eyes dancing. 'Then, I shall call you Claudio when we are alone—and only then.'

Abruptly the air between them changed. 'Say it again!' Claudio's eyes were ablaze.

'Claudio.' She could barely breathe.

His gaze had dropped to her lips, and strangely, she could feel something there, almost as though he were touching her.

'Again!' he demanded.

'Claudio.' Her heart was pounding, her knees decidedly shaky, and her innards had melted in a most unexpected manner.

He groaned. 'To hear my own name on your lips… I have used your name a few times in error. Forgive me. But may I?'

She nodded. 'Isobel. Or Izzy, which is what my sisters call me.'

'Izzy.' He tried it, then shook his head. 'No. It has your fire, but Isobel is better. More romantical.'

'You think me romantical?'

'Most certainly. Romantical. And passionate. You live in your body in a way that many people do not, I think.'

The look that accompanied his words sent flames licking through her.

What is happening to me?

She swallowed, but for the moment words eluded her.

'You were saying…?' he prompted.

'Oh, yes. I was recalling the first time we met, and how much has changed since then.'

He frowned. 'My behaviour was not what it should have been. I apologise.'

'For what?'

'For causing you discomfort. I should not wish you any vexation or distress—no, not for an instant.'

His eyes blazed with intensity, and her heart melted.

He thinks me romantical, and yet I have never heard anything so romantical as the words he has just uttered.

Determined to try and conceal his effect on her—for it was both disconcerting and fascinating—she laughed lightly. 'I am no delicate flower, I assure you.'

He frowned. 'You are, and you are not. I see your beauty and your determination. I sense the strength within you. So maybe not a flower, then. Perhaps you are a tree in blossom.' He smiled. 'We have a special tree at home—*der Dorflinde*. You remind me of the *Dorflinde*, Isobel.'

'The village linden tree,' she translated.

He raised an eyebrow. 'You speak German?'

She confirmed it, adding—in his language, 'I have heard of linden trees, but I do not believe I have ever seen one.'

'But you speak German perfectly!' He shook his head. 'Honestly, I never expected to find—' He took a breath, continuing in a much more superficial tone, 'Lindens are not common here, I understand. Where I come from they are important. Strong, beautiful, and with the sweetest-scented blossom. Traditionally, courts were held under the protection of their branches.'

What had he been going to say just now? To find *what*?

Knowing she could not quiz him, she asked simply, 'Courts?'

'Yes, courts as in justice. But also courts as in court-ing.' He leaned closer, and her breath caught in her throat. 'There is even an old love poem called "Under der Linden".'

'Do you know it?'

Throwing him a challenge with her eyes, she hoped he would accept, as in this moment she wanted nothing more than to hear a love poem on his lips.

'"*Under der Linden*,"' he began, his voice deep and resonant, '"*an der Heide…*"'

She translated in her mind.

Under the linden, on the heather,
Where we two rested.
There you might find—beautiful together—
Pressed flowers and grass,
Beside the woods in the valley.

His voice tailed off, and her entire body was consumed with longing. In this moment she wished for nothing more than to find a secret place under a tree and lie there with him in the sunshine. Vaguely she knew she needed more than just his kiss but did not know exactly what. All she was certain of was that kissing him was *necessary*.

His mind seemed to have gone in a similar direction. 'That first day, I asked you for a kiss and you said no.'

'I did.' The entire world seemed to pause, as her attention remained riveted on him.

'And if I asked now?'

She swallowed. Now that he had said it, caution threatened to overwhelm her.

Remember what happened to Rose. Remember what the Chorleys tried.

'A kiss,' she began, 'may be thought to be more than a kiss.'

His brow was furrowed. 'I would not wish for anyone to misinterpret…'

Disappointment speared through her. He could not have made it plainer that he was offering nothing more than a kiss.

But that is all I am asking for, is it not?

She was all confusion.

She tried again. 'I mean to say, if someone saw a maiden kissing a gentleman, they might misinterpret what they were seeing.'

His brow cleared. 'Ah! I understand you. What the Chorleys tried was reprehensible, and I do not believe for an instant that you would ever attempt such a thing.'

'Indeed not!' she declared hotly. 'However, in this instance I was also referring to the need to protect the lady's reputation. She, too, might be compromised and forced into a marriage she did not desire.' Briefly her mind flicked to a couple of gentlemen she found abhorrent.

His eyes widened briefly. 'I see... I see.'

What? What does he see?

This conversation was not going as she expected. 'And so,' she continued with determination, 'a maiden should only kiss a gentleman if she wishes to, *and* if she can be certain they will not be observed. And since débutantes are never alone in company, I suspect it would be nigh on impossible.'

'But not hopeless!' He sent her a sideways glance, and a delicious shiver ran through her. 'There was some talk of a masquerade at Vauxhall...'

She gasped. 'I am shocked you would even suggest such a thing. Young ladies, I am informed, must never set foot in Vauxhall, which I am told is a place for all manner of vices.' She frowned. 'Not that I know *precisely* what they might be. But I am certain my sisters and I would never be permitted to visit such a place.'

'You must remember that I, too, am new to London. I did not intend to offend. Very well. No Vauxhall.' Placing his other hand over hers, he squeezed it gently. 'Then, I shall take this as a test of ingenuity. For, Miss Isobel Lennox, my wish to kiss you is unabated.'

Unable to speak, she simply nodded. Fire was blazing through her—a fire that needed his lips on hers.

'And your opinions? If they are unchanged, I shall endeavour not to speak more of this. But I believe—I hope—that perhaps you *do* now wish to kiss me?'

She took a breath. 'I do.' *There!* She had said it aloud, and to her it sounded like a vow.

Their eyes caught and held, depriving her of the power

of speech. Mutely, she nodded, and his eyes kindled again with desire. 'Isobel!'

Voices from behind reminded them both that this was neither the place nor the time. Grinding her teeth together, Isobel walked on, her entire body thrumming with frustration.

Chapter Ten

'And so, if I can find an opportunity, I am determined to kiss him. And nothing you can say can deter me from this, Anna!'

It was the morning after the trip to Greenwich. Izzy and Anna were ambling southwards through the Green Park, and Izzy's mind, body, and heart remained focused on Claudio.

'I shall not even try!' was Anna's response. 'I know you too well, Izzy.' She sighed. 'But be careful. Remember what happened to Rose.'

'All may yet be well with Rose. Ashbourne intends to offer for her, as you know.'

'That is true, and she may accept him. But Rose went away because she did not wish to *force* him to offer for her. I would not wish for you to face the same fate.'

Izzy shuddered. 'Decidedly not! Which is why I must not kiss him unless I am certain we will not be discovered.' Her eyes danced with glee. 'It will be such an adventure, to kiss a man!'

'Especially to kiss a prince! But tell me, is this simply an adventure to you? Or are you… Do you still feel…?

'I still have a *tendre* for him, if that is what you are asking. Indeed, it seems to be going deeper and deeper into me.' She frowned. 'It is most disconcerting, but it feels as though he is *part* of me. Is that not odd?'

'Izzy, I hate to be the one to say this to you, but the chances of a prince marrying a lady with a small dowry and no known parents—'

'It is impossible. I know it! But I have quite given up hope that we shall ever discover the truth about our parents. Without knowing who Mama was, my quest to discover the identity of our papa cannot even begin.' She shrugged. 'I am entirely resigned to being an unsuitable bride for anyone of consequence. Which is why all I want from the prince is a kiss. Just one kiss, and then I shall tie myself to Mr Kirby or Mr Fitch and be perfectly content with my life.'

Anna looked dubious at this, and so Izzy pressed on along the flower-bedecked path, changing the subject. 'I do hope we hear from Rose soon. Not knowing is killing me!'

Thankfully, her sister allowed the conversation to be diverted, and as they continued through the park towards the Buckingham House gardens, Izzy was conscious that she was steering them towards the mansion where Claudio even now was resting. Claudio. Not Prince Claudio. Just… Claudio.

They would not see him, she knew. Despite that one morning when they had met him in the park, Izzy knew that gentlemen invariably stayed out late and rose even later. But to know that her feet were even now taking her closer to where he was? That was enough.

Claudio woke, turned over in his comfortable bed, and stretched. Once again, he had returned home early. Once again, he was awake at a time more suited to his life back in his father's principality, rather than the late hours held by the *ton*. Rejecting the uncomfortable notion that this meant he did not belong here, he rose, making straight for the window.

Isobel. For the hundredth time he went over in his mind the events of yesterday. His name on her lips. The way she had looked at him.

She wants to kiss me!

The thought made him feel like a colossus, a god, a king. He, who had enjoyed kisses and more from many a woman, had never before felt so...so *überwältigt*!

No English word would do, but he tried them out. *Overwhelmed. Dazzled. Astonished. Overpowered. Defeated.* She was everything, and he was overcome by her. Aphrodite? Yes, and more. Never had he known anything like the frustrated desire which was these days his constant companion.

And alongside his body's frustrations, Isobel had also left his mind in turmoil. Last night while out with his friends he had been too distracted to be fully part of their usual pattern of cards and wine, inane raillery giving way to ribald buffoonery as the night progressed. He had left, discontented and distracted. Because of the war raging within him. A battle between euphoric confidence and crippling doubt.

Despite wanting to kiss him, Isobel had made it crystal clear that she would not want to be trapped into marriage with him. A lady might be 'forced into a marriage she did not desire', she had said. Yet Lady Kelgrove had told him Isobel and her sisters needed to marry.

It made no sense unless, somehow, Isobel had seen through his princely regalia. Seen the unworthiness beneath. Seen that he was a fraud. Born to royalty, yet never having earned his position. Drinking, gambling, sporting... She had depth, and energy, and *purpose*, somehow. Yes, he knew she was a lady, limited by her sex and her class just as much as he, yet she seemed *whole*. Sure of who she was.

She would kiss him but not marry him. So…

A motion below in the gardens caught his eye. Two women had just appeared, turning a corner to enter into the pretty wildness below his window. In an instant he took in the details—embroidered muslin gowns, parasols—ladies! He looked closer, noting slim figures, identical golden locks…it could only be Isobel and her sister. Transfixed, he stood frozen, trying to discern their features. No. They were as yet too far away. The gowns! The maiden on the left wore a muslin printed with tiny blue flowers. The other? His heart leapt. Yellow flowers—the motif in her signature hue.

Isobel!

Had he conjured her up through his intense thoughts and feelings?

It all had taken only a few seconds. Now, with dawning horror, he realised he had been observed. As one, the sisters' hands flew to their mouths in shock.

Instantly, he dived back, leaning against the wall beside the window, his breathing shallow and his heart pounding. He was naked, and Isobel had *seen* him. His body, belatedly reacting, had begun to respond in a predictable manner, but his mind was spinning. *She is here!* What should he do?

Reluctantly, he acknowledged that by the time he had dressed and ventured outdoors she would be long gone. And besides, he had to hope that he had not been recognised. They had been far enough away that he had been unable to divine their features, so hopefully they had not divined his. Yes, surely they could not know it was him? His mind was awhirl. Golden Aphrodite in golden sunshine.

And it is me she wants to kiss.

* * *

Still idly chatting, Izzy and Anna entered the pretty gardens around Buckingham House. Members of the *ton* were always welcome there, the queen being relaxed about such matters, and the gardens were one of Izzy's favourite walks. The fact that *he* was there, sleeping somewhere nearby, simply provided an added thrill.

'I cannot believe the Season will end soon,' Anna was saying, 'for it seems like only yesterday that we arrived!'

'I know what you mean, and yet it also seems as though we have been here for an age,' Izzy offered thoughtfully. 'So much has happened—'

She froze, the thought lost, for movement at one of the first-floor windows had caught her eye. There, right in front of them, completely naked, was a man. Young, strong, and well-proportioned, he stood there as if greeting the day and seemed unaware of their presence. Even as her eyes widened and her hand flew to her mouth in shock, Izzy had recognised him. It was Prince Claudio, she was certain of it. Fair hair, the right height and build, and more…she *knew* him. Between her artist's eye and her smitten heart, she knew it could be no other.

'Oh, my goodness!' Anna sounded as shocked as Izzy felt. As they watched, Claudio abruptly moved away from the window, perhaps realising he could be seen. 'That man was naked!'

'He was.' Izzy could not help but giggle a little. 'The first naked man I have ever seen in the flesh.'

And entirely fitting it should be him.

'Why, have you seen other naked men?'

Izzy snorted. 'Of course! Now, do not look at me like that. My study of art has led me to peruse the great masters of painting and sculpture. You also must have also seen reproductions of Michelangelo's *David*. And what of all those classical paintings?'

'The paintings,' Anna replied primly, 'usually have a fig leaf or drape of fabric to hide the, er...'

Izzy chuckled. 'No fig leaf today, that is for certain.' She adopted a thoughtful tone. 'And I am not sure a fig leaf would be adequate to the task. It was much larger than the ones I have seen on classical statues. The shape of it was most interesting, do you not think? The way it—'

Anna clapped her hands to her ears, half laughing. 'Stop! No, it was *not* interesting, Izzy! Indeed as gently born maidens we must never let it be known that we have seen such a thing!'

'Ah, that is a shame, for really it was fascinating to see how it nestled there, amid—'

'No more!' Anna turned. 'I want to go back home now. If one of the queen's hedonistic sons wishes to parade around naked, then that, I suppose, is his privilege. But I do not have to look at his—at *him*, I mean!'

Izzy took this in good humour, inwardly relieved for Claudio's sake that Anna had not recognised him. 'Oh, very well. But you must admit that what we saw was a fine specimen of manhood.'

'Do you mean the man? Or his—?' She shook her head, laughing outright. 'Now you have me joining you in this madness, Izzy. Lord, who would have thought moving to London would expose us to such an education!'

'But we must always be ready to learn, Anna. Lady Kelgrove has the right of it, you know.'

'Why? What is her view?'

'She often says that young ladies should be taught about such matters—the marital bed, childbirth, topics that no one will speak about to us. We have brains for thinking, too, and are not such fragile creatures that we would swoon from hearing the truth!'

'But how can you know you would not swoon, when you do not know the truth?' retorted Anna, with inescapable logic.

'If Rose marries the viscount, we could ask her! For she would surely tell us.'

'You know,' said Anna slowly, 'that is not the worst idea you have ever had, Izzy!'

On they went, jesting and teasing one another, while inwardly Izzy saved every detail of the memory and allowed her pulse and thudding heart to gradually return to normal. Claudio in all his glory had had a profound effect on her and would not be forgotten.

An hour later, having washed, dressed, and broken his fast, Claudio strode down the ornate hallway in Buckingham House to the queen's quarters, determination in every nerve and sinew. The queen was a female relative. Surely she could advise him? Having been admitted to her suite, he was disappointed to find her surrounded by her ladies, and with at least three servants standing mutely to the side in case they should be needed. After a frustrating half hour he finally suggested a walk in the gardens, and to his relief she agreed.

Her retinue accompanied them, of course, but he was able to walk with her a little ahead of the others. If he kept his voice low, then he should be able to speak freely. The problem was he now was unsure of what to say. The queen, seemingly oblivious to his dilemma, prattled on about the weather, the gardens, her dog, while pausing frequently to deadhead roses and geraniums as she passed.

'I was speaking to Lady Kelgrove yesterday. She adores the Lennox girls,' declared Her Majesty in a casual manner.

'She does?' Strangely, for a man of four-and-twenty, abruptly Claudio felt like a boy caught stealing sweetmeats from the kitchen.

She sent him a sideways glance. 'Out with it, Claudio! You might as well tell me. Is it Miss Isobel?' She frowned. 'Or the Chorley creature?'

'I…' Feeling as though he should not admit this, he sought refuge in generalities. 'I cannot say. But…you are a woman.'

'I am.' A gleam of humour lit her eye.

Persisting despite deep discomfort, he managed to continue. 'I seek counsel from you. Wisdom, if you are content to share it. About how the minds of women work.'

'Ah, the eternal question from men. But you intrigue me! What is your specific question?'

He squared his shoulders. 'How should a man respond to a woman—say, a young lady—who indicated she would welcome a kiss but would not welcome marriage?'

The queen chuckled. 'Not Miss Chorley, then! Very well. A man should *admire* such a lady even more than he already does. Let me ask a question of you, Claudio. Have you ever wished to—er—kiss a girl and *not* wished to marry her?'

Dozens of times.

'Well, yes. But—'

'But nothing. Women are not so different to men, after all.'

'But young ladies, *débutantes*…?'

'What? Did you think they would all take one look at your princely title and swoon at your feet?' She harrumphed at the notion. 'A true lady is not blinded by such things as titles or parentage. A true prince ought to be the same.'

Her words pierced him like arrows. So it was possible

for ladies—like gentlemen—to want kisses only, with no hope for marriage? Well, naturally, he knew that there were many such women—widows, willing servants. Had he not enjoyed bed sport with many of them? But the Marriage Mart was such an important enterprise for young ladies of the *ton*, it was strange to acknowledge that a débutante such as Miss Isobel might not wish to marry him.

'Did you think,' the queen continued, briskly pulling dead flowers from a rosebush, 'that because Miss Chorley tried to entrap you, Miss Isobel Lennox would do the same?' She sent him a keen glance. 'No, she has too much strength of character for such a trick. And furthermore, she is too open, too *honest*. One knows exactly who she is after just a few minutes in her company. My advice? Kiss the girl, and enjoy it. But do not *think* of compromising her, or you shall have me to answer to!'

'I should not dream of it!' he retorted. 'Not that I would not *wish* to, but I myself am not ready for marriage, and so...'

'You are nearer to readiness than you realise' was her response, 'but I am glad to hear you are more honourable than my own sons, who have struggled to give me a legitimate grandchild between them, despite their tomcatting.'

He did not take the bait, instead diverting the conversation to her social engagements. 'I know you do not often host large events, but I had heard that young ladies are not permitted to attend Vauxhall, so I wondered if perhaps—'

'Ha! You seek my assistance in creating opportunities! Very well, I shall plan a light masquerade—a *bal masqué*—but no more than kisses, mind! And you shall assist me. But do not get found out!'

He agreed with alacrity, expressing his gratitude in forthright terms.

She patted his hand. 'It will do you good, you know.'

'What will?'

'Having to woo her properly.'

'But I have no intention of wooing any lady! I am too young for marriage.'

If I could have only one kiss from Isobel, then I would be satisfied.

'You may believe so, but that does not make it true. Now, about this masquerade ball, let us plan it together.' She chuckled. 'I shall be a demanding queen and require all the ladies to wear white, even the older ones. Or wear a rosebud, perhaps…' Ruthlessly, she pulled a wilted flower from its stem, discarding it. 'Let me think… The gardens, naturally. A civilised version of Vauxhall…*not* a ridotto, of course. Everyone must behave with propriety… Half masks, white for the ladies, black for the gentlemen…'

'Excuse me, miss. My lady has need of you.'

Izzy looked at the maid blankly. Having positioned herself so that her small easel was facing away from the door, thankfully any servant entering her chamber would not be able to see the shocking image that Izzy had been sketching for the past two hours. Ostensibly a study of da Vinci's *Vitruvian Man*, in reality her inspiration was the glorious sight she had seen earlier.

'Hmmm?'

'In the drawing room, miss.' She paused. 'There are letters lately arrived. Something from the palace. And letters from Scotland.'

Now Izzy was attending. 'From Scotland?' She rose, closing her sketchbook. 'I shall come at once! Thank you, Mary.'

Hurrying to the drawing room, her mind was racing.

The information in those letters was important not just for Rose but for all three of them—Lady Ashbourne, too.

'What news?' she asked breathlessly, entering the drawing room, at the same time taking in the expression of delight on Lady Ashbourne's kind face. Anna was there, too, and currently engaged in reading a letter. Further missives—unopened—sat on the low table beside Lady Ashbourne.

'They are to marry! Which I must say I *knew* just as soon as I saw my nephew's determination on the day he decided to follow her. Travelling all the way to Scotland. And in the old coach, too! No, it was more than duty or a sense of honour. He loves her, and I knew it in here!' She tapped her generous bosom. 'Anna, show her!'

Anna handed her the letter, a tremulous smile on her face. 'Oh, Izzy, it is true! He says they are to marry in Elgin— and look at the date! They are already married by now!'

My dearest aunt...

Izzy read the letter, her eyes flying over the viscount's words.

Delighted...
My affections are returned...
Truly happy...

'How wonderful! A love match!' Izzy picked up the other letters. 'This one is for us, Anna. From Rose!'

The final letter, from Mr Marnoch, was addressed to Lady Ashbourne, and so Izzy handed it to her.

Rose was just as delighted as the viscount, it seemed, and her sisters were left in no doubt about her feelings for her now-husband. All three ladies expressed their joy, read each of the letters multiple times, and even—it had to be admitted—shed a few happy tears.

Having called for tea to settle her exalted nerves, Lady Ashbourne shared another missive with them. On top of the wonderful news of the recent nuptials, they were also invited to a masquerade ball at Buckingham House.

'The queen's ball is likely to be the event of the Season,' she declared. 'I suspect Her Majesty has waited until now in order to ensure it is the last major event before Season's end.'

Season's end. Must I accept a proposal that night?

The thought was lowering. Refusing to allow such a shadow to discourage her on a day of such happy news, Izzy responded brightly. 'It says all ladies must wear white. Our court gowns will be perfect! I still love the beading, the way it catches the light. I had begun remaking mine, but perhaps we should ask the dressmaker to adjust—?'

'Oh, no!' Lady Ashbourne looked horrified. 'You cannot attend a ball in a made-over dress!' She grew thoughtful. 'And something else. I am minded to keep the news of James and Rose's wedding to ourselves for now, my dears.'

'But why?' Izzy wanted to shout from the rooftops about her sister's joy. 'Is it—I mean, since we do not know about our parentage, will this marriage harm the Ashbourne reputation?'

'Lord, no! A good marriage is the making of all of you, my dears. My nephew has shown that he values Rose's *character* above her *name*—or lack of it—and so, if we handle this correctly, we may silence those who would criticise you... But the handling is important. Yes, I think it best if we allow James and Rose to make their own announcement once back in London. And besides,' she chuckled, 'will it not be delightful to hold such a wonderful secret to ourselves for a little while?'

'I suppose,' replied Izzy doubtfully. They had to trust Lady Ashbourne's superior knowledge of the *ton*. Still, at least Rose was happy. That was the most significant part of all of this.

Chapter Eleven

In truth there was something delicious about holding such a secret, Izzy had to admit, as she dressed for the Queen's Masquerade Ball, ten days later. Rose was happy, and being sister-in-law to a viscount might serve to counter some of the criticism levelled at Izzy and Anna for their unknown parentage.

True to Lady Ashbourne's request, Izzy had not breathed a word about Rose and the viscount to anyone. It had been difficult at times to resist the temptation, particularly when people like Lady Renford and Mrs Thaxby continued to adopt a sneering tone towards her. The Chorleys, thankfully, continued to give her a wide berth—unlike the prince, who was decidedly showing her some marked attention.

In one sense their conversations were perfectly innocuous—they discussed books, and philosophy, and politics, as well as history, and even a little gossip. She found him to have a well-formed mind, quite at odds with his hedonistic friends, who could discuss nothing but sport and fashion. But there was more: deeper conversations where they allowed each other to see something of their true selves. He told her of his upbringing, and she shared with him something of her life in Elgin.

I know him now.

It had become a habit for him to sit with her, dance with her, or walk with her at whatever events they both attended, and he also had slipped into a pattern of asking her plans for the next day—she knowing that, unless promised elsewhere, he would endeavour to attend the same events.

'Oh, miss, you look beautiful,' Mary cooed, fastening the final tiny buttons on Izzy's white satin gown. It had been fashioned from the masses of fabric from her court gown, Izzy having taken the scissors to it herself, sewing it into the more modern straight silhouette. Lady Ashbourne had had to be persuaded, deploring made-over gowns as a sign of poverty. However, given the queen's decree that all ladies irrespective of age must wear white to her ball, she had reluctantly conceded that the glittering, beaded fabric could not be bettered. Also, she had mused, it did no harm to remind society of the Belles' success at their presentation.

With this in mind she had once again loaned Anna and Izzy the same diamond tiaras as they had worn at court, this time without the feather and lappet headdress. The effect, Izzy acknowledged, was delightful. Raising a gloved hand, she touched the glittering tiara reverently.

'Thank you. Now I just need my fan. Lady Ashbourne said earlier that she has our masks.'

Having accepted the fan from Mary, she glided downstairs, feeling decidedly princess-like. Anna arrived a few moments later, followed by Lady Ashbourne and her maid, a cluster of masques clutched in her ladyship's hand.

'Girls, you look delightful!' Smoothing her own gown, she added, 'It has been an age since I wore white, but I must say I like it! We matrons are not normally afforded the opportunity. Now, take one of these each, and try them.'

Izzy took a half mask, allowing Lady Ashbourne's personal maid to tie the strings behind her head, then rearranging her coiffure to cover them. The masks were of white satin to match their gowns and were lavishly decorated with embroidery, beads, and feathers. No sooner had Izzy donned the mask than she felt *different*. Yes, anyone who saw them together must realise they were looking at two of the Lennox girls, but there was a certain freedom provided by assumed anonymity that sent the excitement of *possibility* thrumming in Izzy's veins.

I feel daring!

Which of course was exactly why young ladies were not normally permitted to attend masked balls at Vauxhall. The combination of anonymity and dark alleyways had led to many a young lady being compromised. A shiver ran down Izzy's spine at the very notion. No, she had no intention of being compromised or even ravished—whatever that involved. But tonight she had every intention of kissing a prince.

Following the others out to the carriage, Izzy was unsurprised to see clear skies and a glorious sunset. Tonight would be perfect. She just knew it.

Claudio stepped through the glazed doors and onto the western terrace, drawn by the golden rays of the setting sun. The stage was set. All around, the queen's servants were making the final arrangements for tonight's masked ball—tables, chairs, floral displays… Soon the flambeaux would be lit, and over the next hour darkness would fall, slowly, gently, cloaking them in invisibility. His black half mask dangled from his hand, the metal beading reflecting the evening glow.

Making one final tour, he declared himself content. Organising the ball with the queen and her staff had been strangely satisfying—a reminder of the duties he had chafed at in his father's court.

I missed this—being purposeful.

If tonight's ball was a success, then he could justly claim some responsibility. The notion pleased him.

'Your Highness.' A breathless page was hurrying towards him. 'The queen desires your presence. The first guests are arriving.'

'Very well.' Securing his mask, he made his way back inside to the large reception room where the queen would receive her guests and where they would be served with food and drink. The musicians were already outside on the terrace, the dancing area a cleared square of ground below. On three sides there were walkways which, as soon as darkness fell, would no doubt be used by intrepid couples seeking the cover of darkness. With a little luck and ingenuity, he was determined to be among them, Isobel by his side. And then…

'Claudio!' Arrayed in white and gold, the queen allowed him to kiss her hand. 'I am so glad you asked me to do this, I declare I have not been so entertained in an age!' As she spoke, the doors opened, the major-domo announcing the first guests, and Claudio prepared himself to greet them one and all. It being a masquerade, none gave their true names, but instead used pseudonyms such as Madame Incognita and Lord Inconnu. When two golden-haired beauties accompanied by an older matron finally arrived, his attention was transfixed.

'I am Lady Hera,' declared the matron, 'and these are my charges, Athene and Aphrodite.' She indicated with a hand which was which. Athene made a polite curtsy, while Aphrodite… Hunger flashed in Aphrodite's blue eyes as she glanced at him, before she adopted a more acceptable expression. *Lord!*

'Ah,' said the queen. 'No doubt Artemis is off on a hunt, is she not?'

'Indeed, Your Majesty,' replied Lady Ashbourne. 'But we do believe she will return before long.'

As the queen and her friend spoke further of Rose, Athene-Anna joining in, Claudio stepped off the dais, extending a hand. 'Fair Aphrodite! Will you dance with me?'

She dipped her head. 'I shall, Lord—' She tilted her head questioningly.

'Tonight, I believe I must be Ares, God of War and Aphrodite's one true love.'

Taking his hand, she curtsied gracefully. 'Ares,' she breathed. 'Ares the valiant.'

Lady Ashbourne and her charges were the last guests to arrive, and so together Ares and Aphrodite walked across the room, lost in a sea of masked revellers. The air was feverish, the company enjoying, it seemed, the freedom of privacy in a crowd. Outside the last rays of the setting sun sent warmth across dancers and musicians alike. A quadrille was already underway, and so Claudio stood with his Aphrodite to await the next dance, talking softly and savouring the moment. Tonight, if she remained willing, he would find a way.

Izzy closed her eyes briefly, savouring the warmth of the setting sun on her face, the warmth of his strong arm sensed through her glove and his jacket. Like all of the gentlemen, he wore black, with white knee breeches, a snowy cravat, and a waistcoat of white and gold. Mr Brummel had long held that gentlemen should wear only black coats in the evening, and tonight Izzy could only agree with him.

Claudio looked dangerous, other-worldly, enticing... To her he had never looked better—apart from the fact she could only see the bottom half of his face. Still, this held unexpected benefits, for her gaze was constantly drawn to his lips. How had she never noticed before how perfect they were? Their colour, their shape—the lower lip full and beautifully carved, the contrast between the strong angles of his jaw and the soft curves of his lips causing the most delicious flutterings within her.

Turning his head, he looked at her, his eyes glittering behind his mask. Leaning towards her, he murmured in her ear, 'If you keep looking at me like that, then I shall kiss you right here in front of everyone!'

She caught her breath. 'No, you must not!'

He laughed. 'Of course I shall not! Not here, leastways. After dark.' The promise in his voice sent a shiver through her.

They danced la Boulangere together—a perfectly civil undertaking—and yet Izzy had never been more conscious of him. His warmth beside her, the hunger in his gaze each time he looked at her... Honestly, the anticipation of his kiss was the most delicious sensation she had ever experienced. And since the reality might turn out to be something of a let-down, she could not imagine sharing spittle with another person to be in any way pleasing—then *this* was the moment of peak enjoyment. This was the moment she must remember forever.

At the end of the dance he saluted her, his lips pressed to her satin glove. 'Until later, my Aphrodite,' he murmured softly, and her lips curved in response.

'I look forward to it!' she declared boldly, locking her gaze with his. With satisfaction, she heard him catch his breath, but before he had time to say more she spun away.

Nearby a lone figure stood scanning all of the dancers, his left hand playing with a signet ring on his right. She shuddered, walking in the opposite direction.

Tonight I can avoid my dull suitors was her gleeful thought as she dived into the crowd.

Two hours later supper was served inside, and Izzy made a show of putting a few things on her plate, though in reality she was too agitated for food. Her pulse was tumultuous, her attention fragmented, and she—like many others—was constantly scanning the crowd to try to figure out who was whom. Except in her case, she was looking for a specific man: blond hair, tall, strong form, wearing a waistcoat of white and gold. She had seen him a few times after their dance, dancing, sipping wine, or conversing with a gentleman or lady.

But tonight he is mine!

Fierceness rose within her as she imagined claiming him in front of everyone, wrapping herself around him and feeling his arms tighten about her. Yes, she would claim him tonight—just not in public. Smiling, she turned to respond to the plump matron beside her, agreeing that the queen had outdone herself with such a marvellous event.

Aphrodite and Athene were everywhere—and nowhere. Yet they had not, Claudio noticed, stood together. Not even once. This was highly unusual, for the Belles often gravitated towards each other at events. Chuckling inwardly at Isobel's ingenuity, he realised that most people could have no clue which of the slim, white-clad maidens held the surname Lennox. Fair hair, tiara, identical masks and gowns, yet never together at once, revealing who they were. If any of the guests had been trying to keep track of them, it would have been almost impossible, since no one could say at any time which of them they were seeing, or even whether they were looking at one of the triplets.

Yet he knew. The tiaras were different. And she even *walked* differently to her sister, her movements always purposeful, always fired by the restless curiosity within her. Vitality. Spirit. *Lebenskraft*. Truly, he had never known anyone like her.

There she is!

His heart leapt as he spotted her, seated at a supper table and making conversation with a plump lady next to her. Keeping her in view he seated himself at a nearby table, noting that outside it was now fully dark. After supper he would make his move.

'Excuse me.' Rising, Izzy left the supper table, making her way to the ladies' retiring room as it was likely to be quiet just now. In fact it was entirely empty apart from the serving maids stationed there to assist with toilette or sewing repairs, all the ladies currently engaged in enjoying the delicious supper provided by the queen. Emerging afterwards, she felt her heart leap as she saw a familiar figure walking towards her. Prince Claudio!

'Hail, golden Aphrodite!' His voice was soft as he invoked their first meeting, back in a hallway in Grantham.

This time she allowed her eyes to smile. 'Hail, Lord Ares.' She had reached him, and he stood stock-still in the centre of the deserted hall. 'Now will you let me pass?'

He remembered, too. 'First, a kiss!'

She caught her breath. 'Here? Now?' Someone might come upon them at any moment. Reluctantly, she shook her head. 'Too dangerous.'

'I agree. I shall meet you at the statue of Hermes in a few minutes. Do you know where that is?'

She nodded. She knew every corner of the royal garden. The statue of Hermes was at the very end of a shady path, perfect for a dangerous encounter.

'Very well—but only a kiss, mind!'

He chuckled. 'As I mentioned previously, your manner often reminds me of the queen. Strong women, both of you. I like that.' Stepping back, he motioned for her to pass, and this time she deliberately brushed against him as she did so, enjoying the shocking feeling of his warm body against hers.

He had not moved, and she refused to look back, simply relishing the picture she had in her mind's eye of him frozen there in the hallway.

I did that to him.

The sense of power was heady, intoxicating.

Without pausing she walked straight through the supper room to the terrace beyond, looking neither left nor right. Straight through the dancing area she glided, feeling as though she were truly Aphrodite, with the power to turn men's heads and leave them longing for her. Well, it seemed to be true of one man, at least. And he a prince!

Calmly, elegantly, she moved gracefully down the dimly-lit path, the velvety darkness enveloping her in a warm cloak. On either side, small flambeaux lighted the way, the gaps between them enveloped in inky darkness. Reaching the statue, she stepped off the path into the shade of the hedge, concealing herself there lest someone else appear unexpectedly. Now all she had to do was wait.

She lifted her eyes to the heavens. A thousand stars twinkled approvingly towards her—a diadem of stars, a cascade, a shower of silver light. As her eyes adjusted to the darkness, she saw that there were not a thousand stars. Ten thousand, a hundred thousand, a *million* stars—and all of them combining to provide exactly the right amount of light, strong enough to see him, gentle enough to protect them from prying eyes.

Her breath caught, for her ear had detected the sound of someone approaching. She watched him approach, every step confirming the familiarity of his shape, his gait. He passed a flambeau and she briefly saw his face, that jawline she had sketched so many times. Might she, tonight, touch his face, learn it as best she could through gloved fingers?

He had arrived. As he turned his head left and right she stepped forwards, feeling as though this one step was the most daring action she had ever taken.

Their eyes met, his glittering in the dimness of the night, and she shook with the power of his gaze.

What is this thing between us?

No words were exchanged between them. Instead he walked to her, took her hand, and kissed it. As if reading her mind he placed her hand on his cheek, and she thrilled to feel the warmth of his skin through the fine fabric of her glove. His own right hand continued upwards, his knuckle caressing her chin, her jaw, her cheek. Now he was trailing his fingertips over her face to her ear, and she gasped as a sudden sensation ran through her. Skin on skin. With his hands on her face and her hand touching his, she hardly knew what sensation to listen to most closely. Of its own volition her other hand came up, and finally she traced his beloved jaw, his cheekbones, every moment a miracle of discovery.

Now his thumb was tracing her lower lip, and she gasped as the movement brought her insides to life in a novel, unexpected, and entirely delightful manner. Leaning closer, he nuzzled her face with his, and she responded, enjoying the sensation: the warmth of his breath, the silkiness of his skin interrupted by rough stubble in places. *My, how thrilling!* Never had she experienced anything like it. She knew only that she wanted his lips on hers, wanted it more than she had ever wanted anything in her life.

Being Izzy, she did not hesitate but boldly moved her face to align her lips with his. A surprised groan sounded in his throat, making Izzy's knees somehow soften. Afraid she might swoon—not something she was prepared to accept— she slid her hands to his shoulders as she had during their waltz, even as he slanted his head a little, moving his lips on hers. She gasped, and suddenly she was in his arms, her body pressed to his and his arms encircling her so tightly she could feel the buttons on his waistcoat. And either he had something unexpected in his breeches, or his manhood was significantly larger than when she had seen him naked at the window. A delicious hardness was pressing into her nether regions, and even as his lips moved on hers, his hips swivelled a little, making her gasp again. This time he was ready, and his tongue darted into her parted lips, connecting with hers and adding to the maelstrom of sensation pulsing through her.

Lost, she kissed him with all the passion that was in her. She would devour him, and he her, and together they would die of bliss. Desperately, she pulled at her gloves, managing to wrench one off, and now her hand could enjoy even more: fistfuls of his hair, the smooth skin of his neck, his strong back and shoulders... It was for this that she had been born. This man. This kiss.

His hands were roving now, releasing her a little to sweep across her breasts, cupping, squeezing. Boldly he swept a hand inside her bodice, exposing a nipple to the cool night air. Shocked, she could only close her eyes as he rubbed his thumb over it, backwards and forwards until she thought she might die from pleasure. But she knew nothing, for a moment later he replaced his thumb with his mouth, at the same time hitching up her skirts to caress her bottom with his bare hands. Entirely undone, all she could do now was cling to him and try to remain upright.

Now he was upright again, and her legs felt cool air all around, and his hands on her bottom were pressing her to him, closer, closer as they kissed again, feverishly, fervently.

Once more he groaned, taking his hips away and releasing her skirts, leaving her bereft. In vain did she thrust her own hips forwards, but he was evasive.

'Hush,' he murmured. 'Hush, my Aphrodite. We cannot.' His arms were around her again, and their chests were connecting, but his hands were no longer enticing and inciting her to madness. Now they moved up and down her back in soothing strokes, his lips on her cheek, her jaw, her lips— featherlight kisses that ached with tenderness.

Tears started in Izzy's eyes. She, who *never* cried! It was all so much, so beautiful. Truly, this moment was for her life-changing, and her heart knew it.

'Ah, hush now, *Liebling*,' he said, kissing her tears. '*Alles ist gut.*'

All is well. Is it, though?

A fleeting thought, lost almost before it had appeared.

'I should not have—this was supposed to be only a kiss.' He shook his head. 'At least I stopped before... I apologise, Isobel.'

'No!' She put a finger on his lips. 'Do not apologise, Claudio, for that was truly wonderful.'

She felt him smile. 'Do you know—' he kissed her fingers '—that this night is for you? Only for you?'

Confused, she could not answer.

'The stars, the darkness, the ball itself. You are the goddess at the centre of it all. There is magic in you, for you have bewitched me.'

His kisses slowed, then stopped. They simply stood there, wrapped in one another's arms. Izzy had never in her life known such happiness.

'We should go back.' She voiced what they both knew. 'If we stay too long we might be missed.'

'And of course you would not want that.' Was it her imagination, or was there a hint of hardness in his voice? Trying to read him was impossible, for there was not enough light for such subtleties.

'No. And the ball is not only for us—for me. There are over a hundred people there who believe it is for them as much as anyone.'

'But it was I who asked the queen for a masquerade… for you, Isobel.'

She swallowed, lifting her face to his. 'Truly?'

'And now I must kiss you again, for how can I resist when you look at me so?'

He was as good as his word, and once more Izzy lost herself in him, now poignantly aware that this was ending, and that she would never know anything like it again. Ever.

Eventually they had to stop, and Izzy steadied herself before going back to the ball, Claudio waiting a few minutes before himself returning. He had replaced her glove, kissing her hand front and back before he did so. She could still feel the imprint of his lips in her left palm, and closed her fingers protectively, as if to keep it there for all time.

Making for the refreshments area, she took a glass of punch, made brief conversation with a couple of masked ladies, then went with them back to the dance floor. As she went through the performance—dancing, talking, going home in the carriage—she was aware that she was no longer truly present, for her soul remained in that other world, the world of his lips, his arms, his words. The world of the stars and the velvety darkness and the enchantment. Soon enough, she knew, reality would intrude, but until then she would hold onto the magic for as long as she could.

Chapter Twelve

'Well? Did you get your kiss?' The queen's gaze pierced Claudio uncomfortably, and he stammered an answer in the affirmative. Her servants were nearby but hopefully would not understand their conversation in German.

'Hmph!' she declared inelegantly. 'Well, I must say it was worth it for me, regardless. My ball was an undoubted hit!'

This was safer ground. 'Indeed, it was! Everyone seemed to enjoy it prodigiously.'

'I am surprised you noticed, Claudio, for you seemed to have eyes only for Miss Lennox. Do not think I did not perceive it!' She patted his hand. 'I approve, by the way. A most suitable choice, for I care not that her parents are unconfirmed. She is clearly a well-brought-up young lady…and with enough fire in her to manage you, Claudio!' She chuckled at her own wit. 'Miss Isobel's character shows her breeding, and your fascination with her shows that you see it, too.'

'But I have not made any choice! As I have said before, I am too young to even consider—'

'You are four-and-twenty, Claudio,' she said firmly. 'Most ladies are married with little ones at that age. And if more gentlemen were sensible enough to find a good woman and settle into marital harmony at four-and-twenty, then the *ton* should be a happier group!' She sighed. 'My own dear husband was but two-and-twenty when we wed, and I have observed that marriages where the couple are both young to start with do remarkably well. You grow together, you see.'

He frowned in puzzlement. 'Then, you do not believe there is a requirement for the man to be...' he sought the right words '...fully formed?'

She snorted. 'Absolutely not! The requirements are simply two things: affinity and constancy—or passion and purpose, if you prefer. Knowing oneself fully and understanding the other person—those take a lifetime.'

Loath to argue, he simply let it go, but her words sat uncomfortably with him, for in truth they strengthened an uncertainty now raging within him. Was he truly too young to wed? What if he married, then regretted it?

Instantly denial blazed within him. He could not imagine regretting marrying Isobel. She was...she was everything. But he himself was a part-formed thing, unsure of himself, who he was, where his future lay. What if the hedonistic side of him came to dominate?

Eldon—despite his predilection for bed sport—had never married, nor had Hawkins, whom Claudio had never seen truly sober. He shuddered.

Is that my future?

Abruptly, he felt a wave of fierceness run through him.

I am glad they are bachelors!

Men such as Hawkins and Eldon could never make a wife happy. Indeed, the wives of such men could only ever be miserable.

So why do I count such men among my friends?

Questions raged within him, doubt and uncertainty clouding his mind. The queen's words had given him much to think about.

Of one thing he was certain, though. Never had he experienced anything like the desire and tenderness he had felt last night. His mind, heart, and soul were full of Isobel. He had not lied when he said he felt bewitched by her. No other maiden earned anything more than a fleeting look from him now. He could acknowledge that some of them were attractive—beautiful, even—without feeling an ounce of attraction for himself.

His overwhelming feeling today, though—as well as elation—was shame. Having promised the queen he would do no more than kiss Isobel, he had nearly ravished her, right there in the gardens. Worse, he had made the same promise to himself and had broken it within moments of being close to her, protected by a cloak of darkness. What sort of man was he, to succumb so readily to lust when Isobel deserved every respect? Yes, she was beautiful, and maddeningly desirable, but he had three years on her, and experience. He should have been better at controlling himself. One thing was certain: it could not happen again. Not because he did not wish it to, but because he had very little confidence in his ability to stop next time.

To everyone's surprise and delight, James and Rose—now Viscount and Viscountess Ashbourne—arrived in the late morning, sparking great celebration in Ashbourne House. They looked entirely happy, and Izzy noted a little enviously how their eyes followed one another at all times.

What must it be like to marry someone you love and who loves you in return?

Having achieved her aim of kissing the prince last night, and it being better than her wildest imaginings, Izzy understood now that he had spoiled her. No man could ever compare to him. His looks, his lively mind, his warm heart, and now, his fiery kisses that had left her in an eternal state of longing. She would never be his bride, never sit by his side with his ring on her finger, letting the world know that they belonged to one another.

On the occasion of her marriage, Rose had received from their guardian a pair of earrings that had belonged to Mama, as well as a letter from her. They read it together, shedding a tear at their mother's beautiful words, and bemoaning again the lack of information about her origins or the identity of their father. Izzy, having believed she had become accustomed to being an orphan of dubious parentage, momentarily railed against the cruelty of her circumstance.

Had I been the daughter of a known, respectable couple, might the prince have considered me?

But no, such daydreams were useless. Her fate was as it was, and she must not dream of the impossible.

'We shall visit Lady Kelgrove first,' the viscount declared. 'Rose and I have discussed it, and we believe it makes sense. She is highly influential, and we all have a fondness for her. If we can achieve her approval for marrying in Scotland, then it will make it easier for the rest of the *ton* to follow.' He took Rose's hand. 'Not that I should care about any disapproval, for marrying Rose has been the best decision I have ever made.'

The happy pair left for Lady Kelgrove's townhouse a couple of hours later, and Izzy, Anna, and Lady Ashbourne— who had now officially become the Dowager Viscountess despite, she said, believing she was far too young for such a title—made ready for the evening, being promised at a soirée at Lord and Lady Renton's. However, before dinner had been served, they received an unexpected but urgent message bidding them all come to Lady Kelgrove's mansion immediately.

'Oh, dear! I do hope nothing has befallen her, for I do

have a great affection for Lady Kelgrove!' Lady Ashbourne looked troubled and fiddled with her reticule the whole way through Mayfair, but when they were ushered into the drawing room by a rather bewildered looking footman, Lady Kelgrove was there to greet them. Worryingly, she did look rather pale and was clutching a handkerchief in her crabbed hand.

Has she been crying?

Rose and James were there, too, and Rose had definitely been crying. The butler stood by the fireplace, wringing his hands. Never had Izzy seen a butler in a state of agitation, but there was no other way to describe it, and butlers were *never* agitated.

Cutting across Lady Ashbourne's distressed greeting, Lady Kelgrove bade them sit. 'Which of you is Annabelle, and which Isobel? Wait.' She held up an imperious hand, looking from one to the other. 'You are Anna. And you are Isobel. I should not have needed to ask, for I know you well.' She closed her eyes briefly. 'Naturally, I know you both.'

Inwardly Izzy's mind was racing.

What on earth is happening?

'It seems,' began Lady Kelgrove, steadying herself, 'that the earrings currently being worn by the new Lady Ashbourne belonged to your mother, Maria.'

All of the hairs at the back of Izzy's neck were suddenly standing to attention, and she could not breathe.

'I recognised them instantly,' Lady Kelgrove continued, 'for they were a gift from me to my granddaughter, Maria.'

Maria Berkeley?

Could it possibly be—? But how?

'A granddaughter,' Lady Kelgrove continued, the slightest hint of a quiver in her voice, 'whom I was informed had died of smallpox at eighteen years of age. Brooks—' she waved a hand towards the elderly butler '—has informed me in the last hour that Maria's supposed death was a lie concocted by my husband after Maria ran away.' She smiled tremulously. 'I am your great-grandmother, my dears.'

Much embracing followed, and copious tears. Lady Ashbourne declared herself delighted and reflected, giggling, that those who had sneered at the triplets would get quite a shock in discovering the girls were of the Kelgrove line. They stayed for dinner, abandoning all engagements for the evening, and agreed that while the news of Rose's marriage was to be shared, for now they would keep their discovery about Maria Berkeley to themselves.

Lord, the ton does love a secret! thought Izzy, her mind still reeling from today's news.

Still, it was fitting that Rose and James announce their own good news. As Lady Ashbourne pointed out, the sight of them would put paid to any suggestion there had been something havey-cavey about the nuptials.

'For,' she said, 'the two of you are smelling of April and May, and this is clearly a love match!' She preened a little. 'And I can say with perfect truth that I knew you were to be married, and it was better done in Scotland where you grew up, Rose.'

'And *was* there something havey-cavey about it?' asked Lady Kelgrove sharply.

Lord Ashbourne held his hands open a little. 'I was seen kissing Rose by Lady Renton's footman, which is why she went away to her guardian and her old school.'

'And you did not offer her marriage?' Lady Kelgrove's brow was furrowed, her shoulders stiff. Indeed every inch of her signalled displeasure.

'I did not get the chance! She was gone before I even knew we had been seen. I followed her immediately—that is to say, two days later, once I was made aware of the situation—and was greatly relieved when she agreed to be my wife.' The look he threw Rose made Izzy's insides melt with joy for the two of them.

He adores her!

'Hmph. You should have offered for her the moment you put her reputation at risk. And *you*—' she pointed a stabbing finger at Rose '—should not have run away.' A wistful expression appeared in her eyes. 'And nor should my Maria.' Her expression changed. 'I must warn you, girls, that I find myself hungry for information about my darling granddaughter. Tell me again, how did you come to have your colours—the blue, the green and yellow, the pink?'

Anna explained that the midwife had tied coloured ribbons around their wrists as each of them was born, and that Mama had kept the colours initially so she would always know which was which, then because each of them liked having their own colour.'

'She even had songs for each of us,' added Rose. 'Mine was ring-a-ring o' roses.'

Lady Kelgrove looked to Izzy. 'Greensleeves,' she said with a shrug.

Her face crumpled. 'I used to sing Greensleeves to her when she was young.' She swallowed hard, then looked at Anna.

'Ah, Mama created a song for me—perhaps she could not think of a suitable nursery rhyme. I mean, *Little Boy Blue* would not have been welcome!'

'Indeed not! So what is your song? Can you remember it?'

Anna glanced mischievously at her sisters. 'Well? Shall we?'

Izzy rose instantly, remembering every word, every

action. They stood together, grinning, then Anna started her song.

'The Lady Blue she points her shoe,' they chanted in a singsong tone, each pointing her right foot as though beginning a dance, simultaneously dipping in a sweeping curtsy, just as though they were wearing huge panniers.

'You find the line to find the kine,' They swept their right arms out as though following an imaginary line. Izzy could almost see the herd of cows she had always pictured in her mind.

'The key is three and three times three.' For this they weaved around each other, the three of them changing place three times each.

'The treasure fine is yours and mine,' and they finished by forming a circle, clapping hands together and against each other's palms.

Laughing, they returned to their chairs, acknowledging the smiles and applause of their small audience.

'Thank you, my dears.' Lady Kelgrove again made use of her handkerchief. 'I can honestly picture Maria's enjoyment as she created this for you. A silly little ditty, but it has her sense of mischief.' She sighed, 'I only wish she had come to me.'

'Do you think,' Anna offered, 'that she ran away because of our father? We were in February the following year—'

'And we came two months early,' Izzy added.

'So she was not with child when she ran away. She disappeared almost a year before you were born. Where could she have been, for a full year? Ah, Maria, Maria. What was so dreadful you could not trust me with it?'

There was a pause.

Izzy swallowed against a sudden lump in her throat. 'I

must ask…do you know who our father might be?' Perhaps, after all, she would find the answer to her own quest.

'I have my suspicions, but let us speak of it at another time. The important matter now is that we have found one another. That is to be celebrated!' She thought for a moment, then slammed her stick on the floor. 'I have it! I shall host a ball for you here, my dears,' she declared briskly. 'A ball at which I shall announce your identity. It will give me great satisfaction to shock the likes of the Thaxbys, Lady Renford, and others. It will have to be next week, for everyone will leave London soon for the summer. Ha! The queen may believe her ball to be the last significant event of the Season, but mine will outshine them all!'

Lady Ashbourne instilled a note of caution. 'You do realise, my lady, that announcing this will add to speculation that Maria might never have wed. Running away, her own father cutting her off…'

Lady Kelgrove snorted inelegantly. 'I do indeed realise it, but I care not. These girls are not to blame for any errors made by their parents, and my patronage added to yours—plus, of course, Rose's recent marriage—will ensure they will suffer no longer for the previous vagueness regarding their parentage.'

She repeated this theme numerous times during dinner, adding that she should have realised the triplets were Maria's daughters, for she had taken to them instantly. 'And you, Miss Isobel!' she declared, making Izzy start and eye her rather warily. Since the events of last night at the Queen's Masquerade Ball, she was half expecting someone to suddenly declare she and Claudio had been seen—as had happened to Rose and James. Lady Kelgrove, however, was on an entirely different tack.

'I was speaking of you recently to Prince Claudio. I described you as headstrong, obstinate, and opinionated. Just as I like you!' She nodded approvingly. 'I see now that you get those gifts from me. Use them well!'

'I am not sure everyone would see such qualities as gifts.'

She was speaking to Claudio of me? Lord, I should love to know what else was said.

But the conversation moved on, and her curiosity remained unsatisfied.

There she is!

Lady Ashbourne had just entered the Renton drawing room, followed by the Misses Lennox. Claudio's eyes widened.

Three of them!

Miss Rose had returned, then. He was glad, for Izzy's sake. The viscount was also with them, and Claudio was reminded that something in him had wanted to make a friend of the viscount. Yes, and Garvald, too. Instead, here he was, standing listening to empty-headed nonsense from Hawkins and Eldon. His eyes roved hungrily over Isobel.

What a beauty she is!

It struck him now that he had absolutely no notion what to say to her tonight. How to *be* when he was around her. What had taken place between them had been so profound, so affecting, that it would be practically impossible to behave with any sort of normality. And yet, he must. They both must. To give any hint of what had occurred would lead to the most vulgar of speculation, and Isobel must not be exposed to any such distress.

Pretending to laugh at something Hawkins had said, Claudio glanced towards the Ashbourne–Lennox party again. Isobel was talking with one of her sisters in an animated way, and his heart turned over just at the sight of her.

A flash of delicious memory came to him: the liberties he had taken with his hands and his mouth. The memories, though, were laced with something that felt suspiciously like shame. Yes, she had been willing—he thrilled each time he recalled the passion within her. But that did not excuse what he had done.

Here she was in a society drawing room, dressed in the pale colours of a débutante—a lady to be respected, admired, treated as an innocent. And she *was* innocent, of that he had no doubt. Yet he had behaved as though she were an experienced tavern wench or a Cyprian. He felt like a despoiler, someone without honour.

If Papa knew what I had done...

And so, when it was finally time to greet them all, he found himself to be tongue-tied, taciturn, reserved. Inside, all was turmoil. She was close enough to touch, yet he could barely look at her. Self-loathing, a familiar enemy, reared its head within him. Isobel was a goddess, and he the mortal who had dared to touch her. He would never be the same again.

Making his excuses as soon as he was able, he encouraged his friends to leave earlier than planned, then spent the rest of the night in a disreputable tavern drinking enough to fall down. Enough to forget.

Izzy watched him go, feeling confused, bereft, bewildered. While of course he could not have alluded in public to what had taken place between them—no, not so much as by a look or a glance—still, she had hoped for something more than *this*. He had been withdrawn almost to the point of rudeness. Even Lady Ashbourne had commented on it, wondering aloud if something ailed him. Izzy knew better.

It is me. I am his ailment, she thought fancifully, imagining herself taking a sweeping bow to the entire assembly, before announcing *Good evening, everyone! I am Prince Claudio's ailment.*

He was clearly regretting his actions in the garden, which in turn was now making Izzy question hers. What had seemed so wonderful—the passion and tenderness she believed she had sensed between them—now seemed overlaid with the taint of corruption. Anger surged through her. These past weeks she thought she had found a friend, yet his actions tonight had shown her clearly that she had been mistaken. He was evidently no friend to her.

All through the evening she worried over it, railing between fury and pain even as Lord Ashbourne made the announcement about his marriage, and the crowd thronged about him and Rose, wishing them happy.

Claudio should have been here to be part of this.

Catching the thought she frowned, questioning her assumptions. He had shown a preference for her company in recent weeks, it was true, yet tonight he had treated her as though she were a near stranger. Was it possible he had befriended her only to persuade her to commit indiscretions at the queen's ball?

Surely not.

Normally Izzy counted herself a good judge of character, but with him all logic was overset, and perhaps she could no longer trust her instincts. What did she know of princes or lords? Having always had an impulsive streak, had it on this occasion veered towards recklessness?

And had he, his object achieved, moved on to try to captivate another? His set was known for wenching, as well as for drinking, gambling, and sport. Were they now on their way to visit courtesans? And would Claudio do to some unknown woman what he had done to her?

Her mind reeling and her stomach sick, she managed to smile and please her way through the evening, vaguely remembering afterwards that someone had mentioned Mr Kirby was to return to London on the morrow.

Lord! Fitch, too, would be back. Having avoided him at the masquerade, she had been relieved to hear of his latest trip to the country to visit his mother. He seemed to visit his dear mama a lot, which was no doubt a good thing. But now he was returning. With only a week left of the Season, either or both of her suitors might well propose marriage, and her mind was in the clouds. She could not think about it now. Her head was beginning to ache, and it was all too painful.

Thankfully Mary was waiting at home to help her undress, remove her uncomfortable hairpins, and offer her a tincture. 'It is this heavy weather, miss. My head has been pounding all day. If we could only get a thunderstorm, then all would be well again!'

Izzy, naturally, did not contradict the girl, but once the maid had gone, she blew out the last candle and cried herself to sleep.

Chapter Thirteen

'What day is it, Jenkins?'

'Monday, Your Highness.' The valet's voice was neutral, with no hint of criticism. It mattered not, for the self-critical voice within Claudio—the one held at bay by wine, ale, and beer—was beginning to reassert itself.

You are a disgrace, it said. Foul. Worthless. Drunken sot. Despoiler of gentle maidens.

Monday? The soirée at the Rentons had been on Wednesday.

Have I really been drunk for four days and nights?

'My engagements?'

Jenkins listed today's invitations while Claudio hoisted himself carefully into a sitting position, the room spinning slightly as he did so. Last night he had made it back to Buckingham House before midnight—hardly surprising that he had faded, since he had been drinking since breakfast. Tentatively, Claudio looked towards the window. The midday sun was bright but not as painful as Claudio had feared.

'And tonight, you are promised to Lady Kelgrove's ball. Shall I cancel everything for today again, Your Highness?'

'Lady Kelgrove is hosting a ball? I do not recall...'

'The invitation arrived only yesterday, Your Highness.'

'And I accepted it?' Madness, for the Lennox sisters

were certain to be there, given the mutual fondness between them and Lady Kelgrove. Dimly, he recalled meeting Ashbourne in one of the clubs and congratulating him on his recent marriage to Miss Rose.

Lucky bastard.

The valet stood his ground. 'Er...yes, Your Highness. In fact your exact words were "Accept and be damned!"'

Claudio swallowed. 'I see.'

Might as well go.

He would have to see her sometime. Why not tonight?

'Breakfast, Your Highness? Or ale?'

Claudio shuddered. 'Ale? No. I have had enough ale to last me a lifetime.' The very thought made him feel sick. 'A bath, and then some beef, eggs, and rolls, please. And tea. Yes, tea.'

Jenkins bowed. 'Very well, Your Highness. Er... Her Majesty has requested your presence today, if it pleases you?'

The sick feeling in Claudio's stomach intensified. 'Yes, of course.'

An hour later, hair still damp from his bath, Prince Claudio sauntered into the queen's apartments. After the usual greetings he took the seat she offered and accepted refreshments. She eyed him closely, and he managed to maintain equanimity. At moments like this she strongly reminded him of his father.

'How do you like your tea, Claudio?' Her tone was deceptively mild.

'Oh, as it comes,' was his reply, his air of unconcern probably not fooling her for an instant. He had seen his red-rimmed eyes in the mirror and knew his dissipation was visible to anyone who knew where to look for it.

'What are your plans for today?'

As he listed his chosen engagements, she tilted her head to listen carefully.

'And then,' he continued, 'this evening I am promised to Lady Kelgrove's ball.'

She snorted. 'Well, I must say I am glad to hear it! She may have announced it only very recently, but all of the *ton* holds Lady Kelgrove in great respect. It would not do to miss it.'

'No, indeed,' he answered mildly, and she flashed him an irritated glance.

'No doubt she will give prominence to the Lennox girls, for she continually reminds us all that they are her favourites.' She sniffed. 'Before she knew them, they were *my* diamonds first, of course!' Taking a sip of tea, she continued, with a nonchalant air, 'Of course, the youngest Lennox girl's marriage to Ashbourne has changed all their fortunes.'

Now she had his attention. 'How so?' His expression was neutral, but there was a tightness in his shoulders that had not been there a moment earlier.

She shrugged. 'They will be seen now as more marriageable. Although the Season is almost done, so the time is short. Some may still sneer at their lack of parents, but I would not be surprised if Garvald came up to scratch and offered for one of them.'

'Garvald? The *Earl* of Garvald?'

'The very same. A man of taste, and wit, and intelligence. The girls themselves of course may not realise this and settle for a plain mister.' She shrugged. 'Ah, well. With the Season at an end, those who remain unbetrothed must choose from the options available to them, I suppose.'

'But Garvald is not seeking to marry, is he?'

'I rather suspect he is very close to it.' She raised an eyebrow. 'You sound surprised.'

He frowned. 'How old is Garvald? Do you know?'

She considered the matter. 'Let me think… Three—no, four-and-twenty. And he is among the most liked of gentlemen, far more so than the dissipated wastrels at the edge of the *ton*. I am sure you have noted it.'

Just four-and-twenty?

He swallowed, making a noncommittal answer, but she was undeterred.

'Many young men face a crossroads, Claudio.' Her gaze became unfocused. 'One path is brightly lit and enticing, with promises of drink, sport, and a lifetime of irresponsibility. The other has neither glitter nor glamour but holds depth, warmth, and enduring satisfaction.' Her words were disturbing him greatly, and his mind was awhirl.

'Despite my husband's madness, I have never regretted my choice, and together we have lived a relatively quiet life—so much so that the king has earned the soubriquet Farmer George.' She shook her head slowly. 'A quiet life, but a happy one…despite everything.'

He left soon afterwards, her message having been received loud and clear. Garvald, a sensible, sober man of just four-and-twenty, was more admired than the likes of Hawkins and Eldon, whom she had described as—what was it?—'dissipated wastrels'. The memory of her words pierced him.

I chose wrongly. I chose badly. And now it is too late.

'No, can you lift it a little higher, please?'

Izzy stifled a sigh. Mary, her usual maid, was sick, and so another of the housemaids was dressing her hair. *Poor Mary!* Strange to think that in the months since she had arrived in London, she and Mary had come to an understanding about the way she liked her hair done, among many other preferences.

I am a lady of the ton *now, apparently.*

'Is that all right, miss?' The maid sounded anxious, and Izzy stifled a sigh.

'It will do just fine. Thank you.'

It had been almost a week since the masquerade. Five days since she had even laid eyes on him. He had attended none of the *ton* gatherings since leaving the Renton soirée so abruptly. A throwaway comment from one of the other gentlemen had given her to understand that the prince and his cronies—she refused to call them his *friends*, even in her mind—were not out of town but rather had been drinking in clubs and taverns for the past few days. And to think she had judged Claudio to be a man of sense, of reason, of sensibility and feeling! Clearly, he was nothing better than a tavern drunkard, despite his princely title. And looks. And manner.

Her mind went back to their very first encounter, in a hallway in Grantham. Yes, her first impression of him must have been correct. He was a wastrel, a seducer, a man who would not hesitate to use his royal title for his own sordid purposes. Her more recent error of judgement had been monumental, and now she was being punished for it. When she thought of the liberties she had allowed him in the queen's garden, she burned with mortification. Clearly, once he had achieved his sordid aim, he had vanished, leaving her wretched.

The sense of hurt and betrayal was not becoming any easier to bear. The pain within her was like a living thing, scalding and piercing as it twisted and writhed. Worse, her foolish heart still retained an affection for him that was as unwelcome as it was idiotic. Not seeing him was agony. Yet seeing him in the Rentons' drawing room and realising he was ignoring her—that had been a thousand times worse.

Will he be there tonight?

The thought had plagued her these past days, each time she entered a drawing room or a ballroom. Each time, the answer had been *no*. Yet that did not stop her imprudent heart from hoping. Even though she *knew* he was not the person she had imagined him to be. Even though he had rejected her in the plainest possible way.

Her head ached, and her heart did, too. And it was not getting any easier. In fact, it seemed to be getting worse, for tonight her very bones were aching, and it hurt to move her eyes. And the new maid had tied her half stays too tight, making it difficult to breathe. Yet still she smiled and pleased, greeting Lady Kelgrove with genuine warmth, and enjoying the elderly lady's air of repressed excitement. Tonight, she would claim the Lennox sisters as her own long-lost great-granddaughters, and she was clearly relishing the prospect.

'Tonight we shall shake them up, girls. Just wait and see!' Lifting her quizzing glass, she studied the triplets from head to toe. 'Delightful! You are a credit to your mother, my dears.' Discomfort rippled through Izzy at the words. Would Lady Kelgrove still say that if she knew what Izzy had been doing in the dark with the prince?

'Now,' Lady Kelgrove continued, 'go and enjoy yourselves. I shall make the announcement at supper.'

Izzy tried. She really did. She made her curtsy to the queen and made empty conversation with a dozen or more ladies and gentlemen. Mr Fitch was there and informed her with an air of sadness that his mama had advised him he was too young for marriage.

'I have taken her advice to heart, Miss Isobel. I, er, do hope no young lady will suffer hurt by the withdrawal of my attentions.'

Relief flooded through her. 'Indeed not, Mr Fitch, though it shows you in a very good light to think of such a thing. And I do think it is important for you to listen to your mama.' They parted amicably, and with relief on both sides, and Izzy continued to circulate amid the large crowd.

Thankfully Rose's marriage had caught the attention of the *ton*, and Izzy lost count of the number of people coming to congratulate again the new Lady Ashbourne, who was now appropriately decked out in a gown of deep rose-pink, a shade that would never have been permitted for an unmarried lady. It was her first event dressed in such a way, and she had been in alt earlier when the first of her new clothes had arrived.

Despite Rose's evident happiness and success, to Izzy all seemed flat, and empty, and meaningless. And the warm weather was not helping. One moment she was shivering, and the next suffocating with the heat. Even dancing was difficult, for her legs felt as though they were made of lead. It hurt to move. Everything and everyone was irritating her, and she wished only to return to the haven of her bedchamber at home.

An excited babble reached her ears, and she turned to see what had caused such consternation, her eyes meeting the gaze of Prince Claudio, who had just arrived. Late, but he had arrived. Instantly she looked away, trying to ignore the sudden thunderous tattoo of her heart.

Be calm, she told herself.

He had to reappear eventually. It still did not change who he was or what he had done.

'Yes, of course!' Mr Kirby had come to claim her for the next dance and willingly she went, flashing him a bright smile. Subtly, as she moved through the figures of the dance, she tracked the prince's progress around the edges

of the dancing floor, the people he spoke to, helplessly observing the way his coat of grey superfine enhanced his cool
colouring... He was spending quite some time with Garvald, she noted. Not his usual company. But then, his own
friends were not here, so he probably had no choice but to
converse with some of the more sober, thoughtful gentlemen. He would no doubt leave before long, the ball being
rather too staid for his liking, she thought, briefly wondering if he would be here for Lady Kelgrove's announcement.
He probably would not care.

He does not care.

'...if I might speak with you later. In private.' Her attention snapped back to Mr Kirby. Red-faced and earnest,
there was no doubting his meaning or his intentions. Unlike with Mr Fitch, there was no controlling mother in the
background to rescue her this time.

Lord! Here was a new riddle. Before Rose's wedding and
Lady Kelgrove's revelations, Izzy had been in danger of
being banished back to Scotland next week, her one Season done. That was no longer the case, Rose having assured
both her and Anna that they could live with the Ashbournes
for as long as they wished. Lady Kelgrove, too, had invited
Izzy to come live with her, stating that Izzy was one of the
few people she could tolerate.

'Aye, and your husband too, once you are wed,' she had
added, and it had taken all of Izzy's self-control not to emit
a sceptical snort. Now that she *need* not marry, she was not
sure she would ever *wish* to. And, despite her plans of just
a couple of weeks ago, she now knew she could never, ever
marry Mr Kirby. Or Mr Fitch.

I must tell Mr Kirby.

A ripple of guilt ran through her. The man could reasonably argue that she had encouraged him for, to be fair,

she had. He was awaiting her response, and now the dance had brought them together again.

'I will speak with you, Mr Kirby. But I must warn you that my situation…has changed recently.'

He looked crestfallen. 'I see.' They parted again, and when they returned he had squared his shoulders. 'Very well. On the terrace, perhaps, after this dance?'

'Ten minutes after.' She needed to go to the retiring room, for her head was throbbing with pain, and she felt decidedly strange. For the first time she began to wonder if she was in fact ill, rather than just heartsore. Her mind flicked to poor Mary, laid low with what Cook suspected was influenza. Yes, that could be it. She stifled a sigh.

Wonderful. Just wonderful.

Claudio laughed at something Garvald said. The man had a dry wit that was both entertaining and admirable, and Claudio was now regretting not making a friend of him from the beginning. The Season was nearly done, and he was only now discovering the true value in the people around him. The queen's revelation that he and Garvald were similar in age had astounded him.

A man of taste, and wit, and intelligence, eh? I could have been described so, perhaps. Had I made different choices.

Here, then, was another way to be. Personable rather than raucous. Unafraid to show one's intelligence. Garvald was a little shy and had seemed standoffish to Claudio at first.

I was distracted by gilt, when all the while gold was before me.

Gold. He had been subtly observing Isobel since his arrival. What to do? She crossed the ballroom, and Claudio watched her go, realising she was making for the retiring room. Remembering their previous encounters in various hallways, there was an inevitability to it, perhaps. A symmetry that might help him. Lord knows he needed all the help he could get.

As he made his bow to Garvald and moved subtly towards the corridor, giving her time to complete her ablutions, his mind went over their previous encounters. The inn in Grantham. The library at the Wrights' ball, when first she had behaved as though she might like him, a little. The hallway in Buckingham House, where they had arranged their garden assignation. And now this. Claudio had no idea what he would say to her, only that he needed to speak to her where others could not easily hear them.

Damnation!

Two footmen stood in the hallway at either side of the ballroom door, two more farther down near the retiring rooms. Of course the wealthy Lady Kelgrove would have many more footmen than any household would consider reasonable. Taken aback, he had not yet recovered when she emerged from the room set aside for ladies, walking towards him with a frown and drooping shoulders. He waited, holding his breath for the moment she would recognise him.

There!

Pausing for the briefest of instants, she then continued towards him at a faster pace, chin raised, and an expression of determination on her beautiful face.

She went to pass him, and he took her hand.

'Unhand me, sir!'

She is angry. Livid, indeed.

In a cajoling tone, he attempted to reach her with humour. 'Now, now, Miss Isobel. You know that my title is *Your*

Highness, not *sir*.' Retaining her hand, he gave a sweeping bow—a royal bow.

She was unmoved. 'Titles should be earned, not given. You are no prince. Indeed, I am not sure you are even a gentleman.'

His jaw dropped. 'If this is because I left the Renton soirée early, I—'

She held up an imperious hand. 'You may do as you please. I care not.'

Conscious of listening ears all about, he dropped his tone. 'I assure you, Miss Isobel, that despite what you may believe, I am a gentleman. And yes, a prince, too! Now, please allow me to apol—'

Her lip curled. 'Let me pass, for I am promised to speak with someone.'

He frowned but could not make sense of this. Letting it go for now, he focused instead on her superior tone, still trying to connect with her. Surely, somewhere inside, was the Isobel he had laughed with? The Isobel who had become his friend? She looked flushed and was clearly agitated. Giving her a humorous look, and ignoring the growing feeling of dread within, he teased her. 'And you, I suppose, are the Queen of Sheba?'

She dipped her head. 'I may be.' Throwing him a scornful look—a look that seemed to sear into him like a brand—she added, 'In comparison to persons of no honour, I suppose I must be higher in true rank.'

Anger flared within him, and he dropped her hand. No honour?

How dare she?

'No honour? I have been a man of honour my whole life. My father, my friends, all could vouch for—'

She cut him off again. 'I know nothing of your father, but I can tell you this. You have no friends, Claudio. Do you think that the likes of Hawkins or Eldon would bother with you if you were not a royal? They are cronies, hangers-on, leeches. They care nothing for you. They are nothing but sycophants who would be gone in an instant if you were not a prince.'

As she spoke, he felt the colour drain from his face. Each word was a knife wound, stabbing him with hurt, leaving white-hot rage in its wake.

How dare she say such things to me?

'Well, at least,' he shot back, 'I *have* a father. Yes, and I had a mother, too. I should hate to go through life with no name, no history, no parentage.'

Too far.

He saw it in the stricken look in her eye, heard it in the gasp she uttered. 'No! Izzy, I am sorry. I should not have said it. Please—'

She was ice-cold. As though he were not even speaking, she turned, gliding serenely away from him. For the rest of his days he would remember the sight: her back, her golden hair, the way she moved…away from him.

Have I lost her?

Izzy entered the ballroom in a daze. Claudio's words were worse than hurtful, worse than cutting. He had attacked her very soul, or so it seemed to her. To hear such sentiments from anyone would have been devastating, but the fact such condemnation had come from the very man she—

She refused to finish the thought, conscious that she needed to survive the evening for just a little longer. A waltz was underway, and her mind tried to take her back to another waltz, another night. But she would not think of it, of what she had lost, for it was clear now that he had never been hers in any way.

Mr Kirby was standing by the terrace doors on the far side of the room.

Oh, Lord! she had quite forgotten her assignation to speak with him. Catching her eye, he gave her a meaningful look, and she nodded. As he stepped onto the terrace, she began crossing the room, avoiding the eye of anyone who might delay or detain her. After the waltz, she knew, supper would be called.

I shall speak with Mr Kirby, allow dear Lady Kelgrove to make her announcement, then go home.

Duty. Honour. *La politesse.* These were morals drummed into her by all of the important people in her life. The Ashbournes. Lady Kelgrove. Her sisters. Mr Marnoch. The Belvedere teachers. Mama.

She would not even have to feign illness to escape, for she genuinely felt dreadful. Her head was now thumping as though tiny creatures with a thousand hammers were labouring inside. Her legs were decidedly weak; she could not have danced now even if she wanted to. And she had begun to shiver as though she were outside in the winter snow, rather than in a sweltering ballroom at midsummer.

Concentrating on every step, she managed to reach the terrace. As her eyes adjusted to the gloom, she saw Mr Kirby was there, waiting for her, and as she approached her heart was sore at the sadness she saw in his kind eyes. Other people were there, too, she vaguely noticed, but in this moment she had one task, and one task only. To disappoint this man—a good, kind gentleman—who had done nothing wrong except believe her when she had encouraged him.

'Mr Kirby.' She gave him her hand, and he kissed the back of it. Moved by regret and compassion, she allowed him to keep it. He would not misinterpret her action now, she knew.

'You said you had something to say to me, Miss Isobel.'

'I did. I do. I must apologise, Mr Kirby, but my circumstances have changed. I thought I might marry you, if you asked me. Or Mr Fitch. But my sister's marriage means now that…' She now searched for the right words.

'That you may look higher for a husband. I understand.' His voice was tight.

Pushing away the image of Claudio in his full princely regalia, as she had seen him during the presentation of débutantes, she shook her head.

'No! Well, yes, but not because of position or title.'

He thought about this for a second, then nodded slowly. 'Your heart is engaged. I had wondered about it.'

She gave him a sad look. 'Hearts may do what they will. Marriages are for more than the passing wants of the heart. Companionship, friendship, children… I think we could have shared these things.'

'I know we could.' His tone was low.

'But that is not my reason.' She squeezed his hand. 'The truth is that I no longer need to choose a husband this Season. My sister and her husband have invited me to live with them.'

'I am glad for you.' He swallowed, managing a smile. 'And I hope we can continue to be friends.'

'Of course!' Without thinking too much about it, she pressed her lips to his cheek for a fleeting instant.

Now his smile was genuine. 'I thank you for your honesty, Miss Isobel. I—' His eyes widened in confusion, then dawning horror, as he looked at something over her shoulder. Turning, she gasped as she saw the prince bearing down upon them, his face contorted in rage.

* * *

Conscious of the footmen's fascination, Claudio coughed, adjusted his cuffs, then returned to the ballroom—just in time to see Isobel disappear through the doors leading to the terrace. Pushing his way through the crowd, he made his way across the room in double-quick time, murmuring vagueness at those who tried to detain him with meaningless utterings.

I must put this right!

With the focus of an arrow, he made for the terrace, driven by regret and something that felt suspiciously like fear.

I cannot lose her. I must not lose her.

Stepping through the doors he paused for a moment, letting his vision adapt to the dim light. To his left, a group of matrons were fanning themselves and seemed deep in conversation. To his right—

He froze. Isobel was there, her pale gown and golden hair dappled with moonlight. She looked ethereal, other-worldly. And standing with her was Kirby, and he was holding her hand and speaking to her in an earnest manner.

No!

Terror raced through him. Everything fell into place.

Lady Kelgrove telling him a few weeks ago, 'From what I know of Miss Isobel, she is practical enough to know she needs a husband.'

The queen's words yesterday, that the Misses Lennox might not realise their fortunes had improved with Miss Rose's marriage and might 'settle for a plain mister'.

Isobel's cutting words earlier had contrasted people with titles who did not live up to them, like himself, and those whose honour was apparent from their deeds. So even if she knew she might attain a titled husband, she might yet choose Kirby. For his character.

He went cold as he now recalled Isobel's other words a few moments ago: 'I am promised to speak with someone.'

This, then, was an assignation, so that Kirby could make his proposal.

If she accepts him, I have lost her forever.

Even as all these thoughts were flashing through his mind like so many lightning strikes, he was striding across the terrace. As he did so, Isobel leaned forward and kissed Kirby on the cheek, driving rage, pain, and loss through Claudio.

I am too late.

And he had no one to blame but himself.

My stupidity. My tardiness. My failure.

At the last moment Kirby saw him, his eyes growing round as saucers. Now Isobel was turning, trying to see what had startled her suitor. She opened her mouth to speak—and Claudio stopped it with his own mouth, firmly planted onto hers. There was no plan there, no thought, just a howling chasm of loss and pain and need within him. Kirby might have won her, but Claudio would kiss her one last time. After this, his life was pointless, anyway.

Her mouth was hot, her lips sweet as honey. But she was frozen, unresponsive.

Isobel!

Izzy froze in shock. Claudio was kissing her, and she was drowning. His arms held her firmly, his chest pressed against hers, and his mouth was moving, begging her to respond.

She could not. Instead, influenza chose its moment to strike. Blackness overcame her, and her body sagged in a deep faint. As the dark waters overcame her, her last thought was that at least he had kissed her again, even though this time he was motivated by anger.

Remember! she told herself. Remember!

An age later—a year, perhaps, or maybe a day—she heard voices. Ladies' voices.

'He just marched across the terrace and kissed her! I saw it with my own eyes!'

'Shocking!'

'Which one is it?'

'Miss Isobel, I understand. Certainly Mr Kirby called her Isobel, before he went to get assistance.'

The blackness came again, interrupted by an acrid smell, making her cough and awaken. Opening her eyes, she saw three matrons and a serving maid who was waving hartshorn under her nose. The acrid smell stung, bringing hot tears to her eyes. Above them—far, far above—the stars. Memory returned in an instant.

I am on the terrace. Prince Claudio...!

'Now, now, my dear,' one of the ladies soothed, patting her arm. 'You have just had an ordeal. These gentlemen think they may do as they wish!' She tutted, shaking her head. 'Still, you have won a prince for yourself. That ought to cheer you up.'

This made no sense. Struggling, Izzy got up into a sitting position, realising someone had placed her on the stone bench on Lady Kelgrove's terrace. Looking left and right she realised Prince Claudio was nowhere to be seen. Behind the ladies, wringing his hands and looking distressed, was Mr Kirby. She met his eyes, attempting a tremulous smile, and he exhaled in relief. Inside, the gong sounded.

'Supper time!' declared one of the ladies. 'I expect you may wish to go home, Miss... Isobel, is it?'

She nodded abstractedly. 'Yes. Isobel.' They exchanged

knowing glances, which Izzy could not understand. 'And no,' she continued, 'I must see Lady Kelgrove at supper before I can leave.'

'May I bring you something to eat, Miss Isobel?' asked Kirby.

'No, but thank you.' His compassion and care were important, somehow. The ladies were saying all the right things, but the expression in their eyes was one of glee, rather than kindness. *Why?*

'Stay with her,' one of the ladies instructed the maid, who nodded. 'We shall go in. We do not wish to miss out on our supper! Miss Isobel, once you are feeling a little better, you may come inside. It is a little cooler out here, so it will be more comfortable for you.'

Izzy managed a nod, her brain sluggish and her body strangely numb. Kirby and the maid stayed with her, while she breathed and sat and thought of nothing. It took great determination, for her mind was all chaos, but she managed.

After what felt like an age, she took a deep breath, then lifted her eyes to Kirby. 'I should like to go in now.'

'Are you certain?'

She confirmed it and took his arm, remembering to thank the maid. He took her to her sisters, who were seated with Rose's husband and Lady Ashbourne. Supper had ended, and the servants were clearing the tables.

Rose, eyeing her closely, frowned. 'Are you unwell, Izzy?'

She nodded. 'I think I have caught the influenza from Mary. I feel dreadful.'

Instantly both sisters were all concern, offering to take her home instantly. Lady Ashbourne, too, although she gave Izzy a keen glance. 'You wish to stay for Lady Kelgrove's announcement, do you not?'

Izzy nodded. Amid all of the events of the past hour, that was the one thread she was hanging onto. Lady Kelgrove deserved all the drama she desired for her announcement. And the triplets' presence was essential for the heightened drama. Besides, Izzy herself needed this small triumph amid all of the pain and horror of her mind, her body, her heart.

'Very well. But we must leave immediately afterwards.'

Lady Kelgrove was soon ready. Without even glancing in their direction, she had her butler strike the supper gong again, drawing all eyes to her.

'My lords, ladies, and gentlemen,' she began, her voice slow and assured. 'I thank you for attending my ball tonight. As you will know, it has been some years since I hosted such an event, but tonight I have a special announcement to make.' A murmur of interest rippled through the crowd. 'Some of you may remember my granddaughter, Maria Berkeley, who died many years ago. However, I have recently discovered that the manner and timing of her death was not as I had been led to believe, through smallpox when she was eighteen. No.'

Pausing to allow this to sink in, she waited. Once the crowd was again entirely silent, she continued.

'In fact, Maria ran away from home that day. My dear husband decided to put it about that she, too, had fallen victim to the smallpox that was rampaging through the village. But it was not true.'

'She is alive?' Mrs Thaxby looked astounded, and Lady Kelgrove shook her head. 'I have just said she died, but in fact that occurred a number of years later.' Addressing the crowd again, she continued. 'Before she died she made arrangements for her children's care.' Lady Kelgrove smiled. 'Yes, I have great-grandchildren. Three of them, in fact.

Maria arranged for them to be placed in the guardianship of Mr Marnoch in Scotland, a gentleman to whom I owe a debt of gratitude.'

At this, a couple of people seemed to realise what was happening. Lady Mary Renford's jaw dropped, her head swinging towards Rose. Miss Phillips's, too.

'Come and stand beside me, girls.' Lady Kelgrove threw out an arm, and Izzy rose with her sisters, making their way through the tables to the top of the supper room. 'I present to you my great-granddaughters: the new Lady Ashbourne, Miss Lennox, and Miss Isobel Lennox.'

I am now the lowest in ranking among my sisters, Izzy noted absently. *Rose's marriage has put her first. I am happy for her.*

It was just…her mind could not continue, struggling as it was to hold any thread of logic, sequence, or understanding.

Applause rang out, thunderous to Izzy's ears. There was cheering, too, from some quarters and much excited chatter. And then it began—just as at their presentation to the queen at the beginning of the Season, the triplets found themselves surrounded by well-wishers.

There is a symmetry in that, Izzy thought dazedly. *Beginning and end.*

To be fair, one or two—Lady Renford, Mrs Thaxby— seemed to congratulate them through gritted teeth, but most of the others seemed genuinely pleased for them. And Lady Kelgrove was in alt, a sight Izzy was glad to see.

Strangely, there was something unusual about how people were looking at her. Or was she imagining it? Tittering behind fans, arch looks… And had that lady really just murmured, 'It seems Prince Claudio has made his choice'? No, her imaginings must be running riot.

But why was Lord Ashbourne looking so grim, listening to quiet words from a middle-aged gentleman with a saddened demeanour?

Surely, this is a happy occasion?

But her mind was gone again, dancing away before she could apply any rigour or logic.

Of Prince Claudio there was no sign.

Perhaps he left after...after...

'I think we can leave now,' declared Lady Ashbourne. 'Isobel, how are you feeling?'

She is referring to my illness. Nothing else.

'Unwell, my lady. Dreadfully unwell.' Nausea had now begun to swirl within her. 'I think I might be sick.'

'Lord, not in Lady Kelgrove's supper room! Quickly, let us go outside. We can leave from the garden.'

'My sisters should stay, though. It would be best for Lady Kelgrove...'

'Yes, of course! Now, go!'

The nausea was manageable, allowing Izzy to make brief farewells on her way to the garden doors. Lady Kelgrove was sympathetic and appreciative of the fact Izzy had waited for her announcement. 'Now, go, child. The Dowager Lady Ashbourne will take care of you, I know.'

They left, and an hour later Izzy was in her bed, shivering with cold and glad to close her eyes. 'I shall be better in the morning, no doubt,' she told Lady Ashbourne, 'for I am *never* sick. I shall defeat this in double-quick time. Just wait and see!'

Chapter Fourteen

Claudio felt confused. The church clock in front of him had just struck eight. Morning or evening?

Having left the ball directly from the terrace, he had stridden through the districts of Mayfair and St James's for hours, trying to work through the anger, remorse, guilt, and fear pulsing through him. Unable to calm himself through endless walking, he had eventually found a grubby tavern. After only two mugs of ale he had put his head down on the table and slept fitfully for an hour or so. On waking, he had paid his reckoning and stepped outside into bright sunshine.

Looking about, he saw tradesmen and servants bustling about their business.

It is morning, then.

A new day. A fresh start. Yet there was nothing fresh about Claudio's heart. Or his head. Over and over he recalled Isobel's words to him. Her curled lip. Her clear disdain. As a prince, he had never before seen disdain from anyone. And this had been earned. Justified. He felt raw, exposed.

She sees me. And she does not like what she sees.

Isobel was right. Eldon and Hawkins had never been his friends. He had no one.

She had seen him naked, though she might not have realised it at the time. Now he was naked in a new way. His soul had been ruthlessly exposed and found wanting.

Now more memories returned. The pain in her eyes when he had hit out at her with words designed to hurt. He had hurt the woman he loved. Deliberately. Knowingly.

Yes, he himself had been suffering at the time. But he had no excuses. On he walked through the lanes and thoroughfares of London, dodging milk carts and butchers' wagons, street hawkers and jarveys. A hearse almost ran him over, which was strangely fitting. By ten o'clock he had achieved a reasonable state of numbness. By noon, reluctantly, he set his feet towards Buckingham House.

What to do? How could he possibly put this right? He groaned aloud as a new memory drew his attention. Instead of speaking to her, trying to apologise again, he had ended by kissing her in front of the man she was probably betrothed to. And she had not even responded, for she was already lost to him. Never before had he kissed an unwilling woman. He had been so sure of her response, so arrogant...

Self-loathing rose in a wave within him. He was nothing, worse than useless. A failure to his father, to the queen, to himself.

A carriage was waiting just outside the gates. He passed it, not particularly looking, for his mind was most definitely elsewhere, and he had no vitality for noticing. A moment later, he was hailed by someone and he turned to see Lord Ashbourne descending from the carriage, just as a cloud passed over the sun, rendering the day suddenly dull and grey.

Bracing himself for social discourse, Claudio managed what he hoped was a polite smile.

'Your Highness.' Lord Ashbourne's bow was shallow, his face tight.

'Lord Ashbourne.'

Something is not right here.

The hairs were standing to attention at the back of Claudio's neck.

What can he have to say to me?

Better in the morning? How wrong Izzy had been.

In the morning she was worse, much worse, with sickness, fever, and aching bones. Her mind, too, was fevered with no ability to think straight or even form clear thoughts. The doctor was sent for, and he poked and prodded her with hands that were cold, while Izzy wished him a hundred miles away.

'Influenza!' he declared, to no one's great surprise. Rose and Anna were banned from the sick room, for fear they would also succumb, and Lady Ashbourne arranged for a daywatch and nightwatch of maids to tend to Izzy's needs. These were not many, for Izzy simply lay there, tossing and turning feverishly at times, and needing only cool cloths on her forehead when overheated and a hot brick by her feet when she shivered. She could not eat, for even the lightest of soups brought on sickness.

'Tisanes,' the doctor had ordered. 'Tisanes and teas. She must drink.' And so they gave her tisanes. Every half hour, or so it seemed to her. The only time she put her foot to the floor was when she needed the chamber pot, and the maids had to support her—just as though she were a child. That was good, for as a child she held no responsibilities. She had no heart to be broken and no memory to make her feel things she did not wish to feel.

'I have been waiting for you.' Lord Ashbourne's tone was clipped, his face pale. He cast an eye over Claudio's rumpled grey coat from the night before. 'I see you have not yet been home.'

'Yes? Is there something I can do for you?' Even as he spoke, Claudio's mind was working feverishly.

Isobel!

Had she told Ashbourne about his harsh words last night? Or his kiss later? Surely Kirby would not have spoken, for he would not wish any rumour to sully the good name of his affianced bride?

'I shall not waste your time with preamble.' Taking off one of his leather gloves, he slapped it across Claudio's face. 'As Miss Isobel's closest male relative, I challenge you to a duel for her honour.'

All the blood had drained from Claudio's face. 'Her honour?' His mind was befuddled. 'But why?'

Ashbourne's eyes blazed. 'You think it nothing to kiss a maiden in full view and not immediately offer to marry her? Instead you walked away, left the ball entirely.' His scornful tone made his opinion clear. 'No.' Ashbourne held up a hand. 'I care nothing for your excuses. Name your second!'

Who will stand with me?

A series of names flashed through his mind, but there could be only one man—save Ashbourne himself, under other circumstances—whom Claudio would want as his second.

'Garvald,' he declared grimly, and Ashbourne nodded. 'Very well. I shall ask Phillips to call on him. I shall see you at dawn tomorrow.'

Then he was gone, leaving Claudio in a state of shock. Helplessly, he watched Ashbourne's carriage until it was out of sight, his thoughts disordered and his heart sore.

I shall die in the morning, then.

He had no intention of firing at Rose's husband, for to

injure such a man would hurt Isobel. And besides, he was in the wrong. He could not, in good conscience, defend himself, for he had done precisely what Ashbourne had accused him of.

It mattered little if he died, after all. No one would even miss him.

Prince Claudio's suite was the most luxurious in Buckingham House, save those of the king and queen and their many offspring. Both the bedchamber and drawing room were opulent and well-furnished, with paintings hung upon the walls and the best of carpets, curtains, vases, and statuary as embellishment.

But the suite also contained a third chamber, accessible only by using a discreet handle in the drawing-room panelling. This room was small and windowless, but spotlessly clean. Here the prince's clothing was stored, washed, and mended, and here Jenkins slept, ready at all times to respond to the small bell, should His Highness have need of him.

And His Highness did have need of him, Jenkins was certain. Something ailed the young prince, but Jenkins was not privy to the details. All he knew was that when Prince Claudio had arrived two hours ago, he had been in a strange mood. Discarding his clothes from the night before, he had bathed and taken to his bed without so much as a bite to eat. And he had not been in the least bit foxed, Jenkins was certain. No, he knew his charge well enough after all these months serving him to know that he was sober as a judge, and just as inscrutable.

As he went about his duties—washing the prince's linen shirt and cravat, methodically cleaning his coat and knee breeches, polishing his boots and cleaning his dancing shoes—all the while Jenkins's mind was racing.

Something is not right.

Breaking off from his work to straighten and stretch, on impulse Jenkins decided to leave the suite, despite his sense of duty reminding him he should not. Seeking out the queen's personal maid, he quizzed her about the evening before. Had anything unusual taken place at Lady Kelgrove's ball?

'Aye, you could say that. Her Majesty told me the Lennox triplets have been claimed by her ladyship as the daughters of Miss Maria, Lady Kelgrove's granddaughter. Such a to-do! Long-lost family, and the girls all now heiresses to a sizeable fortune!'

Thanking her, Jenkins returned to his post, pondering how this news might account for the prince's strange mood. Rumour among the queen's servants held that he might have had an assignation with a young lady during the masked ball, and one servant had sworn he had seen one of the identical Lennox girls in that part of the garden.

So has he a tendre *for one of Lady Kelgrove's greatgranddaughters?*

Yet why should this make Prince Claudio unhappy? For he *was* unhappy, of that Jenkins had no doubt. Unhappy, and unsettled, and with signs of chaos beneath the surface. If he wanted to marry a Miss Lennox, her happy connections should make that an easier task, surely?

Sighing and returning to his tasks, Jenkins continued to ponder over the riddle. Something about Prince Claudio's demeanour was reminding of something or someone else, but he could not figure out who, what, or when. Yet all his instincts were calling upon him to pay attention, and so he would.

*   *   *

'Come, now, Miss Isobel, and let me change your bed.'

Izzy was vaguely aware that her fever-racked body had soaked the sheets, and that they were really uncomfortable. The problem was that she was unable to move. Helplessly she lifted an arm to the maid, and between her and the housekeeper they managed to lift Izzy into a nearby chair. Her head ached, her throat was agonisingly raw, and she knew she would need to be sick again before long. The maid put a fresh nightgown on her while the housekeeper changed the bed, while Izzy clutched her sick bowl, shivering and sweating all the while.

How can I be both red-hot and freezing-cold at the same time?

Thankfully she was then allowed to lie down again, a willow-bark tisane dutifully swallowed despite the pain.

Sometime later she became aware that her bed was on fire. At least, that was how it felt. The flames were in her, on her, all around her. And why were firm hands holding her ankles?

Something is in my mouth.

Gagging, she opened her eyes, trying to bring her hands up to her mouth, but her wrists, too, were being held. Shocked, she met the eyes of Mrs Coleby.

'Thank the Lord!' the housekeeper declared, letting go of Izzy's right hand and right ankle. 'You can let go, Sally. And Jane, take that spoon out of her mouth. The convulsions have ended.'

Convulsions?

I had convulsions?

Izzy had heard, of course, that one could put a wooden spoon in the mouth of a fitting child, to prevent them from accidentally biting their tongue, having been called upon to assist occasionally when younger girls at school had been unwell with a high fever. It had never happened to her, though. Not until today. And she was now certain that it was the worst advice ever.

After that the doctor came again, and vaguely Izzy knew this was not good. Twice in one day.

Is it still today?

Forcing her eyes open, she managed to see his grim expression, the concerned looks he was exchanging with Lady Ashbourne.

'Her fever is too high,' he muttered. Then there was something about seizures…but Izzy had lost the ability to understand. Letting go, she sank back down into blackness.

'Your Highness.' Then again, more loudly. 'Your Highness!' It was the blasted valet.

Blearily, Claudio opened one eye. 'What the devil do you mean by this, Jenkins?' he muttered. 'Can you not see I am sleeping? Or at least I *was*.'

'I apologise, but the Earl of Garvald is here to see you. He insists on being admitted.'

Claudio sighed. 'Very well. He will have to give me ten minutes. What time is it?'

'Eight in the evening, Your Highness.'

He sat up.

I shall not sleep again in this life.

'I shall wear the blue coat, please.' He thought for a moment. 'And the white and gold waistcoat.'

'Very good, Your Highness. Knee breeches?'

'No. Buckskins, if you please. I do not mean to attend any engagements tonight.'

Twenty minutes later, his valet having taken some time to speak to Garvald and to help him into the requested clothing, Claudio left his bedchamber for the drawing room that was part of the suite allocated to him by the queen.

Garvald was there, pacing, but stopped when Claudio came in. 'Your Highness!'

'Call me Claudio.' He gave a tight smile. 'You are to be my second, after all.'

'It is t-true, then?' The earl ran a hand through his dark hair, clearly agitated. 'I could scarce believe it when Phillips called.'

'What has been agreed?'

'Dawn. Hampstead Heath—a well-known spot. And… er…pistols.'

'That I had surmised. So much cleaner than a swordfight to the death, do you not think?'

Garvald seemed momentarily bereft of speech. 'I—I cannot understand why you are so calm about it.'

Claudio shrugged. 'Shall we meet outside here before dawn? What time?'

They agreed on the arrangements, Garvald offering to bring his carriage and to arrange a doctor. Claudio waved this away. 'If you must.'

'You know,' offered Garvald a little more conversationally, 'when I was at Oxford I ran wild.'

Claudio raised an eyebrow. 'You did? I cannot see you as a wild young man.'

'Oh, but I was.' He grinned. 'Perpetually drunk, wenching, gambling. It was the first time I had ever had any freedom, you see. My poor mother must have been in despair at my antics—at least, those she heard about.' He eyed Claudio closely. 'It does not mean I am a bad person.'

'Of course not.'

He is not me, though.

The earl was a sensible, sober gentleman, who no doubt

enjoyed a drink and a flirtation as much as any man, but he had not Claudio's reputation. He had not done to anyone what Claudio had done to Isobel.

At least my father is not here to share my shame.

'I must write some letters. I shall see you as agreed.'

'Wait.'

Claudio paused.

'It is the role of the seconds to try and see if the duel can be prevented, if an accommodation might be reached.' He took a breath. 'I understand Lord Ashbourne has taken exception at an insult to his wife's sister.'

'Miss Isobel, yes. He says I kissed her in the presence of witnesses and did not afterwards offer for her hand.'

'And is that true?'

'It is.'

Garvald's eyes widened briefly, then grew hard. 'And do you intend to offer for her?'

Claudio shrugged. 'My understanding is that she is betrothed to another. To Mr Kirby, in fact.'

Garvald was frowning. 'Something is not right here. If she is betrothed and the betrothal stands, then her reputation will withstand this. I must speak with Ashbourne.'

'As you wish.' Claudio, not wishing to think of her wedding to Kirby for as much as an instant, brushed this off, and Garvald left soon afterwards.

Standing before the mirror in his bedchamber, Claudio forced himself to look at his own reflection. Shame rose within him like bile, but he squared his shoulders. The very least he could do was to go to his fate with acceptance. He had brought this upon himself through his own dishonourable actions, yet he would do his best to face the consequences like a true prince.

* * *

Lady Ashbourne was there again. Vaguely, Izzy could hear her giving instructions.

'Above all, the doctor has said we must prevent the fever from harming her. When she is feverish you must sponge her down. Yes, and open the window, too!' She lowered her voice a little. 'And if she has more convulsions, you must send for me at once.'

'But, my lady, we were always told to keep the window closed in a sickroom.' The maid's voice was timid.

My bedchamber is now a sickroom.

'Well, I trust Dr Crawford's opinion. You will do as he says.'

'Yes, my lady.'

Claudio sat down to a delicious dinner with the queen, setting out to entertain and charm her, so that she might not realise anything was amiss. She had been at Lady Kelgrove's ball, of course, but seemed not to have heard about his actions on the terrace. Not yet, at least. Instead she had other news for him. Astounding news. The Lennox sisters were the great-granddaughters of Lady Kelgrove herself!

Claudio was astonished and inwardly delighted for them. No more would his beloved Isobel suffer the cruelties of those who whispered in corners about the triplets' lack of parentage. Of course, he himself had been the most cruel, throwing it angrily in Isobel's face. Still, his punishment was on its way, and he was resigned to it.

Afterwards, sitting at his desk, he spent the dark hours of the night writing letters—to his father, his brothers, the queen, and Isobel. It was quite the most difficult thing he had ever had to do. Just how many ways could he find to apologise to them all for his failings and foolish acts?

Glancing at the clock on his mantel, he stood. *It is time.* Gathering up all his failed drafts, he placed them in the grate and set fire to them with a taper. Then, tucking the completed letters into a small folio, he looked around his suite for the last time, before heading out into the darkness.

'Oh, Izzy! Izzy! Please live!'

Vaguely, Izzy realised that Anna and Rose were with her, and that Anna was crying.

But why?

Anna *never* cried.

'Girls, girls!' It was Lady Ashbourne.

The Dowager Lady Ashbourne, Izzy's mind briefly reminded her.

'You should go now. I do not want either of you to catch it as well!'

'Absolutely not!' Rose's tone was firm. 'We know what the doctor said.'

'We lost Mama and could do nothing for her.' Anna spoke quietly, her voice ragged. 'We will stay with Izzy until we know she will be well.'

A deliciously cool cloth was placed on her forehead, and she moaned at the wonderful sensation—a tiny moment of relief amid an agony of pain and discomfort.

'Hush now, Izzy, we are with you.'

Someone squeezed her hand, and somewhere deep in her soul, Izzy felt the love of her sisters.

I am not alone.

Jenkins woke, briefly confused. Why had he left a branch of candles burning? And why was he lying on top of his truckle bed, fully dressed? Then he remembered, and rose swiftly, realising the sound that had awoken him had been that of the prince leaving his suite. Taking the candles, Jenkins emerged into the prince's drawing room, his mind furnishing him with recollections of half-heard exchanges from the day before. Jenkins had tried to eavesdrop unashamedly, but all he had heard were snatches of conversation—something about Ashbourne, and Kirby.

Perhaps they are all going early to a race meet or a cockfight, and I am foolish to be concerned.

The prince had been writing letters when he had dismissed Jenkins and, most unusually, had not asked the valet to remove his boots.

'I may yet go out' had been his explanation, offered with an insouciant air, but it had added to Jenkins's concerns. Why on earth would he want to go out *after* one in the morning? Unless he had meant to leave very early the next day. But if he and his friends were simply going to a cockfight, why would the prince not ask his valet to help with his boots? Ladies might disapprove of such pursuits, but valets had no opinion on such matters. It made no sense.

Glancing towards the desk, he saw that Prince Claudio had made use of the sealing wax, yet no letters were on the desk awaiting Jenkins's collection for sending.

Where are they?

A small fire was lit in the grate, despite the heat of the summer night, and the incongruity struck Jenkins as significant. Drafts, perhaps? Something that might provide some insight into the prince's odd demeanour. Swiftly he bent to the fire, rescuing a small fragment of paper. Only a few words were visible…

…my shame…
…most heartily sorry…
…is for the best…

Not a cockfight, then.

In an instant Jenkins caught the memory that had been dancing around the edge of his mind, and he recoiled in shock and horror.

I must follow him!

Wasting no further time, he moved swiftly through the building, using back stairs and servants' corridors that the prince would not be aware of. Concealing himself in the dark garden, to his satisfaction the prince emerged a few moments later, his face briefly lit by one of the flambeaux at the front door. Drawing up the hood of his dark cloak, he walked stealthily towards the gates, and Jenkins followed.

To Jenkins's surprise, a carriage was waiting outside—a well-appointed carriage at that. Quickening his pace, Jenkins saw a groom open the door to allow the prince to climb inside, heard a male voice greet him. He broke into a run as the groom hopped up behind, reaching the carriage just in time.

'Well, help me up, then!' he said testily to the groom, keeping his voice low.

'And who might you be?'

'I am the prince's valet.'

As he had hoped, no further questions were asked, the groom helping him up to the second perch at the rear of the carriage. Belatedly, Jenkins realised the prince would likely not be best pleased when he realised his valet had followed him.

He might call for me to be dismissed.

Yet Jenkins *knew* he was doing the right thing. As the carriage rolled through the predawn streets of London, he allowed himself to remember that other case, the one from ten years ago. A young footman had drowned in the

Thames—accidentally, they had said. But then, they'd had to say that so the poor man could get a proper burial in holy ground.

Jenkins had always wondered, though. The man's sweetheart had broken with him a few days before, and Jenkins would never forget the young man's strange demeanour on that last day. An unnatural calmness, belying the turmoil that must have been going on inside him.

I am the prince's valet.

Over the years, as part of a team of royal valets, Jenkins had attended to many distinguished guests and visitors, both in Kew Palace and in Buckingham House. Yet never before had he spent so long with a single master, and he had developed an unfortunate attachment to the young prince. Unfortunate, for the Season was almost done, and the *ton* would shortly disperse to their various country estates, leaving Jenkins under the direct orders of Her Majesty's butler. Jenkins foresaw a summer of cleaning silverware and—worse—covering for the valets to the queen's sons.

Jenkins, naturally, was not privy to the prince's intentions, but he guessed the young man would either return to his home on the Rhine, or marry and settle in England. Either way, Jenkins's time serving him was coming to an end, and he discovered he would sincerely miss the young man. Despite his shocking habit of parading around naked with the curtains open, he was a kind and generous master, considering Jenkins's own comfort at times.

Perhaps he simply kept his boots on to avoid having to rouse me at this unearthly hour.

Doubts once again filled Jenkins's head.

Lord! I am a fool, and so he will tell me!

He gasped, and the groom turned to look at him. The first glimmers of dawn were showing, obscured by the early-morning fog that regularly featured at this time of year. The sun would burn it off by midmorning, but for now it was difficult to see more than ten paces away. 'Never say we are making for the Heath!'

'We are.' The groom nodded grimly. 'An affair of honour, I believe. My master—Garvald—is to be second to His Highness.'

It is as I feared, then. 'And his opponent?'

'Ashbourne.'

'Lord Ashbourne? But why?'

The groom shrugged. 'Something to do with a lady.' He chuckled. 'Is it not always so?'

Jenkins's mind was working furiously. Lord Ashbourne had lately married one of the Lennox sisters. Had the prince seduced the young bride? Jenkins could not believe it. From what he knew, Prince Claudio had limited his dalliances to willing tavern maids and the like. No, that could not be it.

He considered the matter. The prince had been acting a little distractedly recently, and Jenkins had already suspected him to be lovesick. One of the other Lennox girls? The one he may have dallied with at the Queen's Masquerade? That had to be part of this.

They had arrived. Through the grey gloom Jenkins saw two other carriages. As the coachman wheeled around to stop between them he realised that one contained Ashbourne and his second, the other a doctor.

Much use the doctor will be, if my master intends to die today!

That could be the only logical conclusion to the words in Prince Claudio's letter.

...my shame...
...most heartily sorry...
...is for the best...

His heart sank. How on earth was he meant to avert such a disaster?

Chapter Fifteen

I am ill. Very ill.

This was the first and only thought Izzy had had since the nightmare had begun. All other thoughts were variations on that theme.

I need the basin—I am going to be sick. I am too hot. Why is it so cold? My head hurts. It is agony to swallow. Why is this night lasting so long?

Despite being exhausted she could only achieve brief snatches of sleep. And every time she opened her aching eyes it was still dark.

Why is it still night?

Anna and Rose were not there. Vaguely, she remembered telling them to go to bed, that she would be well. They had protested, but she was Izzy, and so she insisted with all the determination she was capable of. And they had gone in the end.

'Open the curtains,' she murmured, knowing her voice was weak, but thankfully the maid heard her.

'Now, then, miss, it ain't quite morning yet.'

'Please,' she begged. 'I just want this night to be over.'

'Ah, dear, dear. Very well, but I hope the housekeeper does not slay me for this.' Rising, she crossed the room and opened the heavy drapes. In the candlelight the outside world was black as pitch, but a breath of cool air wafted gently from the world outside. 'Morning will be here soon,' she added in a reassuring tone.

Izzy closed her eyes.

Claudio was numb. He could feel nothing, having retreated into a place deep within himself where there was safety, where reality had no meaning. They descended from their various carriages with identical grim expressions on their faces, completing the usual social greetings just as though they were at a ball and not a duel. Yet the black cloaks they all wore gave the gathering a funereal air, which was entirely appropriate.

Mr Phillips carried a small wooden box containing a pair of pistols, and he and Garvald stepped to one side to examine them, while Ashbourne and Claudio simply stood there. All around them swirled the fog, giving the entire experience a sense of unreality. They were in a clearing in the woods, their world bounded by a cage of tall trees, straight, black, and resolute—massive headstones towering over this place. A place of death.

Surprisingly, dawn was breaking, the greyness lightening every moment. A bird called, then another. They, too, could sense the dawn. As the calls became a chorus Claudio listened, conscious of the beauty of the sound. Never before had he appreciated such a simple thing. Closing his eyes, he immersed himself in the birdsong, just for a few breaths.

Footsteps. He opened his eyes. Garvald and Phillips were ready, Garvald drawing him aside for one last conversation. 'Keep your cloak about you and stand sideways on,' he urged. 'That will make you a harder target for him to hit.'

Claudio did not respond, knowing he intended to ensure that he was as easy a target as he possibly could manage to be.

'Wait—do you intend to delope?' Garvald asked.

Claudio frowned briefly, trying to recall the meaning of the English word. *Ah!* Shooting into the air instead of at his opponent. He nodded.

'Yes. I could not harm or injure her sister's husband.' He handed Garvald the neat folio he had tucked into his cloak. 'Letters for my loved ones, if you please.'

Garvald sighed, taking it and perusing the names on each cover. 'This is a bad business. A very bad business.'

Claudio made no response, and so, shoulders drooping, Garvald walked with Claudio back to the others. After exchanging glances with Phillips, who shook his head, he spoke.

'I ask you both one last time, can you resolve this? Your Highness, can you apologise?'

'Willingly,' replied Claudio promptly. 'Though I do not believe that will satisfy Lord Ashbourne.' He looked his opponent in the eye. 'I apologise sincerely. I never meant to do her harm. But I am, nevertheless, conscious of the fact that is exactly what I have done.'

Ashbourne raised a sceptical eyebrow. 'You are correct. My sister-in-law's reputation cannot be recovered through words. Only deeds.' Rage was apparent in every line of his body, in the harshness in his voice. 'Will you agree to marry her?'

Claudio's heart swelled at the notion.

I should love it above all things.

'Gladly, though I do not believe she would have me. And besides, I understand she is already betrothed to Mr Kirby.'

Ashbourne frowned. 'To Kirby? I think not!' He glanced to the seconds.

'Mr Kirby is out of town,' Garvald replied, 'having departed early yesterday morning, and when I called at the house yesterday I was informed Miss Isobel is unwell, so I was unable to establish the truth of this.'

She is unwell!

Claudio had no doubt that Isobel's heart was sore, not her body.

She has been laid low by my actions. This responsibility I must also bear.

Ashbourne shook his head. 'Yes, she is ill. And no, to my knowledge she is not betrothed. In the absence of her guardian, Kirby should have come to me. Unless…' He frowned. 'It is possible, I suppose, that he is on his way to Mr Marnoch in Scotland.'

Naturally the staid Mr Kirby would wish to do things correctly. And Claudio had no right to come between them, if Kirby was Isobel's choice.

'This is a dreadful muddle,' Ashbourne continued. 'Still, one thing is certain. Each day she continues without a betrothal, and with news of your actions circulating, her reputation suffers more.' His eyes hardened. 'Honour must be satisfied. If she is to marry Kirby, then the responsibility falls to him. But I have no notion of such a betrothal, and so I stand as her closest male relative in London. And no maiden in her right mind would turn down an offer from royalty. I say you dissemble, and delay, and prevaricate, and all the while she suffers.'

There was no point arguing. 'Then, let us do this. Right now!'

Though the final words had been his, Claudio had no regrets. This was how his life was fated to end.

That is it, then. No reprieve.

Slowly Claudio walked with Ashbourne to the centre of the clearing, feeling every step, every breath, every heartbeat.

Just as Garvald was preparing to give the combatants their instructions, a cry rang out from the direction of the carriages.

'Stop! You must not!'

All heads turned as a vaguely familiar figure stepped forward. Recognition dawned.

'Jenkins!' Claudio was astounded. 'What do you mean by this?'

What have I done?

Jenkins was trembling so badly his knees were genuinely knocking. As a servant, he was meant to be unobtrusive, invisible. Never seen or heard unless required by his master.

Well, my master needs me now, whether he knows it or not.

'Your Highness.' He made a deep bow. 'My lords and gentlemen.'

'Who is this person, Claudio?' Garvald sounded exasperated.

'My valet. Speak, Jenkins, and this had better be good!'

'He—I—the queen will be most displeased, Your Highness. If you die, I mean.'

'And what of it?' The prince looked furious. 'Honour, as Lord Ashbourne has already highlighted, must be satisfied.' Dismissing Jenkins with a wave of his hand, the prince turned away. 'Shall we proceed?' They began to walk away, then Lord Ashbourne paused, turning to look at Jenkins, a curious expression on his face.

'Is there more, Jenkins?' he asked in a low voice.

Jenkins nodded. 'Two things. I believe he *intends* to die today. And I believe he is enamoured of the lady.'

Ashbourne's eyes narrowed, then he shrugged. 'Noted.' Then he, too, walked on while Jenkins made his way back to the shadows of the carriages.

'Better than a play!' the groom was muttering, clearly entertained by Jenkins's intervention. Jenkins ignored him.

Claudio was experiencing severe mortification. That a servant would dare do such a thing—follow him to his assignation, then interfere with the actions of his master! Never had Claudio known anything like it. And what was more, he had succeeded in turning this tragedy into something of a comedy. A farce, even. Falling back on his dignity, Claudio schooled his features into impassivity and listened to Garvald's instructions.

'You will each take a pistol from Mr Phillips and stand back to back here. When I give the word you will walk twenty paces at my count, then turn and shoot. Understood?'

Claudio nodded grimly. Randomly selecting one of the pistols, he checked it and weighed it in his hand. It mattered not anyway, for he had no intention of shooting Rose's husband. Isobel's brother-in-law. Ashbourne, on the other hand, was checking his pistol assiduously, ensuring it was primed and ready. Claudio, feeling rather sick, looked away.

Lord James Arthur Henry Drummond, the Viscount Ashbourne, was vexed. Recently married to the wonderful Rose Lennox, he was fiercely protective of his beloved wife and her sisters and had been white-hot with rage when informed of Prince Claudio's insult to Isobel.

How dare he!

Even now, anger surged within him as he pictured the prince accosting Izzy in full public view. Reports had confirmed Isobel had not responded to his kiss, had seemed deeply shocked, and had sunk into a faint. Granted, Izzy had been in the early stages of influenza at the time, but this to James was further proof of the fact Isobel had not wished for the prince's attentions, for who could even *think* of such things while so unwell?

It was also significant, he reflected grimly, that the insult had taken place *before* Lady Kelgrove's announcement that the Lennox sisters were her great-granddaughters. Would Izzy have suffered in the same way if the prince had known of her illustrious parentage? James doubted it. No, the man had clearly believed he could insult Izzy, with no intention of offering marriage, and get away with it.

Checking his pistol, another aspect struck him anew. What of the man's insult to the Ashbourne family, to which Isobel now belonged? His own recent marriage to Rose was common knowledge—indeed he recalled the prince offering congratulations—and yet still Prince Claudio had assaulted Izzy.

Does he care nothing for my family's name and lineage?

Or had the prince believed James to be a *laissez-faire* protector, interested only in Rose? Well, if that had been the case, the man knew differently now. With a fair degree of satisfaction, James recalled how Prince Claudio had blanched when he had slapped him.

Yes, you did not expect me to take an interest in your sordid actions, did you?

The house and line of Ashbourne would be a laughing stock if honour were not satisfied. Ashbourne had no choice but to see this through.

Turning his back on the prince, he awaited Garvald beginning the count.

The next time I see him, I shall shoot him through the heart.

A flash of sanity appeared now in his brain, highlighting the enormity of his intentions just when he needed to be resolute. Never had he killed a man, yet honour demanded it for an outrage such as this.

The count began, and Ashbourne paced slowly in time with Garvald's words, his steps measured, for the closer he ended up to the prince, the easier it would be to hit his target. Oh, he knew the *theory* of what his role required today, and he was no coward, and yet...

'Four...five...six...'

His mind flicked briefly to his beautiful wife, sleeping soundly at home. Thankfully, Izzy's fever had broken a few hours ago, and Rose had climbed into bed a little later, cold and exhausted, murmuring to him of her relief. She had not stirred when he had crept out of their bed an hour ago. He swallowed. The possibility of himself being shot and killed was very real, the knowledge swirling uncomfortably in his gut. Reminding himself that Claudio, and not he, was in the wrong, he hoped the young prince would have honour enough to acknowledge his sin by firing into the air.

For himself, though, he must have no intention of deloping. Honour must be satisfied. Even if, having killed his man, he would have to flee the country. Rose could join him in Paris or Vienna... But such matters were for another time.

'Eleven...twelve...thirteen...'

It was a pity, for he had found himself quite liking the prince before this. Yes, the man had been sporting all around London with the feather-brained, hedonistic duo of Hawkins and Eldon, but James had seen another side to him: charm, and intelligence, and what he had believed to be a sense of honour and dignity. An inconvenient memory now assailed him—of himself kissing Rose in the park, before they were betrothed.

That was different. I loved her, and my intentions were honourable.

He pushed the recollections from his mind, focusing once again on the task at hand.

'Sixteen…seventeen…eighteen…'

As the seconds ticked by and he paced on, Ashbourne's mind was now working furiously. The valet's words were sinking in.

I believe he intends to die today.

From what little he had seen of Prince Claudio's demeanour today, this could well be true. Regret? Guilt? A sense of honour? Perhaps the man was not without merit, then.

I believe he is enamoured of the lady.

If the valet was right about the first, perhaps he was also correct about the second.

So why will he not marry her?

Because of Kirby? Nothing made sense.

Time had run out. Despite the valet's best efforts earlier, the duel had not been prevented. It was time. *Twenty.* Turning, Ashbourne raised his gun, took aim, and fired.

Chapter Sixteen

'Twenty.'

Turning, Claudio pointed his gun into the air and fired, knowing that he was about to feel the fatal shot. In that instant, his thoughts—all disordered just a moment ago—now became clear. In his mind and heart at this moment there was only one person.

Isobel.

At least he had done right by her in this one thing. He had not argued, or evaded, or tried to flee England. He had stayed, accepting his fate. And she did not even know how much he loved her. Not yet, at least. Would Garvald give her the letter he had written? He hoped so.

The sound of a double report rang out, shockingly loud, and the stench of gun smoke filled Claudio's nostrils. When the smoke cleared he was still standing, his heart beating furiously and his stomach sick.

What? Why no pain?

Bewildered, he looked down. His white and gold waist-coat was an easy target, framed by the edges of his dark cloak. Indeed he had selected it for that very reason. Why was there no bloodstain seeping through the fabric? And why could he not feel anything?

'By G-god, Ashbourne, you m-missed!' Garvald's shout held a great deal of relief.

Strangely, Claudio's knees decided to melt away at that moment, and he fell to his knees, the gun sliding from his loose fingers.

Ashbourne missed!

His breathing sounded strange, ragged, and his brain would not work.

'Maybe not!' Phillips was running towards him. 'How do you, Your Highness?' Crouching down, he swept a hand across the prince's chest to check. 'Winged?' He checked Claudio's shoulders and arms, the left then the right.

'No,' Claudio croaked. 'He missed.'

Phillips exhaled loudly. 'Thank the Lord for that!' Rising, he eyed Ashbourne, who was approaching at leisure. 'You never miss! What the hell—?'

'Your pistol pulls to the left, Phillips,' Ashbourne declared mildly, handing the gun to Phillips. 'Besides, shooting a wafer at Manton's is a little different to shooting a man in a duel, do you not think?'

Claudio did not believe a word of it. Rising, he offered a hand. 'I am most heartily sorry for my insult to your sister-in-law.'

Ashbourne took it briefly, his expression grim. 'Honour has been satisfied—for now. But you *will* marry Isobel.' His tone did not allow for dissent. But then, Claudio had no intention of dissenting.

'Agreed.' He grimaced. 'If she will have me.'

'That part is up to you. But you must manage it.' He shrugged. 'You are a prince.'

'And Kirby?'

Ashbourne shrugged. 'Whatever may have been agreed between them, he has not formally sought her hand. In her guardian's absence, I imagine he will come to me.'

Claudio bowed. 'Then, may I formally request your permission to pay my addresses to her?'

'Granted. Once she is well again.'

'Of course.'

Ashbourne rubbed his hands together. 'Now, then. I find myself to be starving. Breakfast, perhaps? At White's?'

They assented and took to the carriages, Claudio still shaken by the fact he was, in fact, still alive and was expected to share breakfast with his opponent. Bewildered, he stole a glance towards the horizon, where a perfect sunrise was mocking recent events, slicing through the fog with hopeful intent.

'I am not dead,' he said aloud, making Garvald chuckle.

'No.' His brow furrowed. 'Though, you should be. Ashbourne rarely misses at Manton's.'

'Then, he deliberately spared me—even though I deserved to die.'

Garvald sent him a piercing look. 'Not many men live beyond the day they are fated to die. What do you intend to do with the opportunity?'

Elation flooded through Claudio. He had been fated to die and yet had lived. He felt renewed, reborn, washed clean of his past. He set his jaw, his voice thick with emotion.

'I intend to *live*, Garvald. To learn, and do, and love. To do more than play.'

'Good man.' Garvald nodded approvingly. 'Playing is still good, though—just…in *moderation*. And with the right company.'

Claudio's eyes narrowed. 'And would you have me? Allow me to be part of your set? Even though I have made so many errors, have wronged Miss Isobel and shamed my family and my name?'

Garvald punched him lightly on the arm. 'I thought you would never ask.'

* * *

Finally.

The next time Izzy opened her eyes there was light at the window. It was morning, and she had survived the night. She felt empty, exhausted. The headache and raw throat had not eased, but just now her bed was *not* on fire, and for that she was grateful. Turning onto her side, she looked towards the window with aching eyes. Outside the world was still wreathed in fog, but each moment brought more light, until finally the sun broke through.

Claudio was stone-cold sober yet had never been more contented. Having spent four hours in White's with Ashbourne, Garvald, and Phillips, eating, conversing, and drinking nothing more interesting than tea, he wondered at how he had ever thought their set to be staid and dull. He had been delighted to discover commonality of thought with the other gentlemen and to learn it was entirely possible to enjoy oneself tremendously while not being drunk.

Raillery there was, and plenty of it, but the humorous slights shared among his new friends were rather more intellectual in nature than the tavern-level insults traded among Eldon and Hawkins's set. Intellectual, yes, but all the more hilarious for it.

Claudio found himself watching and listening, and he realised that here, finally, was a group of men more akin to his character than either the dour courtiers at home or the drunken sots of his previous acquaintance in London. These gentlemen could go from a discussion of Napoleon's latest exploits in Western Russia, to gentle raillery, then on to a discussion of Hume's theory of knowledge without so much as a blink.

The day continued, the clock struck noon, and acquaintances came and went. Hawkins came by briefly, and Claudio rose to speak with him. Having stood for a few moments of empty speech, he informed Hawkins that he had committed to other engagements for the remaining few days in London and also that his summer plans had changed, meaning that he would not now be able to join him and Mr Eldon at Mr Hawkins's country residence as previously arranged.

'Ah, that is a shame! Still, we shall hope to see you in the autumn, yes?'

Claudio confirmed it, reflecting that the autumn was a long way away.

I might be a married man by then, if I can persuade Isobel to have me despite my appalling treatment of her.

Ashbourne's confirmation that Kirby had not formally sought permission for her hand gave him hope, although he knew he would have much to do if he was to court her successfully.

Crossing back to his new friends he retook his seat, then realised with a start they were all looking at him.

'Well?' Ashbourne's brows were raised. 'Have you made an assignation to meet your friends later?'

Claudio shook his head. 'I informed Hawkins that I will not spend the summer with him after all, and that I have other plans for this week.'

'Other plans?' Garvald arched a brow. 'Are you assuming we shall include you?' Hardly waiting for Claudio to react, he instead slapped his arm in an amicable manner. 'Which we are. Am I right, my friends?'

They confirmed it, sending a glow of gratitude surging through Claudio, then outlined the engagements they had agreed to attend. 'Afterwards, we go to the clubs for a few brandies or some late-night wine, but we are not fond of tavern fare, and we have outgrown the need for regular gambling,' declared Ashbourne soberly.

'Although we enjoy a good race meet or card party as much as the next man!' added Phillips, grinning.

'That sounds ideal,' Claudio confirmed, meaning it. 'I look forward to maintaining a more balanced approach to my leisure!' His expression changed. 'But I must ask you to advise me on matters of substance.' He took a breath. 'As you know, I intend to offer for Miss Isobel Lennox.' He gave a wry smile. 'In truth, I adore her, and nothing would make me happier than to win her hand. But as you are also well aware, I have made a complete—what is the phrase you use?—mill...mull?' They nodded at the latter. 'Ah, yes! I have made a *mull* of it, and I think she will not have me.'

'Kissing her without permission in full view of the gossips was not, perhaps, the best strategy,' offered Ashbourne dryly. 'Nevertheless, it happened, and as soon as she is well enough, I intend to inform her of her obligation to marry you.'

Phillips was frowning. 'But—forgive me—can there be any doubt about the matter? If she is not, after all, betrothed to Kirby, then what maiden will turn down a proposal from a prince? She will have you and be the envy of every débutante in London!'

Claudio grimaced.

I am not fit for my title, and Isobel knows it.

'I know how strong-willed Miss Isobel can be,' he offered cautiously. 'Indeed, it is one of the qualities I admire about her. But in this instance I fear it will work against me. I should inform you that she and I had words in the corridor just before the, er...incident on the terrace. I am afraid I said hurtful things to her.'

'And she to you?'

He shrugged. 'That is of no matter. But how am I to overcome the very real anger and antipathy she is likely to hold for me now?'

Ashbourne was frowning. 'So why did you kiss her on the terrace? I can understand that you may have been roused to anger following your argument, but what purpose—' His brow cleared. 'Did you mean to punish her?'

'No!' Claudio closed his eyes briefly, shaking his head. 'Though, I suppose that is what she may believe.' He eyed Ashbourne steadily. 'The truth is that when I went to the terrace Kirby had her by the hand, and I saw her kiss his cheek. After that I—I suppose I wanted one last kiss from her, before she wed him.' He brought a hand to his forehead. 'I was not thinking straight. Indeed, I have not been thinking straight since our argument—and even before.' He tapped his chest. 'All is turmoil within me.' He looked around them all. 'What? What have I said?'

They all bore startled expressions, Garvald now rolling his eyes and Phillips beginning to grin.

'"One last kiss", you said.' Ashbourne looked stern. 'Have you kissed her before?'

Claudio groaned. 'Lord, I should not have said that!' Sighing, he accepted the inevitable. 'Yes. At the Queen's Masquerade.'

'And she was willing?'

He nodded. 'We had an assignation to meet in the garden. She had previously told me that a maiden should only kiss a gentleman if she wishes to *and* if she can be certain they will not be observed.'

'How enterprising.' Ashbourne did not look impressed. 'I begin to understand that the sooner Miss Isobel is safely married, the better!'

Garvald was following a different scent. 'Then, she

wanted to kiss you that time? You have a…a connection, an affinity?'

'I believed so.' Hurt pierced him, dagger sharp. 'But that is gone now. How am I to marry a wife who no doubt detests me?'

They had no answer to this.

'Never mind,' declared Ashbourne. 'You will have a life-time to convince her. Yes, and you have time now to plan how you might approach the matter. She is ill, and likely to remain so for a couple of weeks. It is influenza, accord-ing to the doctor.'

Influenza? 'Then, she is not unwell because of…what happened?' *Because of me.*

'No, of that you are absolved. She caught it from one of the housemaids.' Ashbourne frowned. 'She is quite unwell, actually. The doctor was concerned last evening because her fever was so high.'

Claudio caught his breath. 'That sounds worrying.'

So I might lose her, anyway, to illness. Lord, what is the point of me living if Isobel does not?

Ashbourne nodded. 'My wife refused to rest last night until the fever broke.' He glanced to the clock. 'I suspect she will soon awaken, and I intend to be there when she does.' Rising, he bowed and bade them farewell.

Phillips left soon afterwards, being promised to Lord Renford. His marriage to Lady Mary Renford was fixed for late July, and he and his future father-in-law were building a better acquaintance. A little later Garvald and Claudio departed, Garvald handing the prince his folio of letters when they got outside. Claudio went to take it, but Garvald paused, a curious expression on his face.

'A word of advice, Your Highness?'

'Call me Claudio.'

He nodded. 'Burn all these letters, save one. I know not what you wrote to Miss Isobel, but it might prove useful in your courtship.' His brow furrowed. 'In fact, it might be best if I keep it, for now. With your permission?'

Opening the folio, he extracted the letter addressed to Miss Isobel, then handed the rest over. Taking the folio, Claudio clasped his hand. 'Thank you for being my second. I appreciate it.'

'Any time.' Garvald grinned. 'And no, I do not mean you should engage in any further affairs of honour!'

The next few days passed in a daze of sickness, of aches and pains, sweats and shivers. While Izzy was nowhere near as ill as she had been on that awful night, she was still dreadfully unwell. Sometimes her sisters were there, sometimes Lady Ashbourne. Always a housemaid was with her, tending to her needs. Once she was capable of doing so, she expressed her gratitude to them incessantly, saving all of her grumpiness for Anna and Rose.

Knowing her well, her sisters ignored her petulant complaints, giving her only kindness and patience.

'Look!' Anna declared cheerfully. 'More flowers for you!'

Lady Kelgrove had already sent a large bouquet, which currently adorned one of the polished side tables in Izzy's bedchamber. This bunch was even larger and consisted of perfect red roses and delicate violets entwined with ivy and tied with a simple ribbon. Rose had just brought it and was currently arranging the blooms to her satisfaction.

'How lovely!' Izzy attempted a smile, but the muscles in her face were too tired, so she subsided. 'Who are they from?'

Kirby, perhaps. Not Mr Fitch, for I am out of favour with

*him and his mama. But Mr Kirby is kind enough, even in
his disappointment, to—*

'They are from Prince Claudio!' Rose's tone was bright.

Instantly a slice of pain—different to the physical pains
of illness, yet just as potent—stabbed through her. 'Take
them away!'

'But, Izzy—'

'No! Take them away!'

Rose sighed. 'Very well. I shall bring them back to the
drawing room, where we can at least enjoy them.' A look
passed between her and Anna, a look Izzy knew well.

They are humouring me.

Still, in this moment the only battle she had to fight was
to get all traces of Prince Claudio from her chamber. Would
that she could cleanse her heart and mind so easily.

Having finally plucked up the courage to visit Ashbourne House while the ladies were at-home, Claudio was
close to regretting it, for the Dowager—the Viscount Ashbourne's aunt—was clearly vexed with him. Oh, she was
all politeness, but there was none of the warmth that had
characterised their previous conversations.

Isobel's sisters had sensed it, too, departing after only a
short time using the pretext of bringing his flowers up to
Miss Isobel. After they had gone he had politely quizzed
the elder Lady Ashbourne about Miss Isobel's health, and
while she answered readily enough, all the while her eyes
flashed with anger.

'Yes, she was dreadfully ill,' she continued. 'Influenza
is a terrible, terrible illness, and she has suffered greatly.'

Claudio swallowed. 'But she is recovering, you say? She
will be well again?' Lord, how difficult it was to feign polite

concern when inwardly his gut was knotted as he awaited news of his beloved.

Lady Ashbourne sniffed. 'I daresay. And no thanks to those who would wish her harm!' She glared at him. 'Including those who would harm her reputation!'

'My lady,' he began, 'I am glad you have referred to this, for I must be honest with you. May I speak plainly?'

She assented, regal as his cousin, the queen, and he spoke. He had no plan, no prepared speech. He simply spoke from the heart, being careful to omit any mention of events on Hampstead Heath. Duels were not for the ears of ladies, for they tended to abhor such things.

At first her ladyship was unreadable, then astonished, then exasperated.

'Oh, for goodness' sake! Never—' she sent him a fierce look '—have I heard such folly! Or at least only rarely. You young men! Why, you are just as bad as… But never mind that.' She sighed. 'And now it is all a muddle, and she will not have you!'

His heart sank. 'I know. And yet, because of my impetuous actions, she must. But I want no unwilling bride.'

Lady Ashbourne knew Isobel. As did he. Her strong will and stubborn character would not be easily persuaded. *She will not have you.*

'And my nephew?' Her ladyship eyed him keenly.

'Lord Ashbourne has insisted I marry her.'

She gave a nod of approval. 'Quite right, too.'

'And it is my dearest wish. But my own stupidity means—'

He broke off as Rose entered, carrying the same bouquet she had left with not long before.

'Izzy will not—Oh! Your Highness, I beg your pardon. I had not realised you were still here.' Her cheeks were flushed with colour as they all realised what she had been about to say.

'And yet, here I am,' he replied dryly. 'Miss Isobel will not have my flowers in her chamber?'

Rose bit her lip.

'I see.' He stood. 'I shall call again tomorrow, with your permission, ladies?'

Rose agreed politely, but with a hint of a furrow in her brow.

The dowager fixed him with a direct stare. 'London begins to empty,' she stated casually, 'but we are fixed here until such time as Isobel is well again.'

'Understood.' Ignoring the concerned glance Rose was throwing at her husband's aunt, he bowed and made for the door. The dowager understood what must happen to mend Miss Isobel's reputation. Hopefully she would persuade the Lennox sisters of the same.

Chapter Seventeen

$\backsim\!\!\infty\!\!\sim$

As Izzy's health improved, her temper did not. As if it was not already hard just to *breathe* without coughing, to swallow without lifting her shoulders in pain, to move her legs and arms without groaning, now her family were all trying to send her mad, she was sure of it. First Lady Ashbourne—the elder Lady Ashbourne; it was impossible to remember that Rose now had that title—then her sisters. One after another they tried to make her speak of the prince, and Kirby, and the thing that had happened on the terrace.

So people know.

Well, it stood to reason. Now that her brain was beginning to function again, she recalled the gleeful interest of the ladies who had witnessed everything, the interested looks she had been receiving in the supper room.

'I had to go away, Izzy.' Rose was eyeing her steadily. 'All the way to Scotland, because my reputation was at risk. And James and I were only seen by a servant! The prince kissed you in full view of some of the greatest tattlers in the *ton*.'

'And?' Izzy glared at her. 'He is the one who has behaved abominably, not I!'

'But can you not see? He must marry you now.'

'Oh, must he?' She fixed her sister with a hard stare.

'And when you were told James had to marry you, you chose to leave rather than force him in such a way.'

'But that was different! I loved James and did not wish him to marry where he did not love.'

Izzy nodded, as a pang went through her. 'Exactly. No one should marry where there is not love.'

I want no cold-hearted prince as husband.

Rose frowned. 'But Mr Kirby? Mr Fitch? The last time we spoke, you were deliberating which of them to accept.'

Izzy gave a short laugh, which turned into a fit of coughing. Afterwards, she lay back on her pillows, exhausted. 'I have no need to marry now, for so long as I can make my home with you, Rose, I need no husband.'

Moved, Rose took her hand, assuring her that of course Izzy could live with them for as long as she wished, but that dear Izzy must consider her reputation.

Snorting at this, Izzy felt another wave of weariness overcome her. Squeezing Rose's hand, she closed her eyes. How weak she was, that even a conversation could exhaust her so!

Phillips was leaving for a visit with the Rentons prior to his wedding, and the gentlemen had gathered in White's for their last meal all together until the autumn.

'You will come back a married man, my friend.' Ashbourne was clearly delighted. 'I am sorry to miss the wedding, but we cannot yet leave town.' Claudio's ears pricked up as they always did at any mention of Isobel, no matter how indirect. 'The doctor is pleased with my sister-in-law's progress and hopes to permit her to travel in a week or so.' He grimaced. 'I fear he may recommend Brighton or one of the other watering holes—all of which will be full to the gills. London-by-the-Sea is not my idea of a restorative summer.' He frowned. 'No, I must try to persuade him that a country retreat would be more efficacious.'

Phillips was eyeing Claudio. 'So do you intend to spend the summer at Kew with the royals?' he asked, making Claudio grimace.

'I suppose so. While I greatly admire the queen, her children are not, perhaps… Still,' he said as he lifted his chin, 'it is the least of my worries.' He frowned, glancing at Ashbourne. 'I hope the doctor will agree to your taking Miss Isobel to your country seat, wherever that is. If it is anywhere near the royal residence, perhaps I may call on you?'

'Naturally, although—Miss Izzy's health permitting— we shall not be there all summer.' He glanced at Garvald, who grinned.

'What Ashbourne means to say is that my mother has invited Lord Ashbourne and his entire family—including his wife and her sisters—to my home in Scotland for a party in August, along with some others.' He inclined his head. 'You are most welcome to join us.'

Claudio shook his head. 'Much as I would relish the opportunity—indeed, I can think of no more delightful opportunity—I must decline.' He spread his hands. 'You have been more than generous to me, but I cannot forget that just a week ago I was on Hampstead Heath believing I was about to die.'

They protested, but he would not be moved. It was too soon, he knew, to trade on their goodwill, and much as he wanted to cement a friendship with them, instinctively he felt it would be wrong to accept the invitation Garvald had just been pressured into offering. Despite the opportunities a country house party would offer, from here forward he must be guided by his conscience. This was his new life, his second life, and he was determined to behave as he ought. Even if it cost him in the short term.

Ten days after Lady Kelgrove's ball, Izzy came downstairs for the first time. For the past few days she had been spending most of her time in a comfortable chair by the window. While her body remained weak, thankfully her mind was now mostly free of the cloudiness which had beset her since falling ill. It was now mid-July, and London was hot, bereft of the *ton*, and dreadfully odorous. Lady Ashbourne insisted on keeping the windows closed, for the stench from the streets was overbearing.

Grateful, Izzy had brought her sketchbook to the drawing room, having first ensured all her foolish drawings of a certain unprincely prince had been pulled from it. On the verge of destroying them, something had held her back, and so she had contented herself with secreting them in a drawer.

They shall serve as a reminder of my foolishness, she had told herself.

Currently, she was sketching dear Lady Ashbourne who, when not sermonising about reputation and marriage, was still a darling. Drawing was Izzy's relief, for while engaged with pencils and charcoal, she had no thought for anything outside the present. And so she was quite astonished when Lady Ashbourne suddenly rose, declaring,

'Visitors! How wonderful!'

Izzy lifted her head to see the door open and two gentlemen entering. Instantly her heart began to thump wildly with anger. While she had no argument with Garvald, the last time she had seen his companion he had been disgracing her in public. Nor had she forgotten his hurtful words in the hallway.

At least I have a father. And a mother, too!

'Your Highness!' Rising, Lady Ashbourne held out two hands to him. He took them, bowing and greeting her with every appearance of warmth. The maids had told her he had been a frequent visitor to the dowager during Izzy's illness, and she had no doubt been the subject of many conversations.

'Miss Isobel.' His brow was creased as he studied her face, and fleetingly she wondered if she looked terrible. 'I am glad to see you so much better. I was concerned about you.'

My, he is clever!

His expression held just the right amount of warmth and worry to be credible, and yet she knew better.

'Good day,' she offered, inclining her head in a greeting that was not quite an insult. 'And Garvald!' Allowing a natural smile to break through, she greeted the earl with perhaps more warmth than was strictly necessary, just in case Prince Claudio had missed the point.

They sat, tea was ordered, and Lady Ashbourne and the earl covered up any suggestion of an awkward silence with chatter. Yes, Rose and Anna were shopping. The doctor had agreed the Scottish air would be just the thing for Miss Isobel, and they were looking forward to visiting Garvald's home. How was his dear mother?

Unusually for her, Izzy was at a loss. Enormous feelings were running through her—of hurt, and loss, and grief. But most of all she felt anger. She turned towards it. Yes, anger was safe. Picking up her sketchbook, she began slashing lines on the page—the fireplace, Lady Ashbourne's chair, an impression of side tables and paintings and the ornate clock on the mantel.

He was seated near her, and the entire right side of Izzy's

body was tingling with awareness. Then he spoke and oh! her foolish heart thudded with joy. 'I remember you told me you enjoy drawing, Miss Isobel. May I see?'

Meeting his eyes, she was attempted to deny him, to throw up her head and flounce from the room, but something held her back—perhaps a vestige of *la politesse*, perhaps the realisation that she was suddenly as weak as she had been five days ago and could not trust her legs to carry her. Wordlessly she handed him the sketchbook, watching his face as he flicked through the book, viewing her work. And all the while she was hating herself for hoping for a compliment from him.

She was not disappointed. 'But these are astounding! Look, Garvald, this study of a vase. And this—one of your serving maids, I presume?'

'Yes, that is Mary who then gave Miss Isobel the influenza! But our Izzy is mightily talented, is she not?'

Garvald agreed, and together the gentlemen perused the book, pausing over her studies of Rose and Anna.

'Astonishing! The differences between you are small, yet I think this one is of Miss Lennox, and not your youngest sister?'

Izzy nodded. 'Yes, that is Anna.' Even though she was out of charity with the prince, she could not help but be pleased at both gentlemen's response to her work.

Prince Claudio turned to the next page. 'Your presentation!' His eyes roved over the scene, where Izzy had attempted to capture both the elegance of the room and the sense of a huge crowd within it. 'That you remember these details so well, yet surely you cannot have returned there recently?'

'Oh,' Izzy said as she waved this away. 'My drawings are out of sequence in the book. I usually open the book at a random page and just start drawing. That was one of the first sketches I made when we came here.' Clamping her mouth shut, she regretfully realised that had been much too long a speech when she was trying to show him by word and deed that she despised him.

They continued to go through her book page by page, praising each drawing, and in doing so showing insight into her work. Proportions, lines, expressions… The details they noticed showed perception into exactly what she had been trying to achieve with each piece. Despite herself, she could not help but feel a little gratified.

Dropping her gaze to the book, she watched Claudio's smooth hands as he turned another page.

I could draw those hands…

Both gentlemen gasped at the same time, and Izzy froze in horror. There in all his naked glory, was the prince at the window. Yes, it was clearly him, and yes, he was naked.

Her eyes flew to Claudio, who met her regard, something like stupefaction in his expression. Seemingly unable to speak, he simply gazed at her. Similarly voiceless, her hand flew to her face, while with the other she wrenched the book from his grasp.

'Let me see that!' Lady Ashbourne, sharp as ever, had realised something was amiss. Taking the book, she shrieked, 'Lord save us!'

Snapping it closed, she eyed Izzy and Claudio grimly. 'Well, that puts an end to it. I shall leave you both alone now, and when I come back into this room, you had better be betrothed. Do you understand me?'

Never had Izzy seen Lady Ashbourne so angry.

'But, Lady Ashbourne, this is not—'

The lady put up a hand to silence her. 'I do not wish to hear one more word from you, miss! Come, Garvald!'

Lord Garvald bowed. 'Gladly.' His eyes were dancing with amusement.

Oh, Lord! Could this moment get any worse?

Apparently it could. No sooner had the door closed behind them than Claudio dropped to one knee before her, taking her hands in his.

'Isobel! I—'

'No!' Wrenching her hands away, Izzy took two steps back, gripping the back of a gilded chair. 'I do not wish to hear what you have to say!'

He rose, looking pale but determined. 'Nevertheless, you will hear it. Isobel—Izzy—I know I have made a mill of it—'

'Mull.'

'Excuse me?'

'A mull of it. You have made a *mull* of it.'

He swallowed. 'I have. I have behaved abominably, thinking only of my own heedless pleasure, when all along another life was calling to me. I have been a drunkard, a gambler, and a fool.'

With some difficulty she maintained a neutral expression, but inwardly his words were having a powerful effect on her. She had expected either a determination to marry her despite his best instincts, or a flowery display of false sentiment. What she had not anticipated was brutal, self-critical honesty.

Or is he simply telling me what he believes I wish to hear?

'And the worst thing is that I hurt you. I lashed out with cruel words that I did not even mean. For that night, you held up a mirror to me, showing me myself in all my meanness and baseness. Those men whom I called friends were indeed sycophants, and part of me knew that, but I confess

I liked their attentions.' He shrugged. 'It is no excuse, but as one prince among four at home, I was never myself, I think. Coming here to England was a chance to discover who I truly am.'

'Who are you, then? For it seemed to me you have been showing me your true character all along. The man who chooses Eldon the Lech and Hawkins the Sot for friends.' He winced. 'The man who cared nothing for my reputation or my feelings, only his own anger.'

His head bowed. 'I accept all that you say of me. And it is true that when I kissed you on the terrace, I was not conscious of what it might do to your reputation. But I was not angry with you.'

The second part she ignored for now. 'Lady Kelgrove had not yet made her announcement that my mother was her granddaughter. But for that, my reputation would have been quite ruined. You did not care. And your words to me were very plain. You said you would hate to go through life with no name, or history, or parentage. And you were right in a sense. It has been difficult for us all our lives, but particularly since coming to London. But that is not what you intended. You meant it as an insult.'

'I was angry. I should not have said it.'

She folded her arms. 'It cannot be unsaid.'

'But we must marry. You know it as well as I do.'

'That is not true!' she declared hotly, uncaring that her voice was raised.

We cannot be trapped into marriage like this.

'The gossips will soon move on to a new target.'

'Lady Ashbourne, however, will not. And she, like my cousin, the queen, is formidable. As are you,' he added softly.

'No!' She almost shouted it, so great was her distress. Here, in front of her, was the man she loved more than life itself, talking of marriage, but she must not give in. She must be strong. Her mind flashed back to the library at the Wright house, when Miss Chorley had tried to entrap him. 'I am no Miss Chorley!'

His eyes widened. 'Is that what you think? For I can tell you right now that—'

The door opened, and Garvald marched in. 'From my position outside the door, it seems to me that this conversation is not proceeding as it should.' He handed her a letter. 'On the morning of his death, the prince wrote this to you. And then he did not die.' Turning on his heel he departed, leaving Izzy staring down at the letter in numb shock.

'Death? What does Garvald mean?' Her own recent experience was all she could think of. 'Were you unwell also?' Her brow furrowed. 'Did I, perhaps, infect you with influenza when you kissed me? If so, it is no more than you deserve!'

The prince said nothing, his handsome face rigid as granite.

Her mind was made up. Turning the letter over, she broke the seal and opened it.

My darling Isobel,
If you are reading this then I am gone—killed in a duel by a good man defending your honour.
I have wronged you, and I know my fault, so I shall delope.
Too late I see my errors, but at least I see them. I have wasted the opportunity I was given. Wasted it on wine and cards and people I thought were my friends but who, as you eloquently pointed out, were in fact only hangers-on. Instead of carousing in taverns, I should have been forging friendships with the

honourable young gentlemen of the ton—men like Garvald and Ashbourne and Phillips.

And I should have told you what my heart has known for a long time.

I love you, Isobel. You are my match, my twin, my perfect missing piece. No one but you would dare to tell me such truths as you did that night. You bring clarity, and light, and challenge to my life. You see the man, not the prince, and for that I am eternally grateful.

If you have chosen Kirby for your husband, then he is the luckiest man on God's earth, and I wish you happy.

Please know that I am calm as I go to my fate. I am ready to die. For all the wrongs I have done you. For the foolish choices I have made. For the small chance I had of gaining your affections—a chance I wasted as I have wasted my life. But to die—this will be the one truly noble act of my life, and I am ready.
Forever yours
Claudio

His signature was unadorned. No titles, no flourishes. Not *Prince Claudio*. Just *Claudio*. Stunned, she could barely take it in. A duel? To the *death*?

Lifting her head she met his eyes, and instantly he knelt again, keeping his eyes on hers.

'Isobel,' he said, and his voice seemed to reverberate through her very soul. 'You are my life, my light, and my love. I know myself to be a fool, and I know I do not deserve you. But will you marry me?'

Sinking to her knees before him, she reached for him with both hands. 'You idiot! You might have *died*!' she declared fiercely. 'That would have been the greatest fool-ishness of all!'

His arms slid around her as they moved towards each other. 'How so?' he muttered, his gaze dropping to her mouth.

'Because I need you to *live*!' Then her lips were on his, the letter fluttering to the floor beside them as they surrendered to one another in the most wonderful kiss of their lives.

'Then, you will marry me?'

It was a long time later—Izzy had no idea how long—but they had moved to sit together on the settee, and were now ready to talk again. Their kisses had been frenzied, then gentle, and Izzy had felt tears prick her eyes at how beautiful everything was. The letter—which Izzy knew she would treasure all her life—was safely folded and tucked away in her reticule, the sketchbook safely closed.

She smiled at his words. 'I shall, and gladly! I love you. But I did not know, you see, that you loved me. I would never do what Charity Chorley did—or at least she tried.'

He shook his head. 'Of course you would not. You have honour. A quality I am determined to nurture in myself, having perhaps slid from the high standards I was raised to believe in.' He chuckled. 'But tell me, did her parents really name her Charity Chorley? It is like something from a masquerade!'

There was a discreet tapping on the door, then Lady Ash-bourne entered cautiously, followed by Garvald.

'It has been quiet in here for quite a few minutes, so we dared to hope that perhaps you have—Oh, I can see that you have! Well, thank the Lord for that!'

Smiles and congratulations followed, and Izzy was shocked to realise that her whole conversation with the prince—including all the delicious kisses—had taken only a quarter of an hour. 'Garvald insisted on intervening, you know!' continued Lady Ashbourne, dabbing at the corner of her eye with a lace-trimmed handkerchief. She patted the earl's arm. 'I know not what you said, Garvald, but it appears to have done the trick! Oh, and here are your sisters! Come in, come in, girls, for Izzy has news for you!'

Epilogue

Prince Claudio Friedrich Ferdinand, third son of the Prince of Andernach, married Miss Isobel Lennox in a quiet ceremony in St George's, Hanover Square, a week after Isobel had read his letter. Given the bridegroom's royal status, there was no difficulty in procuring a special licence.

The newly wedded couple spent two weeks in Shropshire before travelling to Scotland to visit her sisters as part of a large party of guests at the main seat of the Earl of Garvald. The following spring they journeyed to Andernach-on-the-Rhine, where Claudio's brothers and father gave Princess Isobel the warmest of welcomes. During their stay they were able to share the good news that Izzy was in the family way, with the baby expected in the summertime.

With the blessing of both families they made their home with Lady Kelgrove—an arrangement which suited everyone, for Lady Kelgrove was delighted to share her life with family, and the young couple had all the privacy and independence they needed in her substantial London mansion as well as in her country estate.

Prince Claudio became universally respected as a man of sense, and taste, and honour, and was known to be firm friends with Ashbourne, Garvald, and Phillips—as fine a group of young men as could ever be recalled among the *ton*.

Izzy, while deliriously happy with her prince, pursued her love of art with a great deal of fervour and commitment, and if she made drawings unsuitable for sharing with guests, she always made sure to carefully keep them in separate sketchbooks.

* * * * *

*If you enjoyed this story,
you can catch up with the previous book in the series*

Miss Rose and the Vexing Viscount

*And look out for the next book in Catherine Tinley's
The Triplet Orphans miniseries
coming soon!*

*Whilst you're waiting, why not pick up her
Lairds of the Isles miniseries?*

A Laird for the Governess
A Laird in London
A Laird for the Highland Lady

HARLEQUIN
Reader Service

Enjoyed your book?

Try the perfect subscription for Romance readers and get more great books like this delivered right to your door.

See why over 10+ million readers have tried Harlequin Reader Service.

Start with a Free Welcome Collection with free books and a gift—valued over $20.

Choose any series in print or ebook. See website for details and order today:

TryReaderService.com/subscriptions